AFFLIC

The Destruction of Souls

By

N M Meyers

CONTENTS

The BEginnINg

The mask around my reality has peeled and within such a short period I have become entangled in matters that are completely beyond me. I feel so lost and inferior against the foes that wish to destroy me and my friends. It all began when I perished at the hands of a creature born of myth....

*

A werewolf, a creature seen only in scripts of fiction and films, broke into my house and destroyed my life. Not only did the beast brutally take my life, but it also injured my mother, my best friend, so gravely that I am still unaware of their fate. I hope with all of my depths that they survived the vicious attack but I just do not know. Death, however, incredulously was not to be my end, instead, I was swept from my torn carcass, from my family and friends to be tossed onto a perilous path. I was informed it was my destiny. I wish they had chosen someone else for such a fate; my newly selected path is simply filled with agony, despair and torture. When I perished I did not ascend to the heavens instead I have been cursed to my very own hell on earth.

It was not all sorrow though, my friend Dion searched for me and took me under his wing. He explained I am part of something called the Magi. They are can access and utilise an energy source from within. It became apparent rather quickly that I was able to use my imagination to gift life to anything I put my mind to (with the practice of course). Apparently no other has been able to complete such a feat, ever. Wonderful... My powers began to develop as I stumbled through the terrifying circumstances accompanied by unimaginable pain. Almost perishing alongside some friends I met on my journey. Despite this, these trials have been beneficial, training my senses, my abilities all the while growing in strength.

I now find myself alone, isolated from my group and in the presence of a most dreaded creature...

ThE jOurRNey – ParT 2

I turn, terror clambering from the depths of my stomach. Through the thickened black smog, a large hairy hand flexes towards me. Knifing claws extend, slicing through the mist with ease. The blood-red eyes glow brightly as the twisted hand draws near, converging on my position...

It stretches for me from within the mist. At this point, terror has taken hold and all rational thoughts dissipate as my emotions whirl from control. The internal darkness lengthens its grip on my sanity with each gruesome encounter, slowly inching its way to the surface, threatening to engulf me. My instincts kick in creating an enormous blast of blue wind which vacates my lungs and takes the beast by surprise. Seizing its momentary disorientation I tare forwards, vision impaired. I search frantically for my opponent, where did it go? I circle the area a couple of times but with all the fog I am not able to see it. I decide that my time would be better spent retreating to help Dion. I turn back. The haze seemingly closes in; it is so substantial I feel as though I cannot breathe. I have never suffered from claustrophobia but in this moment of despair, I begin to panic. My breathing becomes shallow and rapid as I realise I *am* lost.

Which way did I come from? I have no sense of how to get to

Dion. I turn to my left, then my right frantically trying in vain to visualise the path I had taken. I search desperately to see any sign that I had passed through. Clueless and terrified I make a snap decision and stumble forwards. I have lost all bearings and have no idea if I have been graced with choosing the correct path. I can only hope that luck is on my side for once. My head swirls as I walk cautiously. I try not to imagine what terrors could be lurking literally beside me as I stumble around blind.

"I knew something like this would happen," I shake my head. "As soon as we left I knew it was a bad idea. What were we thinking? We should never have left."

A tear escapes, consumed by the fog before I wipe them away.

I shake the thoughts of despair from my mind and concentrate on the dire situation that has ensnared us. I slither along the floor at a lessened pace for fear of stumbling into the unknown. When something finally comes into view I realise that I had taken the incorrect path. In the distance I notice a small dim light, I approach cautiously.

"That isn't Dion," I whisper to myself, my hands pressed across my nose restricting the sounds of my breath.

I exhale more loudly than intended and force my legs onwards. Ducking low, ensuring my form is as close to the ground as possible, I crawl towards the faint glow. The mist closes in around me, tightening its grip, threatening to smother me at any given moment. I ignore the panic and as it rises, I force it back down. I must concentrate on the task at hand.

As I approach, the smog surrounding me reflects the light to a larger scale and I know I am almost upon its source. I rise into a crouching position as I stare around the wall of light before me. Will I be faced with friend or foe? There is only one way to answer that question. I waver a moment as fear threatens to overcome me. My hand shakes. I take a deep breath and push myself through the wall of illumination more forcefully then intended. I crash directly into something.

2

Losing my balance, I topple backwards. A large mass leaps onto my small frame. Huge claws pummel my arms into the ground. A searing pain jolts through my limb as I hear it crunch beneath my skin. A scream escapes before I have a chance to halt it. The black figure pushes its head through the dense fog and I realise who my attacker is.

'Oh no, Lexi! I am sorry, I thought you were....' Leo forces his words into my mind as he lifts his mass from my body.

"It's okay," I interrupt, "we need to find the others before that creature does."

Leo bows his head in reply, or at least I imagined he did.

'I did not harm you?' Leo quizzes.

"No," I lie, "you just winded me."

I raise shakily, pain searing through my right wrist. I wince. We press forwards. As if reading my mind Leo diminishes his electrical light source. Most likely for fear of attracting unwanted attention. We cautiously shuffle onwards. My hand dangles horrifically beside me. It must be broken at the very least especially with the sound it made; I shiver as it replays in my head. Although injured I have not the time to check the full extent of the damage. I block some of the pain and ignore the remainder. I may not be able to afford to waste my energy sources on trying to heal this injury. Our feet pad softly on the ground as we desperately search the surrounding area. The sightless mist still restricts our vision. I can barely see Leo beside me through the density of it, never mind locating the entirety of our group. Regardless of the obstacles we push onwards, our perilous quest before us, to which I have a dreadful feeling will not have a desirable outcome.

When Leo and I cannot locate any member of our group my anxiety rises.

"What if they have been attacked?" I whisper aloud to nobody in particular. "They could be lying on the ground somewhere in this maze, wounded, or worse."

Leo does not speak and silence befalls us. We plod along for a while before the silence is eventually broken by Elliott. I almost jump out of my skin when he speaks, surprising the life out of me.

'Psst, what's that to the far right?'

My heart pounds ferociously against my ribs, I place my shaking hand over it as though that will still it, and breathing deeply I respond.

"I don't see anything."

I stare intently in the direction of Elliott's sighting but cannot see beyond this perilous fog. I shake my head, nothing. I watch intently as we strain to penetrate it. Seconds pass with no sign of movement. Then I spot it. Directly to my right I can make out a slight shadow. It moves from sight a second later. I push my legs into motion. It is almost as if we glide across the path, swiftly yet silently as a ghost would.

I reach the location where the movement took place and lower myself to the ground ensuring my frame is as minute as possible. I take a deep breath and crawl along the floor like a lion stalking its prey. If I was not so frightened I could imagine my stance to be almost comedic. Leo is close behind, readily awaiting an encounter. I swallow hard as I see the shadow for a second time. It shoots off the left before I can establish its origin. I turn left and trail blindly, hoping I am on the correct course and that I am following a member of our group and not that disfigured beast.

Leo bumps into me from behind. I stop dead, close my eyes.

"Leo?" I whisper.

No answer. Opening my eyes I slowly rotate my head, meanwhile trying to contain my terror, to force down the lump which is lodged in my throat. The mist seems to close in once more. Finally, my sight clears a little and I see Leo on the floor.

"Oh no, Leo!" I speak more loudly than intended as my fears spill out, tearing my insides to shreds. A couple of frozen seconds pass before his face twitches. I approach him.

"What happened?"

'Nothing, I lost my footing and tripped. I am sorry,' Leo shakily rises.

I breathe a sigh of relief which sweeps over my entire body, soothing my pounding heart.

"It's okay, let's keep movi-"

I am cut short as something breathes down my neck. My hairs stand upright. My eyes widen as irrational thoughts cause panic, my facial features contorting to reflect utter fear. I gain the courage to turn my head, expecting rows upon rows of razor-sharp teeth to welcome me. My heart skips a beat as Lunar pushes his head towards mine.

"Thank goodness!" I exclaim.

All sense of danger evacuates as I rise and throw my arms around his neck.

"You're okay!"

I am taken aback as something leaps onto my arm. Titan crawls up to my shoulder. I breathe a sigh of relief as I stroke him.

After a couple of moments, I nestle Titan in Leo's fur, which sweeps over the injured horse, acting as a belt, holding him securely. I turn to Lunar.

"What about the others?" I ask hopefully.

Lunar shakes his head in reply as if understanding my question.

Can he understand me? I ponder the question a moment, my features thoughtful.

Alas, I must, unfortunately, return to reality, I need to find the others. They may be in danger; I quiver at the thought, pushing it to the back of my mind. I need to stay positive. We continue onwards.

"Elliott, do you think they are okay?"

' I dunno, they might be if we find them soon.'

I nod my head solemnly.

"This is bad."

Leo and Lunar push their heads into my sides, trying to comfort me. I manage a weak smile before we head into a particularly thick section of fog. My smile fades, replaced by a solemn expression; the mist camouflaging it from my friends once more.

We creep along silently for what seems like an eternity. Something scuttles ahead of us. I cease all movement; halting my breathing, straining to hear something, anything. It seems as though time has frozen, the minutes drag by as I hold my breath waiting for something to happen. My face begins to turn red; I have yet to take a breath I realise, gasping for air, inhaling deeply. After a few moments I decide to press onwards, ears alert to pick up on any sounds.

The mist seems to thin out a little as we approach a large rock. I can now see at least a meter of ground up ahead. This place is scattered with huge misshapen rock formations which we navigate through with difficulty. Leo leaps onto a boulder directly ahead. His ears fold back as he bares his teeth.

'What is it Leo?' I link minds with him.

'It is here, I can smell it,' he stoops low, ready to pounce.

'No, wait!'

He turns; eyes filled with confusion 'What?'

'Let's just see what it does, if it has anyone with it.'

He clenches his teeth, glares down the other side of the rock before leaping beside me. Leo wishes to pounce upon this beast and end its reign of terror once and for all and I completely understand his instincts but if we can avoid confrontation we need to try. If we battle the beast we could very well be injured, vulnerable even lose our lives. If we can locate everyone and escape without a fight then this is what we must do, it is not worth the risk to life.

Leo's rage seeps through his once calm frame; he is furious with our predicament. Lunar ducks behind a large rock beside us. I follow his lead, camouflaging my body between the jagged ends. I peer over the edge. The sharp fragments scrape my skin but I ignore the discomfort. The scrawny beast shuffles around the lower rocks awkwardly. Has it been injured? It seems to move clumsily which could suggest it is as not as able-bodied as we may think.

'Lexi I can overpower it, look how weak it is.'

I hold up my hand to halt his thoughts. I have to agree with Leo it does appear malnourished and weak, I think to myself. I strain my eyes, trying to see through the thin covering of mist.

As it breaks through into the clearing I realise that this is not the same werewolf I encountered initially. I stare intently; this is certainly not the one that attacked Dion. My heart sinks as my fears are confirmed.

The scrawny werewolf hobbles along, it whimpers. Something moves from within the bulk of the mist to the left. A large muscular werewolf bursts into sight and lands at the weakened werewolf's side. My heart stops with the next action. I was hoping they were feral and harsh on weak links to their pack, but it does not attack the lesser beast, instead, helps it. My jaw falls slack as it hooks its muscular arm around the wounded wolf, taking most of its weight. It then assists the pitiful creature from sight. I shiver as two more werewolves emerge from the mist and follow suit.

I begin to shake as the blood drains from my body. My hands become cold as this grey smoke descends over me. Panic rises, grasping my soul and clawing me downwards, I feel myself give in to the terror. We are dead. My breathing becomes audible, uncontrollable, I hyperventilate. Then my whole body convulses as the last werewolf turns back. My tears form as its eyes curiously search the fog. The beast sniffs the air. Its ears prick up as it looks in our direction, following the strange scent it has come

7

across. It seemingly locks gazes with me, eyes lighting up. I freeze. It has found us.

'Lexi, do something, shield our scent, obstruct us from sight, anything!' Leo pushes his head into my side.

I desperately wish to do as he instructs but my body will not allow movement. I just stare dumbfounded as the werewolf clambers the smaller rocks, heading straight for us.

"We're dead," I whisper, loud enough to be pinpointed by a ravenous werewolf.

Leo pushes his tail over my mouth, trying to stop my imbecilic action. His tail muffles the words to an almost silence. I have lost everything, I no longer have my senses, or any control what so ever. I relent to our fate as I simply repeat the words over and over.

"We're dead." The words struggle against the mouthful of fur.

"We're dead," I repeat, my eyes blank.

My sanity strains, partially vacating as hideous images flash before my eyes, our horrendous agonising death we will soon endure. Witnessing my friends being torn apart piece by piece, unable to save them..... The werewolf is at the other end of the rock we are hidden behind.

It closes in on our position.

"Were-"

I am cut short as the werewolves vile breath enters my nostrils. Its sharp fangs directly in front of my face. The werewolves glowing red eyes pierce through mine as it stares into my soul, its evil snigger forms as I stare at it dumbly, numb from all emotions. Its large mass heaves with every wicked breath, its stench gagging me. I find myself incredulously taking note of its appearance. Its head is rather slender and has only one scar. This one scar reaches down from its cheek to its neck though. It reminds me of my friend Ellie. Her image floats around in my mind. It seems like an eternity since the last time I saw her, I miss my family and friends.

Leo interrupts my numbness 'What is wrong with it? Why is it not attacking?'

I shake the smoke from my mind and concentrate on our situation, my sanity finally returning, well partially at least. I stare into its eyes. I close the gap, we are almost touching. The beast sniffs the air once more. Then I see it, the reflection in its eyes, it is not myself as you would expect with our proximity, instead, I only witness the jagged rocks that surround us. The wolf appears confused as it searches for us; I follow its sight, viewing the reflections of its vision.

'It doesn't see us, it only sees the rocks.' I speak to Leo telepathically.

'But how is that possible, did you?'

I shake my head, 'Not me.'

The werewolf examines the air once more before growling and snorting. Green goo oozes from its nostrils and drips to the floor. The beast snorts once more before turning and retreating. I scramble over the rock just in time to see it disappear into the thick fog, following the path of the others. We are safe, for now.

After a tense silence, I finally turn to face Leo, a puzzled look creasing my facial features.

"What happened?"

'I do not know,' Leo states simply.

I stare blankly at Leo. Then I realise what had prevented the beast from noticing us. Saving all our lives from a traumatic end. A smile creeps across my face as the thought crosses my mind. Leo follows my gaze. Standing behind him is Lunar. His eyes glowing brightly against his darkened fur.

"Of course," I slap my head, "It was Lunar!"

The moment I mention his name he shakes his head, the light slowly fades and his eyes become normal once again. With his trans broken Lunar brushes his head against my arm, seeking affection.

"Thank you for saving us," I stroke his head gratefully.

I find myself at a loss for words. One moment we were faced with certain death, having given up, and the next...well this...

Even though we survived that encounter I steal a thought over how our circumstances have shifted greatly from our favour. We were thinking there was but one of these vile beasts and we *may* have stood a chance of escaping this place whole. Now, however, that faint glint of hope has been eradicated as we are confronted by a group of them. Who even knows how many of those things are out there? Hidden within the depths of the dense fog we must transverse through.

"What are we going to do?" I shake my head. "There's no use, were not going to escape are we?"

My mind swirls once more, I close my eyes. Various images transverse my mind acting out different scenarios, each resulting in our grizzly demise. I was not made for this; my fraying sanity cannot handle the immense pressure. Why did I have to be forced onto this path? Surely there are more qualified people than me? I seriously fear that I cannot survive this kind of life.

I become dizzy from the pressure. Reaching out I grasp the rock tightly as I steady myself. I press my fingers over the ridge of my nose, trying desperately to think of what action we should take. They are all depending on me to come up with a plan, a solution, to be their leader and extract us from such dire circumstances, but how can I? I am not a warrior, I am not battle experienced, and I have no idea how to lead this group. What should I do?

'You should take Lunar, search for them from above the mist, it may be better.'

Elliott breaks my train of thought, dispenses my insane images. My mind clears as he manages to force them away.

"It could be risky," I seemingly speak to myself.

My heart pounds within my chest as I mull over the suggestion.

'*Yes, but it might work.*'

"But I can't expect them to risk their lives for me."

I look to Leo and Lunar.

'*They will put their lives on the line for you.*'

My anger begins to rise, bubbling in the depths of my stomach.

"That's my problem," I shout, "they would risk it all for me, protect me at all costs. I don't want them to, they need to save themselves."

A tear runs down my cheek as Leo spreads his dragon-like wings to double the size of himself. He lowers his head to the ground, his right wing following to his chest. He bows before me. Lunar realises what is happening and follows suit. My heart pounds in my chest as both offer me their assistance.

'*I know it's hard, but you have to decide kiddo, what will we do next?*'

DeCiSioN

My thoughts are consumed by dread as I search for an alternate solution. When I draw a blank my heart aches as I conclude Elliott is correct. If we rise above the thickened mist our progress will be much swifter although the risk is greatly increased. We will make infinitely more noise as well as disturbing the fog, possibly even dispersing it, making us visible to those vile creatures.

Leo realises I am battling internally with myself unable to come up with an alternate solution or make the decision to risk their lives.

'Lexi, you can fly with me and Lunar can alter his size becoming almost invisible, we can do this.'

I suck in air and release a large breath. I make my choice.

"I'll ride Lunar, he is quicker and you can tail us to give extra protection," I sigh.

'As you wish,' Leo bows his head.

I leap on Lunar's back, face filled with dread. The knots in my stomach twist and turn as I wonder if this is the correct action to take.

"This is a bad idea," I shake my head before edging him onwards.

He springs into life, jolting over the edge of the rock collection; he spreads his wings and beats them forcefully. We take off and soar skywards. The fog is extremely thick as we ascend and I begin to panic, claustrophobia rearing its ugly existence once more. I feel I cannot breathe. I try to take in the air normally and eventually the fog thins out; I attempt to slow my manic heartbeat but do not prevail.

We peer down through the mist below.

"I still can't see anything," I shout aloud, the wind catching my words, muffling them.

Then Lunar begins to spin. His wings close in around his body as we rotate. His body straightens out like a missile as we coil frantically. I begin to feel the contents of my stomach gurgle within me, I rapidly become dizzy.

"What are you doing Lunar?" I scream.

'Lexi, look!' Leo speaks to me.

I manage to open my eyes and shakily peer to where he is gesturing. I do not notice anything at first.

"There's some rocks down there what am I…"

I cut myself short as the realisation hits me with more force than the wind we are generating. Lunar is extracting the fog through the wind generation. I can see the ground almost clearly now.

I cannot take too much time to marvel at his intellect; as dizziness grips my senses. I fall from my perch, the world darkens and I faint.

My eyes flutter open moments later, I am still in free fall. I notice Leo dead on my tail, he pumps his wings with great effort trying to reach me before I run out of time. He kicks his legs then pins his wings back. His velocity greatens. I manage to make my body as large a possible hoping to slow my descent.

The air forces my body to turn, the ground rapidly approaches as I gulp down my terror. I am only a meter away now, seconds more and I will be shattered against the rocks. My body irreparable, my life ended prematurely, again… I accept my fate and close my eyes.

All of a sudden claws scrape across my back, embedding quite deeply; they grip the back of my skin and clothing halting my fall instantaneously. I open my eyes as a shocking scream escapes my lips, with such force that it echoes from the rocks long after I have ceased.

The ground is an inch away from my face. I reach out a shaky hand and touch it. As if it is not real I lay my hand on it. I throw up my stomach contents. Then I am lifted and hauled onto Leos back. When his claws retract, they rip from inside my back releasing a yelp along with them. His enormous frame is drenched and shaking from the sheer effort and terror.

"That was...... close" I shiver "Are you... okay?"

'Yes,' he pauses, 'I am just pleased I got to you in time, I would never forgive myself if......' he trails off.

A smile forces its way through the shock and I hug him as tightly as I am able.

"Thank you so much Leo, you saved my life!" I babble through streams of tears.

Titan is still nestled within his fur beside me, snoozing, unaware of all the chaos that had ensued. I stroke them both as we ascend once more. My heart still races from the fall. What if Leo was just a little slower? What if he did not manage to reach me in time? I shiver. Leo shakes violently beneath me, pumped full of adrenaline and fear yet utterly exhausted. What can I do to help him? I think a moment. Then an idea comes to mind, I reach out and place my hand on his back, I force the energy transfer, hoping it will replenish his resources. I feel my source dwindle slightly as it enters Leo and after a minute or so he ceases his violent shakes. We pick up speed.

'Thank you.'

"No problem," I smile to myself.

I am impressed, it was only a spark of an idea I did not think it would work, and after all, I am basically an infant to this reality. After a couple more seconds we catch up to Lunar who is still spinning rapidly, a large cloud of fog twisting around him. The black clouds intertwine and gravitate around him, I can barely see through it.

Just looking at his velocity makes me feel lightheaded, I am glad I am no longer perched on him. I turn my attention to the ground. Only a thin layer of fog remains. I can now see anything that walks beneath us. Leo closes in on Lunar, camouflaging ourselves within the swirling mist.

At this moment, time seems to drag; seconds pass as though they are minutes. Then time suddenly stands still as my heart pulsates rampantly making my heartbeat visual. The sight sends me into overdrive.

"Werewolves," I shriek.

We soar above them as if in slow motion. I panic. Then time reanimates, catching up to itself as if rectifying its malfunction. We seem to pick up speed and push past them without recognition. When time seemed to pause I managed to take a rapid headcount. I gulp as I mull over the numbers.

'Oh my, I counted at least fifteen down there' Leo's saintly voice is tainted with worry.

"I counted twenty, maybe twenty-five down there."

The sheer sound of the numbers sends a shudder through my bones. How can we even survive this? With so many werewolves, not knowing if that is even the full extent of their pack? I fear that this is a battle we cannot win. As my emotions wreak havoc on my body, my mind spins, madness stretching its twisted fingers towards me once more. I imagine the fingers almost touching my face.

"Should I allow them to claim my sanity?" I ask aloud, the malformed fingers twisting towards me.

'Lexi, what is wrong?'

I shriek backwards as they wrap around my face, smothering me.

'Lexi, snap out of it!' Leo shouts.

My mind is consumed by the insane terror of these imaginary images.

An electric current transfers from Leo to me. My muscles tense as a screech escapes my cords before they contract. Leo ceases his pulsation and my muscles relax. The insane images vanish from my mind. His actions had the desired effect but he did not bank on my shock. Had the shriek I let loose caught unwanted attention?

I gulp. Peer backwards. My heart settles a little as I see nothing. We glide behind Lunar, searching desperately for the remaining members of our group. I hear a howl up ahead which splinters a shiver down my spine.

Then I see the monster which caused the horrific call. It is battling fiercely with Sapphire. My emotions transverse into energy and I begin to shake. I clench my fist, dislodge the clump of fear caught in my throat and swallow my terror. We break from formation and dart towards the battle. Sapphire has transformed into her skeletal form and splinters bones from her wings toward the beast.

I entice the energy into my functioning left hand, my anger builds as we desperately close in on the battle. My breathing becomes rampant as I erupt with rage.

"LEAVE HER ALONE!" I roar.

My eyes glow brightly as the energy forms into a ball. My hair shoots backwards as the wind velocity surrounding me increases. I force the sphere away and it spirals towards the battle.

I manage to manipulate its direction with a hand, trailing the werewolves' location carefully, ensuring it makes contact with the correct target. I push my hand forwards and the energy sphere gains velocity. It contacts the beast and sparks fly in every direction. The whole area is brightened with blue light. I shield my eyes as we swoop down. Leo lands in the heart of the battle. His chest heaves with the extreme exertion. I leap from my perch and rush into the scene blindly, unthinking. The light finally fades as something crashes into the side of me. Taken off balance I lose my footing and stumble. My foot catches a rock and I fall to the floor, landing on my right arm. Pain sheers through my limb as I realise the severity of the damage.

I pulsate energy into it, shielding myself from the suffering. I have not time to dwell on such minimal injuries. I turn, pushing my body from the ground. When my eyes adjust I search for the battling pair. The immediate area is clear. Then I notice a bundle on the floor to the right.

"Sapphire!" I shout, praying there will be a response.

Nothing, no movement.

I rush to her side, then realise the beast has landed on top of her, forcing her into the ground, rendering her helpless. It is unconscious for now. I shuffle around to the side. Sapphire struggles under the mass of heaving muscle and fur. I send energy into my arms, strengthening them. I push against the beast. The blue aura aids me as I force more energy through. Large bulges of intertwining strands of energy transverse up my limbs, inching the beast a little from Sapphire. She fights to escape through the slight opening. It is not large enough.

Sweat seeps from my body as the strain buckles my knees. I push up once more, locking my knees in place. Pain rips through my injured limb, I redirect some energy to numb it once more. I grunt with effort as blood streams from my side wounds as well as down my arm.

Sapphire remains trapped beneath the beast; I have not the strength to complete the task.

"I won't give in," I splutter.

I struggle under the excruciating weight. With the last of my energy resources, I gather everything I have. Pressing it all towards my arms I force its direction.

"AAGGHHH!" I scream aloud, much louder than it should have been considering our situation.

Then my force greatens and the beast is lifted off Sapphire. I fall to my knees, all energy evacuating my body in an instance. The blue aura spreads down into the ground all around me, dissipating out of sight. My arms shake as Sapphire shuffles awkwardly toward me. She finally manages to lift herself. I glance at her quickly, a couple of broken ribs. They will be tender but nothing too major. Her damage assessed I return to my own struggle. I manage to normalise my breaths before pushing from the floor. I jerk forward; coping with the weight I straighten my legs into a standing position. Dizziness storms through my bodily functions and my surroundings begin to spin. I sway a couple of times before collapsing.

Leo catches me before I drop on to my face.

'Are you okay?' Leo sounds strained.

His chest heaves beneath me. I manage to nod in reply.

Once my head ceases spinning I manage to sit up on his large muscular back.

"Thank you," I stoke him tenderly.

"Sapphire."

My head shoots around sending my eyes spinning. I hold my head, crunching my face trying to fight the dizziness.

'Lexi she is okay after I assisted you she was able to remove herself and escape.'

"So that wasn't all me?"

'It was, I just assisted you.'

"Thank you. Again!" I shake my head "We have to move."

I turn once more. Sapphire is now behind us.

"Come on."

She leaps from the ground, outstretching her wings she takes flight.

Leo and I follow. I desperately search the ground, my mind whirls and I begin to feel unwell. I push it back down, completely ignoring what my body is trying to tell me. I have not the time to deal with such minor

18

issues we need to find the others. They could have be in a life-threatening situation and I must not give up, nor rest until I find them. A couple of seconds later we meet up with Lunar. He shoots towards us, a bright light follows him. I realise after a while what the source is.

"Manara! You're here. Do you know where Dion is?"

The sight of Dion's little companion brings me immense hope. Manara summersaults midair, changing direction. Her wings close in and she whooshes off with great speed. I find it difficult to follow her movements as she darts from one side to the other, so rapidly my human eyes cannot keep up. She merely vanishes from my sight, appearing some distance away.

This only impairs my mind more. I rub my eyes as I train them to concentrate. Suddenly Manara drops down, much like the appearance of a shooting star across the night's sky. Leo adjusts his wings and we follow.

"Please....please let her know where he is," I repeat aloud, hopeful.

As we track her movements I catch sight of him. My heart flutters, but is immediately followed by a twisted sinking feeling. For he is barely moving and extremely close by is a large pack of werewolves. They sniff at the air, trying to trace our location. I gulp. My hand starts to shake as I order my mind to construct a plan.

"Think Lexi. Think!" I wrack my brains.

I am not a leader. I was not created to order people around. I have always been a follower, never taking control of any situation in my life. And now I am faced with impossible choices. How can I make them? Oh, how I wish Dion was here he is so strong and always has so many ideas. I shake my head rattling my thoughts about.

"I wish it wasn't me that has to make these decisions," I whisper to myself.

Then I get an idea. What if I did not need to make these decisions! The idiotic thought crosses my mind and like an imbecile, I act on it. I relinquish control of my bodily functions. I seek solace within my mind leaving my body an emotionless, empty shell.

'Come for advice?' Elliott greets me.

'Yes, well, you could say that.'

I ponder a moment about the connection we share, it is very strange indeed. Although Elliott has no physical body we share images of each other through our minds. This strange occurrence allows me to see him when I disconnect from control which thinking about it also sounds insane... I stare at him directly in the eyes, his features portray his confusion. I am silent as the motions turn in his mind. Then his facial features alter once more, his face draining of all emotion into a scowl.

'No.'

'But why?' I plead.

'Lexi you know I would help you when I can but taking your place, carrying out this for you, it's immoral. It's your battle and I won't do it.'

'How can you say this is my battle, it is yours too. You are a part of me now which means it's ours.'

My anger flourishes.

'Lexi, yes I'm here but if I wasn't there wouldn't be a choice. This random fluke of nature shouldn't have happened and I can't interfere with it. Anyway, what would happen if I ran into trouble? I can't access your energy and use your abilities. I'd be putting you all in danger, my answer is no.'

Elliott's eyes are firm. As his words penetrate I almost slump to the ground.

'You're right. I'm sorry for putting you in this situation.'

'No worries Kiddo.' he smiles.

I concentrate, linking all my senses to my body, I regain control. My face regains its colour as it creaks into life once more.

Thoughtfully I stare at the dire situation below us; an image passes through my mind. My mother. I see her face clearly, along with another person. Ellie. I think of them, praying that they survived that terrible fate. Hoping that somehow they are okay. Even in my absence I still have some optimism that they did survive and have each other for support over the loss of me. My poor mother would have had to witness the horrors that also befell me if she did survive. I shiver at that thought. No parent should ever have to bury their children.

I realise that I have not allowed them into my mind for a long time, not permitted a thought regarding them as it is, simply, too painful. Now I must make what could be a fatal decision, I allow them entrance, for this may be, my final stand.

LoUDer tHAn WorDS

I turn from the worsening situation below to the rest of the group. I see the fear in everyone's eyes, and they see mine. I have limited options and our situation is dire. The air feels thick and my heart begins to race. Before I know it I am speaking to the group.

"Everyone listen, this most probably won't end well and I don't want to put you in danger, but this is your decision. If you decide you can't help, you can stay above and out of danger. If you decide that I won't think badly of anyone. But if you decide to help then I will appreciate it more than I could ever say."

'Lexi I will not leave you. I will be by your side always,' Leo bows his head beneath me.

I look to the rest of them. They all wish to follow me blindly into battle, risking their lives, for me. Each one of them bows their heads in a show of an alliance to me. I stare from Sapphire to Titan. Sapphire has yet to return to from her skeletal form and I can see where a couple of her ribs are broken. Titan is miniature in form, he is still very weak and would not be well suited to a battle. It would be like sending lambs to the slaughter. My mind turmoil's, as I decide everyone's fate.

"Okay Sapphire, you carry Titan. You're both injured you need to stay away from here."

Sapphire snorts at me, unhappy with my decision. I train my eyes onto hers. I stare at her firmly. Then she whinnies and rushes to my side. Her skull pushes against me as she comforts me. I elevate titan from Leo's back, stroke them both before placing him on Sapphire.

Titan is extremely weak and can barely stay on her back. Sapphire's white aura vanishes, titan falls through her bones. I gasp as I reach out to catch him. He falls into her rib cage then stops. I stare confused. Then I realise, the aura has been replaced. She is now carrying him steadily in her rib cage. The sight is very strange and also slightly disturbing but he is laid down comfortably. Sapphire rears mid-air and Titan does not fall from his holding. He is safe and secure.

I order Sapphire to gain distance from this area to escape this terrible situation. She flies away but is still within viewing range. She floats within a large collection of mist, almost fully camouflaged by it.

I close my eyes, hold my head as I try to map out a plan. An eerie silence fills the sky.

"Okay, Lunar do you think you can create some cover for us? Quietly?"

Lunar bows his head before slowly turning mid-air. His spirals gain speed and he quietly directs himself to the mass of black mist floating a short distance away. The instant Lunar approaches, all the thick fog is torn from its holding and is forced into the wind he creates. When he has a large enough gathering of mist he approaches our location.

Just before he crashes into us he changes direction and heads for Dion's location. Lunar manipulates the mist. As he kicks out his rear leg, a large cloud dispenses behind him, completely covering the area from our sight.

"This might actually work!" I smile, confidence filling me for the first time in a long time.

I look towards the pack of wolves; they are none the wiser to neither our presence nor our actions.

My confidence increases as Lunar finishes his task. I cannot see Dion any longer but I have created a mental map as to his whereabouts. I grin as Leo descends into the mist silently.

The fog surrounds us and I am blind once more. Leo pads down softly, slowly reclining his dragon wings. I slide from his back. Manara dims her illumination to a dull glow, just enough to light the area, yet not enough to attract attention to our location.

I crouch low, blindly feeling around the floor. Dion must be around here somewhere. The mist is so thick I cannot see anything beyond it. I push through a large gathering of fog, closely followed by the others. The instant Manara passes through, the whole area is illuminated and I see Dion just ahead.

I rush over to him. His breathing is shallow. I shake him gently, praying he will arouse. Please wake up Dion I repeat in my head over and over all the while keeping an eye out for any unwanted attention. After a couple of agonising seconds, his eyes finally flutter open. He smiles as he sees me for the first time.

I examine his injuries. A pool of blood has leaked from his body. I search for its source and find it on his side. He has smashed into a rock, which protrudes through his side. Pinning him in place, I curse silently.

"Dion I'm going to get us out of here," I sit back a moment, trying in vain for a solution. "Leo what can we do?"

'We are going to have to pull him from the rock. I will be able to lift him from it but you must somehow cease the blood flow.'

My face drains of all colour "I can't that I don't know how, I can only heal myself."

'Well you must try; those things will be closing in on us soon. This is his only chance, or he will bleed to death.'

"Oh no!"

24

'What is wrong?'

"We still have to find one member of the group."

Leos features crease as he thinks. Then his features become gaunt.

'Sparkie.'

I nod my head "how could we forget her?"

Leo's solid stature seems to sink as the realisation hits him.

"Leo, don't even think that! We won't leave her. I have an idea," I turn to my black stallion, "Lunar, can you scout the area for Sparkie? Ask Sapphire to help you. She shouldn't be too far; she would never leave Dion from choice so she may be unconscious. You'll have to carry her if that's the case."

Lunar wishes to remain here where I am under his protection but he also knows I need him for this. He pushes his head against my hand before taking to the air. Within seconds he vanishes from sight.

I ruffle Leo's fur. "Don't worry, we'll find her."

Leo's features soften with my touch.

"Come on let's help Dion."

He is more conscious now. I think a moment.

"Dion you're trapped" I whisper "Were going to free you."

I hold my sweaty palm above his wound. Leo grasps his body with his enormous dragon claws intertwined within his wings. He grips firmly before nodding in my direction. I draw on my dwindled energy resources. Strengthen them as they travel through my arm.

"Okay, 3….2…1..." I whisper.

Leo gently heaves Dion from his imprisonment. He grits his teeth against the agony as the rock tears through his side. The very moment he elevates Dion, blood fountains from the gaping wound. I push forward, hands pressing over the area which only just cover the surface. Blood splatters in my face as I concentrate. I force my energy into my hand, instructing it to enter his body, to cease the blood flow and reconstruct the fibres within his side. I begin to shake as Dion loses more blood. His features are strained and weak, all colour is lost from his face. He loses consciousness from blood loss.

"It's not working!" I panic.

'You can do this Lexi.' Leo soothes.

"Leo I can't do it. I don't know how to..." I begin to cry.

Leo reaches a paw to my hand, touches me. The instant we make contact, a burst of energy travels through my body, forcing my head back, thrusting my chest upwards. I grit my teeth. My eyes glow intensely as the energy travels down my arm and into Dion. Light transverses from my hand, breaking into every direction. I cannot control it. The light begins dispersing the mist. Our cover is diminishing by the second. Leo retracts his paw in awe and fear. I try in vain to cease this spontaneous burst of energy but I am helpless.

I finally manage to peer in Dion's direction. Thin strands of fibre crawl across his gaping hole. They climb over his broken arteries and muscle contorting and connecting.

"Its work...ing!" I manage to choke.

Leo stares at the wound for the first time. He looks from the diminishing fog cloud to the wound. He is silent.

Then I realise why. The progress is extremely sluggish and with each second that passes healing Dion, the more our whereabouts is revealed. I concentrate hard.

"They won't find us," I strain to speak.

Dion's blood ceases as the veins reconnect. The skin then stretches, disgustingly reaching for the other side. The fibres split into worm like creatures. They assemble then spiral upwards. They infuse together then lie flat. The once gaping hole is no more. The skin is fully fused and leaves only a small tender scar.

My energy shows no sign of vanishing. I close my eyes,

concentrate on diminishing the power. Leo is by my side. He replaces his paw on my hand.

'You must calm yourself.'

Leo puts pressure on it. The force is strong and the moment he releases, my body flops to the ground. I open my eyes as the blue aura dims before vanishing. My eyes return to normality as I stare at Leo. I smile. My breathing rampant I try to stand. My legs are shaky but I manage to lift myself. Leo has Dion on his back. He is still unconscious, but he is no longer in danger of bleeding to death.

Leo's face is filled with dread, his train of sight fixated behind me. My heart sinks as I notice the mist around us has vanished in its entirety. I turn slowly to where he is staring.

The packs of werewolves are hustled together. Their backs turned to us. They have not yet noticed our presence.

'Leo, get Dion and yourself out of here. Now!' I calmly speak to him through our mental link.

'No I...'

'Leo' I cut him short, 'Go...!'

'But...'

'NOW!' I shout at him.

His head sinks as he realises I will not allow him to stay. Not with his and Dion's life on the line. I would not be so selfish, I am willing to risk my life for my friends and I will meet my fate if needs be.

'You have all the others to care for as well as Dion, so please just go.'

I ruffle his fur, a tear running down my cheek. It smears a clean patch down my dirty face. I wipe it away. I pat his head and sniff. Pulling myself together I order him to leave for the final time.

He spreads his wings and leaps into the air. He glides up as quietly as his vast wings will allow. I turn to face my fate once more, in the hope they have yet to notice me, praying I can make a swift escape, slipping from their grasp without their perception of my presence.

My heart leaps as I realise they have yet to turn and locate me. I duck low, step backwards quietly. I look behind me; a couple of meters away, a large gathering of rocks. If I can just make it to them then maybe…

I do not get to finish my train of thought as one of the beasts swivels their head, I am faced a set of piercing blood-red eyes glaring at me with evil excitement. My heart rises to my throat before sinking. We stare into one another's eyes and they begin to change colour, a grey mist sweeps over them. As I stare deep into its soul, images flash inside its eyes as if I am viewing a film. This happened to me previously, with Dion. This strange occurrence had completely vanished from my memory until now. The film plays before my eyes. A small boy, down a dark alleyway, frightened. I feel each emotion as I view these strange events. My concentration is interrupted as I hear a growling ahead of me.

Another beast has noticed me. The growling alerts the whole pack as masses of evil red eyes zone in on my position. My instincts spark into life and order me to run. I break contact with the pack and run as fast as humanly possible.

I skid on the smooth floor losing my balance. I rapidly regain my footing. Darting behind the rock collection I slow down. I look around. I am in a maze carved out of the rock I realise. I hear shuffling behind me, I have no other option but to enter this maze and hope I choose the correct path. I stare from the middle path to the left turn. Without much thought, I swerve left and follow the path around.

Left again. Straight ahead for a while. Running flat out. I come to a fork, turn right then left then right, right again. Hoping I am choosing a path which will lose the pack. As my visibility becomes compromised by the darkness I slam right into a jagged rock, piercing the skin on my already injured arm. I hold back my scream. My arm shakes as the warm blood trickles down. I cease the blood flow and numb the pain once more. Instantly regretting piercing my skin as I am sure they will be able to smell the blood.

"This is not good. What can I do?" I whisper to myself, racking my brain.

I turn in a circle. Examining my surroundings. A thought comes to mind. Before me, I have three choices. Left, right or straight ahead. I walk to the path directly in front of me. I close my eyes, imagine a large block of granite, the exact appearance to those around me. I plant it in front of me to join the edges. A breeze blows over me and the image solidifies. When the image sets alight I open my eyes.

The path I had just come from is now blocked. A slab of rock blocking the entrance. I place my hand on the granite. It is solid.

"Should buy me more time," I speak to myself aloud.

'Lexi, what's that?' Elliot speaks.

"What?"

'Shush! Listen.'

I silence myself to listen intensely. I place my ear against the rock I constructed. I hear nothing at first but as I am just about to open my mouth to speak I hear it. Scuffling sounds from behind it. A low growling sound that takes me back to when I first met these foul creatures, when fate transformed my life dramatically. I shiver as I run through the memories.

'Lexi, I'm sorry but you have to go. It won't be long before they figure it out. They're more intelligent than you give them credit for,' Elliott's voice strains with sadness.

I shake my head, "I'll have to leave the trip down memory lane for another day" I chuckle quietly "If we survive that is" I smile manically as my sanity strains.

'You scare me sometimes you know...' Elliott admits as I rush

down the path.

I giggle childishly then think a moment "I actually scare myself come to think of it."

I shake my head and continue with my perilous journey. Left, right, right, right. Then I come to the choice of four paths.

"Which would you chose Elliott?" I talk to the conscious mind stuck within my own.

'Second to the left.'

"Why thank you," I bow in the way he would and take the path he has chosen.

After more differing routes I run out of momentum and exhaustedly cease my movement. The fatigue seemingly returns some of my sanity at least I think to myself. I peer around, on edge, my breathing rampant. Hearing only my sounds I relax a little. Bending over I place my hands on my lap, trying to catch breath.

"Can't…. run……anymore..." I puff.

I walk for a while, petrified they will locate me yet physically unable to exert myself any further. I am lost in desperation. No sign of any immediate escape. I do not know how long I have been in this maze but every sound makes me jump from my skin as if viewing a scary movie, only worse. My life has turned into just that, I realise. Terror around every corner, I shake my head.

"I can't think like that. We need to find a way out."

I look toward the sky, hopeful I will catch sight of a horse or Leo. Even though I know they are either injured or otherwise engaged by my requests. At least they will be safe.

The sound I hear next, breaks me from my train of thought, forcing me to move more swiftly. A howl so close it sends a shiver down my spine as I imagine the foul breath breathing down my neck. My extremities burn as I exhaustedly push them further than I thought possible. I stumble around trying to put more distance between us. Then as if by magic, I find what appears to be the exit to this hellish maze.

Just ahead of me I can see the rocks part and open into a clearing. My legs pump hard gaining energy from nowhere. My heart summersaults as I burst from the maze and onto the rock plain once more. I fall to my knees, almost hugging the ground from delight. Then I feel something wet drip on me.

"Seriously? Rain?"

I turn around and the smile I bore from freedom now vanishes within the split of a second. My heart sinks as the large sets of teeth hover above my head. My mouth opens to scream but no sound leaves my lips. I crawl backwards as the beast tilts its head to the side, an evil twisted grin forming. Its saliva dribbles from its fur and onto the ground.

This beast is rather small in stature compared to the others; also it appears to be weaker. I wonder if it could be an older werewolf from its initial appearance; I could possibly win this battle. I stop squirming and rise, shakily yet standing firm, holding my ground.

I spark a blue current in its direction. It did not anticipate this and the bolt impacts his chest, directly over its heart. The animal doubles over in pain then leaps for me. I evade its attack partially; its claws dig deep into my side, reopening the fresh wound. I numb the pain slightly and rise once more. Blood seeps through my clothing and trickles down my side. I ignore it and concentrate.

I search my surroundings. Just to my right are sharp knifing shards of rock. I force my dwindling energy into my hand which then glows blue. I direct my vision to the rocks and manage to dislodge one. I pull it towards the beast. As if using a sword I swing, slicing into its side. I manage to wound the beast before it grips the rock and pounds it into a thousand pieces.

As it lunges for me once more I close my eyes. Duck to the left whilst the wind blows over my creation. The fire burns and I open my eyes. I clasp the chains within my energy and lasso them toward the beast as it slides across the rock's surface. I snake them around its chest, legs and arms. They tighten and I force it backwards. With my broken hand, I wave the largest shards of rock and launch them towards the chains. The action causes immense pain as my hand flops at the wrist but I have no other option.

The rock pieces slam into the spaces between the chain links and force the beast against the wall. I order them to burrow deep within the rock, pinning the beast to the wall. I implode the edge of the embedded rock and small spikes protrude from the wall ensuring it will stay securely fixed.

The beast struggles with the chains. The rocks strain with the strength of the creature but they hold, for now. I smile with my achievement as the wolf's anger grows with its imprisonment. My breathing deepens as my energy dwindles more. Then the beast stops struggling and just hangs limply from its shackles. It stares me directly in the eyes and seems to smile.

"What do you have to smile about?" I ask as though it can understand me. "I've trapped you, you can't get out," I chuckle with confidence.

'I think you should leave!' Elliot suggests.

"Yes."

I turn assertively. Then I hear it. The fiercest howl to ever pierce my ears. I turn as my heart sinks. I immediately realise the reason behind its smile. It is calling for the others to come. I quickly dispense the beast, shooting a blast of energy directly into its heart. The animals head flops to the side. Its chest rises and falls weakly. I have knocked it unconscious.

"Did the others hear that?"

'Don't wait around to find out, run!!' Elliott's rampant tone sends a chill down my spine.

I regain my senses and turn to run. My legs pick up velocity and my heart flutters with hope as I leave behind all of that death and destruction. For one split second, I think I am clear of danger. How wrong I was…

A FaTe worSE ThaN DeAtH

s I leave behind the maze an enormous mass pounces onto my back, pinning me to the ground. As I impact the granite rock with huge force and my head collides with a shard. It crunches under the pressure and dizziness descends. Dazed I try to scramble away, hauling myself from under the grotesque mass. As my world spins, coupled with dwindling energy levels, I realise I simply cannot escape its grasp.

A red liquid pools around me. My senses vacate as I try in vain to claw them back. My mind is numb as the beast flips me over. The monstrosity has only one eye; the other most likely removed in some battle. Its muscles bulge with every breath. It is enormous in stature. A scared, misshapen nose takes in the aroma of my blood, whilst drool forms a warm puddle on my shoulder.

Its ravenous grin widens as it extends a claw toward me. They lengthen, sharpening themselves into large needle-like shapes. The dark nails turn red as they extend. The beast hovers them above my heart, a black substance seeps from the tips, forming a large droplet. It has the appearance of some sort of tar. I expect the substance to drop onto my chest but gravity does not seem to affect it; it merely gathers, increasing in size.

My sanity threatens and I begin speaking to the wolf.

"What….are you… doing," I splutter.

Its eyes narrow at me. Then it raises my deathblow, plunging the pincers directly into my heart.

A scream escapes my mouth at such volume the werewolf flails backwards, clutching its ears. As it stumbles around I see its eye is bleeding. I scream out in pain, it cripples me. I have never experienced this amount of agony before. I clutch my chest as I try to cease the blood flow. I know not how I am still living after such a fatal blow to the heart but here I am, suffering all the more.

Remarkably my anguish returns my senses; causing more awareness of my pain, but at the same time, allowing me to access my energy. I drag it from within, draw it into my hands. The blue sphere spins as it develops within my shaking grasp. I do not have enough time to finish so I hope this will suffice and force it into my chest cavity.

The blue light blinds me as is expands. I can feel the energy within me; it travels around my impaled heart although it seemingly cannot close the wounds.

I grit my teeth, squeeze my eyes tight as the battle within terrorises me. I roll to the side, my chest feels as though it is on fire. As my senses evade me once more I think I have been engulfed by the flames. I roll around manically trying to put myself out.

The flames grow as I scream. Then through the madness, I feel a hand touch mine. I do not care who the hand belongs to I only need to put myself out.

"Help….. the fire!" I shout manically.

"You're not on fire you silly child. What's wrong with you?"

I hear a woman's voice but do not take the time to study her. A freezing wind blows over me and the fire is extinguished.

My energy is not experienced or powerful enough to heal me. It vanishes and the blood pools up through the holes, it begins soaking through my clothes and pooling around me within seconds. It trickles from my mouth and I splutter.

"Hold on," the woman states calmly.

A young hand hovers above my wound. I look at the woman. She is extremely beautiful. Her eyes turn black and I return my gaze to her hand. My heartbeat slows as I struggle for breath. A black light is transferred into my chest as I feel my heart beat weakly. My head slips to the side and I lose consciousness.

****

Red twisted horns hover above me. I leap from the rock on which I reside and haul myself to the next. I jump for the closest rock but the monster catches me mid-air. It laughs a deep throaty chuckle before releasing me over the edge. I fall...

****

My eyes jolt open, heart pounding as I yelp from fear. Dazed, I stare around blankly. Then my memories rush back, I place a hand on my chest, roll up my clothing. The left surrounding area beneath my Bra is black, the four holes remaining. Bright blue veins bulge disgustingly from the skin. Suddenly a shock of pain tears through my chest and before my eyes the blue veins spread. They crawl across my skin, wriggling and writing. Followed shortly by the darkness that taints my skin.

"Oh no," I choke.

I try to touch the surface but before I can even get close it burns my hand. I pull it back quickly. A small red burn appears instantly. I run my eye over my surroundings. I have not been moved.

"Who was that woman?" I shake my head.

I grit my teeth and drag myself to my feet with the aid of a large rock. I manage to steady my body before I shuffle towards where I exited the maze. I notice the werewolf I previously trapped here has now disappeared. Only the remnants of the rock shards remain.

'Lexi, thank god you're ok!' Elliot exclaims. *'Hey, where are you going?'*

"I need to…Argh!"

I almost topple over as the pain strikes again. I lift my top once more. The black area increases in size slightly after the blue veins crept in. My heart skips a beat as worry strains my features.

"Need to find the others," I push onwards through the maze.

'You're in no state for that, I've never seen anything like that before.'

My anger rages, my voice morphs, deepening. "WHAT AM I SUPPOSED TO DO?" I shout.

My jaw falls slack as I curse myself for allowing my anger to project.

"I'm sorry Elliott. I didn't mean that. If I stay here hoping that someone friendly finds me I will end up dead. I have no doubt those things are still here, I have no other choice but to keep moving."

'Okay but take it easy.'

I manage to salute him "Yes sir."

I gulp in air and continue my perilous journey.

The twists and turns blur together as I struggle onwards, trying in vain to envision my previous path. The pain in my chest flares up. Ignoring it I press onwards quickly. Well as quickly as possible in my crippled state. I do not wish to know how far the infected area has spread, more from fear than anything else.

My breathing becomes shallow. "I need to rest a little while."

I slide down against a rock. My eyes grow heavy. Exhaustion kicks in and I fall into a light sleep. My conscious is ejected and thrown into my mind. I find myself in front of Elliott's image. His ghostly features strained with worry.

'What happened?' I try to connect but I only receive darkness.

'You fell asleep and now you're here, I don't know why.'

'Oh no that can't be good.'

I try to reconnect with my body, nothing happens.

'No it's not working!'

'What?'

'Try and take control.'

'Ok.' He closes his eyes, *'nothing.'*

'No, no, no!' I panic.

Then an idea comes to mind. I tap into my energy. It is extremely difficult to manipulate most likely due to my current state. Once I have control I concentrate. With great difficulty, I manage to engage.

I open my eyes. I struggle to stand but persist and finally manage the feat. My heart pounds beneath my chest.

"I'm defiantly not doing that again" I chuckle dryly.

What if I had not been able to regain control of my bodily functions? Two active minds ensnared within a shell, never able to move again. I shiver at the thought. Shaking my head I push onwards.

After numerous right turns, so many I cannot even count I eventually spot something in this now desolate place. Black fur sends a chill down my spine. I shuffle to the side, hiding from what I think is the worst possible situation I could find myself in, again. The creature does not move for a long time. Searing pain in my chest makes it aware of my presence as I yelp and fall to my knees.

"That's it, I'm finished!"

I do not dare to stare my end in the eyes, I hunch over in agony waiting for my demise. Then I hear something.

"Lexi!" Dion shouts.

I creak my neck upwards just in time to catch sight of him emerging from behind a rock. I manage to smile before it jolts through my chest once more. I fall to the side, clutching my chest. Dion rushes to my aid. He places a hand on my top, pulls it upwards. I push his arm away and roll to the opposite side.

The pain subsides and I roll onto my back, breathing heavily with sweat soaking my face.

"Are you okay?" Dion crawls toward me.

I nod, closing my eyes.

"Can you help me up?"

Dion squats beside me, hooks his arm around my back and eases me from the ground. He edges me toward a large rock and I rest against it.

I am terrified at revealing my chest to him, along with myself catching sight of it.

Dion stares in my eyes, he examines my body and his eyes fall on my chest. The blood-stained holes are a dead giveaway. I try to push past him.

"We should go; those things could still be here."

I manage to get beside him and for a split second, I think he will allow me to pass. Then his arm shoots in front, blocking me.

He grips my top and pushes me backwards. I struggle under his strength.

"Dion let me go."

His eyes are fixated on my chest, his expression blank, emotionless. He reaches for the bottom of my top again. I push his hand down as my anger rises once more.

"Let go OF ME!!" I roar at him in a deepened voice, furiously trying to pull his hand from me.

He shakes his head and looks me directly in the eyes.

I shake from my emotional state and return his stare.

"What happened?" He presses.

"It's nothing, we need to…" I stop myself from ending the sentence as he lifts my top swiftly.

He gasps upon sight of it. I gulp and look down. My whole chest area is now black, it has spread rapidly. He narrows his eyes, confused. He extends his hand to touch it. I grip it.

"Don't!"

He does not break his glare "Does it hurt to touch?"

"I didn't even get that far" I show him the burn on my hand.

He allows my top to fall back down. He walks backwards, holding his head, turning his ring.

I cannot ask the question in my mind as pain seers through my body once more. I keel over, curling into a ball, tensing every muscle in my body.

Dion rushes over, a yellow light surrounds me. The pain does not dull, it intensifies. I scream out in anguish as he pumps more into me. My jaw muscles tense and I cannot speak. He is making it worse. I try to roll from his grasp but he tightens his grip and I cannot pull myself free. Suddenly my jaw frees and I shout at him.

"STOP!!"

The instant he ceases the flow of energy my muscles relax and the pain dulls. My breathing becomes rampant.

"Please help me up."

Dion grips me and hauls me into a standing position.

"I…. Think," I breathe deeply, sucking in air, "you made it worse."

Guilt overcomes his features. "No." He shakes his head "I am so sorry, I…"

I hold up my broken hand halting him. "You didn't know."

I shakily grasp my clothing, my heart pounds as I elevate it. The blackness has now spread to my abdomen and around my sides. I burst into tears as the sight.

Dion pulls my top down gently, edges me towards where he emerged. I now see that the black fur was not a werewolf, but Sparkie. She is unconscious but Lunar is beside her. He rushes over to me, excitement filling him, he bucks playfully.

"He found her, good boy," I manage to stroke him shakily.

"Indeed he did, if he had not I fear she may not be here now, he saved her!" Dion pats him, "he found Sparkie then travelled back to take me to her location."

"Where are the others?" I peer around, nothing but rocks surround us.

"I made them stay behind but we know their location. They are safe."

The pain flares once more, flames burn across my torso. I double over, trying to regain control of myself. I grip onto Dion to cease my legs from failing. As the pain ravishes me, my grip tightens, squeezing his arm with all my strength. His features tighten as he tenses against the pressure of my grip. When the pain dispenses I release his arm. My breathing becomes shallow as beads of sweat escape my pores. As I straighten, Dion rubs his arm tenderly.

"We have to get you some help," he edges me towards Lunar. He holds his head in frustration.

"Look at the state of you! Your wrist is broken, you have deep gashes in your sides and that....." he trails off as tears well up.

I have not seen him this upset before. I stare into his eyes, mixed emotions filling me as they seem to be filling him. Is he falling for me? I shake the thought from my mind and look to Lunar.

41

"He can't carry all of us."

Dion shakes his head "He cannot. He will carry you to safety then come back for us."

"Dion there is no chance I am leaving without you, those things might come back."

"You must."

"The answer is no and that's final."

Dion curses to himself "You are so... stubborn!" He shouts.

"Yes," I half-smile cocking an eyebrow.

We stand in silence for a while, mulling over our situation; what action to take. We think of various ideas, none of which are viable.

"Maybe I can create something with wings and a large enough capacity to carry us."

"That would not be wise, you are in no fit state..." Dion shakes his head whilst twisting his ring.

An idea crosses my mind and I curse that I did not think of it earlier. I search the depths of my mind, trying to locate my connection to Leo.

After a couple of moments, I finally link our minds.

'Leo?' I ask questioningly.

Nothing. I wait a couple of minutes. What if he is too far away?

More time passes as I watch Dion growing more anxious. My chest burns with agony once more and my mind screams out in pain as I try to keep it hidden from him. This is torturing Dion as much as myself. My facial features reveal the pain I try hard to disguise. My anguish subsides and I breathe I sigh of relief.

"I don't know where Leo is…." I pant, "what are we going to do?"

Then I recall a distant memory stored deep within my mind.

"What about the Titanous?"

Dion's face lights up as a smile creases his face. As soon as his delight appears, it disappears.

"It would be too risky. They are too unpredictable; many would sense injury and try to place you in danger out of enjoyment."

I scowl. What will we do? Then I hear it. The vague sound of the air parting as the thin layer of mist dispenses. A soft thud up ahead as Leo approaches.

"Oh thank..." I choke, falling forwards.

Leo leaps to my aid, creating a soft landing on his large back. I struggle against the burning sensation. Finally, it subsides and I push myself upright, my grip remaining firm in case another episode breaks out.

'Lexi, what is wrong with you? Why is your arm turning black?' Leo asks.

My breathing becomes rampant as my hand starts to shake. I inhale a deep breath of air before turning to my arm.

Sure enough, this vile infection has spread to my arm. It has surpassed my sleeve slightly. A tear threatens to escape; instead, I do not allow it to fall. Shaking myself from this trans I face Dion.

"We need to move, NOW!" he half shouts at Leo.

"Leo, can you carry Sparkie?"

Leo bows his head in reply, then bounds over to his unconscious friend. Dion assists the placement of Sparkie upon his rear.

"Lexi jump on Leo."

I peer from Lunar to Leo.

"He can't hold Sparkie's weight as well as worrying if I'll fall from him. Sparkie is heavy enough."

Dion's face creases "What then?"

"We can get on Lunar."

He stares as the horse's frame "He cannot hold two, he is young and weak."

"Lunar," I call him over.

He trots to my side. I pat him before whispering in his ear.

He mimics Leo's previous movement and lowers his head in acceptance.

"He can do this," I reassure him.

Dion hesitates but realistically what other option is there? He gives in and hurries to my side, gently helping me to my position.

When I am finally upon Lunar, Dion leaps effortlessly and perches on his back. He places each arm around the side of me.

"What are you doing?" I push him away, "You'll burn."

"No other option," he grits his teeth against the heat that he can already feel.

"You can't."

His tone changes, toughened and firm "Lexi how do you expect to stay on Lunar when that pain creases you?"

"I can if I..."

My chest sets alight once more and the entirety of my muscles contract. I hunch over as my senses whirl manically. After 10 seconds or so the pain lessens then vanishes.

"Well?" he pauses, "do you honestly think you can remain within safety whilst in that state?"

I shake my head; he is correct.

"I would not expect you to either."

Dion forms a yellow coating over his arms before instructing everyone to take off whilst bear-hugging me from behind.

MuTator ForMArUm

ion yelps as my flesh burns him, the intensity seeping through his barrier. He grits his teeth keeping his tongue under wraps, not allowing too much sound to escape.

As he soldiers on my skin begins to burn. It must be reflecting from his barrier. I writhe with discomfort but try to ignore the sensation. I concentrate. Dion is receiving the brunt of the heat, despite mine increasing, I must not allow it to show. I am stronger than that. I manage to ensnare the scream, forcing it back down. My chest creases me once more, this is something I cannot hide sadly. Dion does not let go, he merely tightens his grip until my episode has passed.

I cannot carry on much longer like this. What will happen when the infection takes the entirety of me? The black skin, bulging blue veins coursing over me, pulsating. Will that finally be my end? What is this virus? What will happen to me? I look around as the questions swirl in my mind. We have departed the rocky pit where I became a burden to the group. I glance around; Titan, Sapphire and Manara have joined our journey.

More questions coarse through my mind.

'Elliott, what do you think will happen to me? To us?'

I close my eyes, concentrate hard. My mind screams with the

various torments currently coursing through my broken body. I strain to hear a reply. Nothing. Either my mind is in too much turmoil or he has not answered me. Either way, my outlook seems bleak. I stare at my arm. The black skin has spread a little more. Dion's arms are burning red under the heat. I am helpless. My mind begins to wonder, what other choice do I have? I welcome the thoughts of normalcy.

My mother and father are together. Ellie is next to them, waving at me. I look to my side, all of my new friends are also with me. Amahté grins cheekily, spreading it across his oval-shaped head whilst tilting it towards me. I ruffle his bald cranium and he jumps onto my shoulder. Sapphire, Lunar and Titan prance around excitedly. Dion strokes Titan and transfers Manara onto his back. She coos happily.

Leo bows his head slightly before I stride towards my family. I run forward desperate to hold my father who was taken from us so swiftly. They hold out their hands as I run toward them. The more distance I cover, the further away they become. I turn around. Dion, the rest of the group, also appear to be moving away from me. As if making me choose which path I wish to take. I stare from my family, normality, to my friends. Although I love them dearly that path is filled with despair and sorrow. I look from one to the other.

Father calls my name and my emotions take control. I rush towards him and my mother. They are still leaving me and after a couple of minutes, are no longer in sight. I halt and pound the ground with my fists, tears streaming as I turn to Dion. I walk towards my friends. They do not leave me and moments later I am beside them. It seems as though fate has chosen my path even if it is filled with twisted horrors. I turn for comfort, the one-eyed werewolf stands beside me, grinning devilishly as it pins me to the ground.

"NOO!" I scream thrashing.

"Lexi calm down. You were dreaming", I hear Dion's comforting voice.

It calms me instantly. I force my eyes open.

"Where are we?" I croak.

"We are at the Houndori," he smiles sadly.

I take in my surroundings. We currently reside in the middle of a derelict temple, long conceded to decay. I touch a stone wall beside me. It crumbles on contact the remnants forced down by gravity. The area is enormous yet I still feel disappointed at the sight. I imagined a magnificent and beautiful place. Instead I am greeted with moss, grime and failing walls.

"This is the temple?" I ask confused.

"Indeed."

"Hmm not as I imagined."

"Oh I am sure it will live up to your expectations, here drink this."

Dion holds out a pink, stodgy drink. I gulp it down without question and wretch as the thick substance worms slowly down my throat.

"Disgusting."

As the substance hits my stomach a strange feeling overcomes me. My eyes begin to twitch rapidly from side to side. I try to focus them but they ignore me and act out on their own. Just as I begin to feel dizzy something appears before me and they cease their movement. I can now focus on the cloud forming before me.

"Magipures at um," Dion speaks firmly.

I stare as the cloud alters shape. It stretches toward the sky growing rapidly. Once out of my sight the top surface begins to shimmer and wave. The cloud touches the ground. Upon impact, it creates the shape of a step.

"You aren't being serious?" I ask dumbfounded breathing shallow.

Before Dion can answer I am doubled over on the ground. I grind my hands into the dirt, squeezing as if it will relieve the pain. As it subsides Dion grips my arm and hauls me to my feet.

"I *am* being serious, we had better hurry."

I stumble onto the first step. It holds our weight to my surprise. Then Dion lifts his foot to step on the next segment. This section is still blowing slightly in the breeze and does not take any shape, yet that of a cloud. I am sure he will fall right through it. Unexpectedly he does not. A second before his foot impacts, a step forms beneath it. I find this very interesting. For, sure enough, each time he advances, the step forms before he makes contact.

"Come on we must hurry, the cloud does not last forever you know. Everyone has to follow this route but Magi must drink that liquid first."

"Can't we just fly up?"

Dion grips my hand more firmly, almost taking all of my weight.

"This is the only way; otherwise the Houndori would be seen."

I roll my eyes, of course. The others follow closely behind, we quicken our pace. We advance up and beyond the cloud layer. Moments later, expectedly, I fall to my knees in agony once more. I feel as though my chest is being ripped apart, my skin tearing from the inside, each strand shredding and twisting.

I can do nothing to cease the scream this time. It erupts from my vocal cords as I try to hold my chest, in the hope of aiding my anguish. Dion swiftly grasps my hands forcing them away from my body. I pull against him, my instincts trying in vain to overcome sense.

"You must not touch it; you will burn away your skin and cause more pain."

I allow his words to sink in, force myself to overcome the instincts which have saved me on numerous occasions; I let my hands flop onto the cloud. I grit my teeth against the tearing sensation within. It will pass soon.

Minutes pass by; this time it does not fade. My breathing becomes rampant as I struggle to hold myself together. Dion must know that the pain is not passing as he scoops me into his arms and runs upwards. Through blurred vision, I catch small glimpses of the world around me. We halt at the top of the cloud. I do not know where we can go from here. Then Dion shouts something inaudible.

We step off the edge. My vision blurs once more. I cannot see anything beneath us yet we do not plummet to the ground. Dion rushes along our invisible path, I am still bundled within his arms; in agony. I slip in and out of consciousness. My eyes flicker open slightly as we pass under a large arched entrance before closing once more.

Something sharp in my side jolts me back to reality. I gasp, eyes open instinctively. A strange contraption is being pressed into my side, I panic trying to pull at it. A ruby red light surrounds me, clearing my vision whilst forcing me to the ground. I manage to focus on Dion's face. A large man is crouched over me. He has long black hair and looks much like Dion in appearance. His nose is slightly pointed with a small scar across the ridge. I focus on his eyes, they terrify me. They are completely black and seem to pierce through my soul.

He places his large hand on my shoulder.

I try to speak but only chocked muffled sounds escape.

"What are you thinking Lyca?"

"I have seen this once before but we were too late, he died and didn't have the chance to tell us what happened." He looks from Dion, to his contraption then back to me. "She must find the strength to speak or I don't know what I can do."

Dion's face is strained with worry and guilt.

"Come on Lexi."

I open my mouth and he leans in hopefully. The pain catches my words. I struggle with them and eventually give in.

"I should have asked before; I just did not want to put too much strain on her. This is entirely my fault," he places his hand on his head and lowers it.

I search the depths of my energy, praying I can manipulate it to assist my speech. I draw upon it. It takes a lot of effort to drag it to my throat. Finally, it reaches its destination. I order it to wrap around my larynx.

Opening my mouth I shout as loud as I can. No sound leaves my mouth. I try again.

"Di....n," I manage to croak.

Dion stares, a smile creeps across his face.

Lyca speaks to me gently, "What happened Lexi?"

I shiver, close my eyes for a moment, gathering my strength.

"Werewolf" I croak painfully.

Lyca's expression darkens. His features tense, as he stares into my eyes.

After moments of silence, he finally speaks.

"No, this cannot be?" He shakes his head confused.

"What?" Dion presses anxiously.

I struggle against the red aura pinning me to the ground, my anguish is great and I doubt my sanity can take much more of this.

"Well, you know how Werewolves infect their victims..."

Dion nods "Of course."

Dion's jaw drops as he lifts my top, staring at the puncture wounds on my chest.

"No...... but..... how?" Dion shakes his head, overwhelmed.

Lyca locks gazes with me. "Did a werewolf impale your heart with its claws?"

I manage a nod, trying desperately to keep track of the conversation. My mind screams within, please just help me!

Dion's face turns white as dread fills his features.

"What can we do?"

Lyca shakes his head, his eyes searching for the answer within his mind.

A tear scurries down Dion's cheek as he almost shouts at Lyca. I do not catch what he says as I begin to lose my hold on reality. My eyes roll around in my head as I shake violently. I notice that the skin on my hand is now black, scattered with vibrant blue veins. As I stare I think about how beautiful they are.

My eyes start to close. Then something jolts me back to this cruel world. The contraption Lyca was pointing to my side is now deeply embedded within it.

The shock clears my senses slightly. Dion pushes Lyca, but he is much larger than him and it has no effect.

"Stop, she was fading, I had to do something to bring her back."

He paces up and down. "There could be one thing we could try."

Hope wells within me and from his expression, Dion's too.

"Mutator formarum."

As the words sink in, his hope filled face turns to anger.

"What are you thinking?" Dion roars at Lyca, "are you insane?"

Lyca remains calm through Dion's rage

"The only thing I can think of is that she somehow, unbelievably, removed the werewolf before it could finish the job. Normally once they have you, that is that, you turn or die... so maybe it left some sort of poison in her?"

He turns to me as I force a nod of approval.

"See that is what happened" he scratches his head before continuing.

"The only thing that comes to mind is to try Mutator formarum. It could counteract the disease."

Dion shakes his head "No, it is too dangerous! You know it has been forbidden with good reason!"

Lyca places a hand on Dion's shoulder

"This should be her choice."

Dion pushes his hand from his shoulder, repulsed, "She does not even know what we are talking about."

Lyca turns to me, eyes fixated, features stern.

"Lexi, concentrate now. If we try Mutator formarum it may counteract the effects or it could cause more pain, end you or worse... but it is the only option I can think of that may work. As soon as the substance reaches your brain you will either perish or transform into one of those wolfish beasts and we will have no choice but to end you ourselves."

"She will die... or worse" Dion interrupts devastated.

"What other option do we have? If the poison does not end her, she will transform into one of them anyway. There is no other choice."

Dion accepts his answer, looks to me for mine.

My mind swirls, and within seconds I make my decision. I will not become one of those monsters. I hold my arm up, stretch one finger out.

"Mutator formarum?" Dion asks.

I nod my head in acceptance as tears roll down my cheeks. The moment they reach my neck I hear them sizzle and dry out, the poison must be very advanced. Lyca releases his hold over me, before pulling me into the sitting position. The heat does not seem to affect him. He supports me, grips my hand tightly.

"Are you sure?"

I shake my head, dread clawing its way up from my stomach.

Lyca ignores my cowardice and extends his fingernails. He holds out my arm firmly. It shakes partially from fear, partially from my anguish. He presses them just below my elbow, digs them in deeply before ripping my skin down to my wrist. I jerk backwards, releasing my arm from his grasp. I fall but before I know what is happening Lyca has gripped me once more.

He inserts his index finger nail into the vein in my wrist. He releases my arm and I try to pull backwards, writhing. When I look to where he entered I realise the skin has fused around his nail, locking it in place. He then swiftly repeats the process on my other arm.

I feel a strange substance journey up each arm. I see the white matter travelling up my left arm, and black up my right. My skin releases the claws and he retracts them.

As each substance travels simultaneously up each arm it seems to dull my pain slightly. When they reach my shoulders the substances travel towards my heart. I watch as they swirl around each other. Then I hear Lyca.

"Sorry about this."

He raises his hands above my heart, claws extended. Lyca whispers "Mutator formarum," before plunging them directly into my heart.

I choke as blood gargles within my now perforated lung. My throat restrictions are instantaneously lifted as I roar out with the intense agony. I thrash around.

"What have you done?" I choke.

The world around me loses focus, my eyes flutter. A sharp object is pushed into my side forcing my focus to return to reality.

"Why?" I hear Dion stammer.

"She must......awake.....a while if she is going to... a chance..." I struggle to interpret the rest as my senses take their leave.

The darkness battles within. I feel every confrontation. I roll over, crunch up in a ball. I tense my hands into a fist, crushing my nails into the skin of my palms, drawing blood.

As I roll onto my back, one arm lands on my chest, burning through my skin instantaneously. Dion rushes forward, grabs my arms. I manage to pull free of his grasp and thrash about wildly. Lyca joins Dion as they take an arm each, cradling my back.

My eyes roll around my head so much I catch a glimpse of Elliott, or so I think. My chest is thrust forwards as my insides are being shredded and twisted.

"How long must she endure this?" Dion's voice strains.

I do not hear Lyca's reply. As I struggle against their combined strength. Suddenly a ruby red light covers my face, I hold my breath. When I can hold it no more I exhale deeply and breathe rapidly. The red light enters my lungs. My eyes roll to the side. A strange sensation overcomes me   as   my   head   falls.   I   am   in   pain   no   longer.

IntERnaL BatTLe

My eyes flutter open. A hand is directly in front of my blurred vision. I grasp it without thought, allowing it to pull me to my feet.

"Ouch," I hold my head, creasing my features.

"Are you okay?" Elliott asks.

I shake my head, "Not really, where are we?"

Elliot peers around, "I'm not sure, but I'm thinking inside your head?"

I frown at him "In my...?"

I take in my surroundings; we are in a desert type landscape filled with extruding rock clusters as far as the eye can see. The land is rugged and rough, with no sign of life what so ever.

"It can't be. Can it?" I mull over the information.

"Last I remember we were in the most horrific pain, then that guy did something and everything went black. Then I woke up and everything was like…" Elliot stares ahead into the distance motioning his arms at the horizon, "…this."

"Lyca was saying something about a battle. You don't think? Do you? Is that what we are doing now?" My face creases in confusion "Surely not, right? Maybe it's just a dream."

Elliott shrugs his shoulders.

I take lead and trudge through the perilous desert we have found ourselves in. Elliott and I do not speak, we only advance, searching for something, anything.

A large rock forms a staircase up ahead. "Hey, you see that?" I nudge Elliott.

"Come on," Elliott pushes forward, rushing up the strange staircase.

I trail behind, less sure-footed than he. None the less we reach the top without any problems. Ahead is a blanket of snow. A blizzard blows the snow upwards. I crease my face peering behind me, a searing desert. I look forward, snow, everywhere.

"Huh?" Elliott shrugs his shoulders before stepping onto the snow.

"No, wait!" I grab for him but miss.

He sinks to his knees, glances back. "It's kind of deep," he smiles.

I turn back once more, what else can I do but move forward and hope for the best? I step off the edge of the rock. The freezing blizzard wreaks havoc on my limbs. When I finally cease plummeting through the layers of snow I realise this will not be simple. The snow reaches the bottom of my waist. I push onwards, each step exhausting. Cutting through the wall of snow with my leg muscles alone consumes masses of energy; I must rest frequently.

This harsh environment takes its toll on both of us. Our bodies freeze, icicles form so swiftly. I glance backwards.

"We haven't made that much progress," my teeth chatter.

"Yes but I can see something ahead, right in the distance."

I squint my eyes, trying to strain vision through the waves of snow. Finally, I catch a glimpse of it. I cannot make out the object as of this moment but there is most defiantly something there.

"I...I see it…" I shudder violently.

Rubbing my arms rapidly, trying in vain to retain some heat.

As we progress the wind picks up speed, dragging the thin layer of snow from the top of the hills. The storm collides with us brutally with such force; it almost feels like the soft, fluffy snow has frozen into icicles which now pound our skin relentlessly.

I offer my hand as a shield for my face, it does not aid me greatly but it eases a little. Our progression is unbelievably slow. With each directional shift in the wind, more drifts accumulate. Mountains seem to form before us.

I glance at Elliott. I can only see a slight silhouette behind the battering storm. At least we are still together, for now. I concentrate on my path ahead. A large drift is forming up ahead. I sigh as I finally reach its base. Our surroundings truly are beautiful, all be it below freezing and arduous, yet I admire the smooth snow in all its glory, I always enjoyed the stuff in my past life. The tiny crystals of the untouched snow glint in the sun.

I fall to my knees, disheartened, as I realise the extent of the climb ahead. The drift is at least two times the size of me. I search the area, praying it does not last the whole length of our surroundings. Surely enough, from the short distance I can see, the drift stretches into the distance, like a large wave.

"I can't make that," I puff to myself.

As I slowly sink within the snow below me, a hand grips my shoulder, encouraging me to my feet. I force my legs to obey and sluggishly return to my previous standing. The snow is above my hips now.

"Come on Lexi, we have to carry on, it's getting deeper very quickly!" Elliott shouts over the howling winds.

"Have you seen that thing?" I shout dumbfounded, "How am I supposed to make it over that?"

"We have to try," he drags me.

I puff aloud, shake my head, "Okay."

Elliott does not hear my reply as he has already pulled ahead of me. I grip hold of my right leg, pull it upwards sharply, removing it from the snow which had engulfed it. I place it in the softer snow ahead. I repeat the process with my left leg, tugging a couple more times before it is finally released.

I breathe heavily as I drag my exhausted body up the ascension. With each step, I seem to slip deeper and deeper into it with it now being up to my stomach. I almost wish I could swim through the waves.

When we are more than halfway up I try to cut through the peak, I push my fully engulfed legs through the snow, creating a path behind. My actions create the desired effect, for a while, until I seem to hit a section of securely compacted snow. I try again to force my legs through the barrier. Exhaustion mixed with a sheer lack of strength forces me backwards. I peer around. Now what? I am very deep and this wall of snow towers over me. I outstretch my arms to their full length with the intent of pulling myself from the ditch and climbing over my barrier.

The moment I place even a minuscule amount of pressure on my arms they instantly sink, the snow claiming them also. I stand back and chuckle insanely. The pressures of exhaustion and the cold strain my senses.

"I made a snow angel."

Elliott once again peers over the edge of my increasing pit. He lies flat on the snow to my left. I stare at him confused. Is he insane?

He then stands up, before lying down in the same spot. He repeats the process a couple more times before testing the area with his foot. Then it hits me. He is compacting the snow, creating a more stable surface to enable me to drag myself out before I sink too far.

I smile at him.

He shouts down to me, his voice a little croaky, "Okay should hold, take my hand."

He reaches down towards me. I grip both hands tightly. He lifts my whole body up and remarkably manages to free me from the trouble I had landed myself in.

I roll over onto my back and catch my breath before thanking Elliott. We make rapid progress this time, careful not to sink too deeply again. The snow sustains our weight more and I only sink to my ankles thankfully; I do not know how long I could have continued like that, with such a strenuous task depleting my energy.

We finally reach the tip of the remaining immense snowdrift. There, planted in the centre of the descent is another set of stairs. I run down the hill at maximum velocity, gravity aiding my speed. I almost topple over but thankfully manage to steady myself, I reach the steps. I place a foot on the first one. Look back before stepping onto it fully.

Where is Elliott? I strain my eyes searching through the blizzard.

"Elliott!" I scream.

No response, the sound of the wind gushing past my ears is my only reply. I begin to panic. I am about to retrace my steps, maybe he has fallen into a hole? I start back when I notice something moving at the tip of the drift. I narrow my eyes, push my head forward, trying to penetrate the blinding snowstorm. It begins the descent and I realise it is Elliott.

I breathe a sigh of relief. He shuffles down the hill more slowly and safely than my crazed speed. As he is about a meter away he stands, smiling and approaches me. I hold out my hand. The moment he is about to make contact, the snow beneath him crumbles and collapses. He plummets down. I panic and try to grasp him. Luckily I manage to get a grip around his wrist. His weight forces me to the ground with speed and I slam hard on the solid steps. My ribs ache from the trauma but I keep a tight hold. It seems that the ground surrounding the step is rather thin I note before making the mistake of peering down the side to see how deep this hole actually is, my heart skips a beat as my blood runs cold.

I gawp in terror; there is no foreseeable end to this chasm. The surrounding ground is jagged and cracked but it looks like Elliott falling through created what seems to be an endless pit. What if I cannot hold on? I would not dare to think what will happen to him.

I gulp, shaking my head. Elliott peers down. A few seconds pass and when he returns my gaze, all colour has drained from his face also. My hands begin to shake. I have not the strength to hold on for much longer.

I contract my biceps towards me. They shake viciously under the strain and merely shoot back to their original position. My body strains against the weight.

Elliott can see the struggle on my features. He gulps before shouting to me "Just let go."

I crease my face in amazement. "What? No! What a stupid thing to say," I stammer.

"You can't pull me up; I don't want to drag you down with me."

My anger rises as the statement sinks in. I find the last strands of my strength. It mixes with my anger and I pull once more. I lift Elliott slightly and he manages to grasp the edge of the step with his right hand.

"Pull yourself up and over me if you can."

He tenses his muscles. Places great tension on my arm as he slowly clambers up the side of the rock eventually he is on top of me. I sigh in relief as he slides from my back to safety. He peers over the edge once more and I hear him gulp.

I lie a while, catching my breath, or so I try to convince myself.

"Thank you, Lexi, you saved me" Elliott places a hand on my shoulder.

I do not respond.

"Are you okay?"

"Yes. Can you help me up?"

I curl my knees toward my stomach and with Elliott's assistance, I am able to stand. My ribs remain sore. I breathe deeply.

I step forward and cringe, holding where my rib cage is.

"What's wrong?" Elliott asks.

"I think I have bruised them" I state, praying that I have not broken something.

Elliott assists me up the stairs and the pain eases slightly as I keep up my speed. When we are at the top of the stairs I notice that we are suddenly surrounded by water.

The water laps against the step, soaking my foot. It is freezing. I shiver.

"Oh great."

Elliott guides me to the edge before helping me into the water. I tense up and yelp as the cold caresses my body. I instantly lose my colour and begin to violently shake.

Elliott slides in after me, also yelling at the cold.

I try front stroke but my sore ribs will not allow it. I turn onto my back, kick my legs instead.

"Will yy-you wat-ttch out for meee?" I shudder.

"Yyy-yes" Elliot replies.

He picks up speed and takes the lead. I cannot see so I rely on his guidance.

Kicking my legs rapidly warms them a little but I suffer greatly from hypothermia; the majority of my body does nothing to keep my heat contained. I push onwards and slowly I lose feeling in my extremities.

The scenery around us is fixated. Not a single ripple of water, nor a cloud in the yellow sky, alter, even the smallest amount. It seems as though we replaying the same scene over and over. My body loses stamina, slowing my pace thus impacting me greatly. We carry on regardless, our eternal stretch of water draining our energy.

"How much further Elliott?" I shout.

Silence. I shout again, more frantic. As I open my mouth again water creeps in, it seeps down my throat and enters my lungs. I cough violently, flailing in the water. The saltwater violates my mouth as I spit out the vile tainted substance.

I mange to turn myself around, staying afloat only by my legs. I search the distance. My colour drains; Elliott is nowhere to be seen. Panic gurgles in the depths of my stomach, threatening to rise and overpower me.

"Elliott!" I scream as loud as possible.

My eyes strain as I try in vain to locate him. Time passes slowly as I drift along on my own. I search desperately for him. Then I see it.

Just ahead, the set of stairs I have been praying for. I redirect myself and swiftly make my way to rest and hopefully, freedom. I quicken my strokes desperate to reach my destination. As I stare above at the unchanging sky I sigh with relief. Counting to ten I manoeuvre myself to face the steps. These rock steps appear to be granite. I admire how beautiful the aesthetic is; a gentle stream flows down the steps and conjoins with the vast stretch of water, gently rippling it outwards. The only water movement I have seen this entire time.

As I begin pulling myself from the grasp of the water I realise there is something I have forgotten. It is in the back of my memory but I cannot seem to place my finger on it. I stall a moment, wavering on the edge. What is it? I rack my brain and my arms begin to shake from the weight of holding myself up. Then it hits me.

"Elliott!" I shout aloud.

How could I forget about him? What is wrong with me? I allow my arms to give way and I slump back into the water.

"Elliott where *are* you?" I speak to myself, anxiety creeping in my tones.

I swim around the exterior of the steps, searching for my lost friend. Then I see it, a small bubble surfaces, it floats around for a millisecond before bursting a little ahead of me. I do not wait for another to surface or for my suspicions to be confirmed. I inhale a large breath before plunging myself into the depths. My eyes ache as the salt attacks them viciously. I ignore the discomfort as I follow the slight bubble trail. I can see nothing other than a meter ahead of me.

The water is shrouded in darkness, impairing my vision greatly. Just as I am about to resurface I spot a figure. It is sinking slowly, lifelessly. I doubt my breath can sustain me any longer, but if I resurface and dive down again he will have sunk further. I need to make a swift decision.

The answer is clear. I dive down, pumping my leg muscles to their capacity. I burst down towards my friend. My lungs strain as my limited air intake affects me. I manage to grasp his arm. As soon as I have a firm hold I swim back up. My legs work even harder and my progress is so much slower with the extra weight but I must not give up.

Air, running out, my body flails in the water. The surface is so far away. Vision impairs, my head becomes light as images flash before my eyes. My family, friends, my life, Dion and then something tears the images in half. An enormous werewolf, it releases a throaty laugh of achievement. It seems to be saying something.

"Even if it is not at our hands, you are doomed," it laughs again.

My body sluggishly churns back to life; I find strength from that evil image. It will not defeat me. My legs begin to kick at the water once more. The surface looms. We burst through and I make a disturbing noise as I engulf the surrounding air. My lungs ache as I try to catch my breath. Strength draining I manage to pull Elliott to the steps. I struggle to haul my mass from the water. Once on the first step, I take a grip of Elliott with my free hand. I heave. My muscles shake before the strain becomes too much and Elliott plunges into the water once more. I manage to keep hold. I dig down deep, deep into the depths of my strength.

"Come on!" I puff as I haul his mass once more.

He edges up a little.

"Yes, yes come on that's it," I stammer.

After one almighty pull, I manage to finally free Elliott from the water's grasp. He lands on top of me. I wriggle from under him and flip him over. My ear on his heart. No beat. Panic takes over.

"Noo!" I shriek at the top of my lungs. I pound the watery step with my fists in a blind rage.

Through my tears springs an idea. I place my hands where Elliott's heart lies. I grasp my other hand on top and pump down hard. I do this numerous times before breathing air into his lungs.

After a couple of attempts desperation sets in.

"I don't know how to do this!" I cry, "please, come back Elliott."

I bury my head into his abdomen; I pound my fist once more on his chest this time, a small spark transfers from it. After a couple of seconds, I feel movement. My action forced him to come back to me. He coughs up the water from his lungs and spits it to the side.

"Oh thank you," I screech.

I launch my hands around him "I thought you were a goner! I squeeze him tightly.

He coughs a little more, "easy on the lungs, you're squishing me kid."

I pull back "Sorry, what happened?"

I search his eyes, which swirl with confusion, trying to find my answer.

He scratches his head, "the last thing I remember is something whispering then I was grabbed and dragged under…"

My face mirrors that of terror yet relief. I do not dwindle on Elliott's words; the thought of a presence under that water, observing, creeping towards us. I shake it from my mind, placing it in a far corner of my psyche.

I help my friend to his feet, allowing him to distribute his weight onto me. We take the steps, side by side, struggling to keep friction against the slippery, smooth surface. Elliott falls back a little, I edge him onwards; he is exhausted.

I count the steps to pass the time as we ascend. Twenty, twenty-one… thirty-five, thirty-six. My breathing deepens as exhaustion takes hold, my limbs grow weary and weak, my muscles ache and shake violently under the strain. We decide it would be wise to rest for a while. I stare upwards; our ascension vanishes into the clouds above. I sigh.

"Are you okay?" I ask Elliott.

"Yes, I'll be fine. How much longer do we have to go?"

I peer upwards; shrug my shoulders "I don't know. I can't see the end."

I sit beside Elliott as we both claw back much-required energy to enable us to push onwards and upwards.

"So how do you think we are holding up in this battle?" I half chuckle dryly.

"Hmmm not so great, but at least were both alive. Who knows what would happen if one of us died. If this really is a battle to fight off whatever is inside you maybe we wouldn't win."

I think over his suggestion a while. I feel his statement is a little farfetched. So he thinks we are battling the blackness spreading through my body and we have to complete all this to beat the disease? And then what? Will I remain in this state or will I be allowed control of my body once more? I shake my head, I still lean more towards the gesture of this simply being a dream, it is strange admittedly, that Elliott is here with me but not as strange as an internal battle…

After a little rest, we finally reach step number seventy-one. This step is extremely important. It is the second to last feat of our strenuous climb. Our bodies are worn and shattered from exhaustion. One large step lies in front of us. I reach up, grasp the edge of the rock. I can only just reach it. I pull myself upwards. My arms shake and threaten to give way. Elliott pushes my bottom upwards aiding me. After a couple of seconds and one large shuffle, I manage to reach my destination. I lie on my back, panting heavily.

"Just…..getting," I huff, "my breath back."

After a couple of moments rest, I heave myself onto my stomach.

"How are we going to do this?" Elliott asks, looking defeated.

I peer over the edge. Elliott is taller than me, therefore, can reach up further than me.

"I'll have to pull you from up here."

Elliott's face creases in confusion. He laughs loudly.

When he finally ceases his laughing fit he looks to me once more. My features are stern. His smile drops and he creases his forehead.

"You're not kidding are you?"

I smile crookedly and shake my head.

"It won't work, you're not strong enough."

"Pft have faith," I almost shout, trying to convince myself more than anything, of my surreal suggestion.

He shrugs his shoulders and stretches towards me.

"Okay, if you can pull yourself up as much as possible I should be able to drag you the rest of the way," I smile, "I hope," I mumble under my breath.

He grasps the slippery surface, jumps from the step, propelling himself just under half of the slab. I instinctively grab his hands, preventing him from sliding backwards.

I would assume we only have a few chances at this before our bodies become too exhausted. I shake my head, close my eyes and heave him towards me. He slides a little. Elliott is trying desperately to gain grip with his feet, but the slippery water washes his holding away each time.

I wriggle into a sitting position. I plant my feet pushing off them I haul Elliott up a little more. After a few exhausting minutes of heaving, Elliott manages to curve his leg up and put it onto the step. He takes his weight and I fall backwards.

My chest heaves as I pant rapidly. Sweat rampages my body, soaking me even more.

I shiver violently from the strain. Elliott shuffles up next to me. "Thank you," he half-smiles.

"For what?" I stammer.

"Not letting go" He closes his eyes.

We lie in silence for a long time, allowing our extremities time to regenerate. My breathing eventually calms and I stare into the sky above. Not a cloud appears in the sky. I realise that we are both lying in the small gentle waterfall which forms directly behind me. Its source cannot be perceived as it appears to just begin life in the air, a little higher than the step.

I reach to my side. "I think we have rested long enough, I want to get out of this place. What do you think?"

"Yes, let's get going."

We both roll onto our sides in unison and haul ourselves up. My limbs ache and stiffen slightly. We edge towards the border. I peer around. I glare at the nothingness... I almost burst into tears.

I simply stare dumbfounded. Scanning the area toughly results in nothing. The slab we are perched on is the end of the trail we have been following. I cannot comprehend where we made a mistake, to land ourselves here, with no way forward. Yet here we are…

Turning to Elliott for some direction I see his head is slumped. He must be replicating my feelings. Then I realise there is something wrong with him. Elliott's eyes have turned entirely black. I reach out for him as his head snaps up in my direction, bones cracking disgustingly.

"What's wrong?" I ask, terror gripping me.

He cocks his head a little to the left, bones creaking with each movement.

"Elliott you're scaring me!" I stammer.

His lips spread into the largest smile. Straight from ear to ear. His head twists in the other direction as the smile grows. It reminds me of something I cannot place my finger on. I stare bewildered and terrified... Then what he does next forces a shrill yelp to leave my lips. Elliott spreads his arms to the side, flaps them like a bird and jumps over the edge. I scream, lunging desperately for him. I was not swift enough to grasp him and he plummets. His figure slowly decreases in size until it is too small for my eyes to pick up. I stare over the edge, distraught, my hand still reaching for him.

For an eternity I remain in the same position. Reaching for my lost friend. Manic thoughts running rampant through my mind. Finally, I manage to regain control of my emotions and force myself to think logically.

Tears stream down my face as I try desperately to make sense of this lunacy. Then I remember that he was staring at one specific spot before. I take his original position, wipe the tears from my face, un blurring my vision I search for answers. I stare as the water ripples around the spot he was fixated on.

"What did you see?" I pound the water in frustration.

As I force the water away with my fist I spot something carved in the granite. The word faith is carved along with an arrow which goes down over the cliff and out of sight. My forehead creases as confusion sets in. I peer over the edge.

"Faith," I repeat to myself continuously.

"Faith, what does that mean?"

I pace around in the surface water.

"To have faith in something you need to have reliance and trust in it."

I scratch my head.

"Elliott leapt over the edge, did he have faith in it?"

Then I slap myself as it clicks into place.

"He did a leap of faith over the edge."

I inch forward, leaning shyly, terrified I peer over. Nothing as far as my eyes can see. I shudder.

"I really shouldn't put my trust in a carving... Right?" I shake my head as if anyone but myself was going to answer that question; I am the only person here.

"No...I can't..."

I search around for another option and after searching for a solution long and hard I realise that other than returning the way I came, there is no other perceivable way from this rock. I swallow hard, trying to dislodge my heart from my throat. My legs begin to shake as I fight with my instincts and my mind. I pace up and down the stone slab, palm to my cheek. No. I cannot do that. How stupid would I be if I simply jumped off? There is no way that is what I am supposed to do!

"What the hell" I shrug, running full speed to the edge.

As I am about to plunge into the abyss below I change my mind and stop instantly. I teeter before losing balance and slipping from my holding. I reach out desperately and manage to grasp a shard of rock. My fingers strain from the weight. My left-hand slips and before I have a chance to replace it, my right hand gives way and I plummet into the depths of the unknown.

I scream at such a frequency my ears ring. I close my eyes, awaiting my crumpled demise. A couple of minutes pass before I open my eyes surprised I have not yet perished. I am greeted by clouds rushing past me as I fall. I glance below, no ground seems to appear. I stare upwards, I see nothing but the beautiful white of the fluffy clouds I have passed through.

Around thirty minutes pass. I am still falling. Will I ever escape my eternal descent? I decided to cross my legs and arms, fearful that if left loosely by my side they would get injured with the velocity.

After what seems like another twenty minutes I become extremely agitated. My mind churns over different possibilities but none feasible. I puff aloud, rest my head in my hand still keeping limbs close to my body. The clouds stop rushing past me and I glance around. Finally, I look down. Nothing more has altered. More time passes before I eventually notice the ground gaining distance on me, rapidly. I panic.

"I knew it! I shouldn't have jumped!"

Fear grips me as gravity forces me on my stomach, I am now falling to the ground, staring directly at my future. I try in vain to turn around; I do not wish to view this. Alas, my fate has been set for no matter how much I try, I cannot turn myself. I accept my destiny. The smooth black floor fills all of my vision.

"A couple more seconds and I will..."

I smash into the ground with such force the rock cracks and shards veer off into different directions, half a second allows me to witness the large pool of blood surrounding me. I lose...

HoUnDS of hELL

yes flicker. Bright lights blind and burn all at once. I close them slightly introducing small amounts of the painful light until my eyes adjust. Every inch of my body aches when not even in motion. I feel as though I have been smashed against a wall, over and over. What happened? My eyes finally adjust and I analyse my surroundings.

The room I have found myself in is large in stature. Rainbows dance where the light reflects across the smooth pearl-like walls. The entrance is to the left of my position. It appears to be crystallized although it is not transparent; I cannot see anything through it. I stare at the frame encasing the door, it is very peculiar. Two hounds stand on their hind legs either side, their forelegs stretched upwards resting on the crystallised door. Nothing more lies in the room apart from a black glass table, chair and a small set of draws beside the bed I have been laid on. The furniture is extremely out of place in this room.

An itch on my head begins to irritate me. I ignore it at first as I examine my whereabouts confused, but the irritation grates on me so I stretch to relieve myself. My arm stops mid-action, something is preventing me from moving it any further. I peer down, puzzled. My heart races as terror sets in. My arms and legs have been restrained. The large black leather straps appear to be those used for a patient of a psychiatric hospital. I tug with great difficulty. Pain shoots throughout every inch of my body and I have no choice but to relent. Sweat runs from my head. My vision is fuzzy and I am disorientated. The world keeps repeatedly fading away before coming back into view.

Something beeps beside me. I turn to my left dazed. A tube has been inserted into my arm. I follow it to a machine that has a bag of neon blue substance contained. It beeps once more, exerts some of the strange substance into the drip. It crawls toward my vein. I tug once more, trying to stop it from entering my body. What is that stuff? My restrictions will not allow my success and after a couple of seconds, it disappears into my arm. The substance burns as it enters and I whimper quietly gritting my teeth.

"What's going on?" I choke, vision blurred.

Something in my mouth impairs my speech. I strain my eyes and find that I am attached to a ventilator. Although the machine differs from those I have viewed before it is most definitely the same sort of instrument. The tube inserts down my throat and is attached to a machine which breathes for me.

I turn back as the other machine makes noise once more. It does not release the blue substance this time. It must be on some sort of timer, the noises alerting you of a certain amount of time passed. Various other machines are beside me. Wires are attached to my chest, my head and my hands. Another tube has been inserted into my other arm but I cannot see to which this one is attached.

There is nothing I can do. I am utterly helpless, I have awoken in a strange room, without any memories of how or why and I am trapped. I could try bursting through my restraints with my energy. That is if I have enough reserved. I concentrate on my left restraint. A weak blue light surrounds the buckle. The restrain vibrates as the end slowly moves. I start to shake from the effort. After a moments rest, I begin again. The light intensifies a little and the leather slithers through the first loop. It inches out from the metallic buckle. Now for the pin holding it in place. Breathing more rapidly I manage to make the pin vibrate slightly. After a few seconds, it pulls free from its holding and my arm is liberated from its shackle. The restraint falls loosely around the side of the bed.

I drag my weak mass into sitting position, with great effort and tenderness I manage to sustain myself. I get to work on the other restraints. Fumbling numbly as I stare at the door, praying no one will enter. I manage to free myself. Feeling around the ventilator I try to decide what to do. I detach the tube from the inserted pipe. I place my hand on it, pull slowly. I wretch, scratching my throat as I pull. I almost exit my stomach contents as I try to force the tube from my throat. I cannot budge it for some reason as if it is stuck. I decide against wasting time trying to pull it out in here. Once I am out of this place I will remove it, but for now, it will have to stay. I transfer a small amount of energy to my throat to try and relieve the pressure of the tube. It almost reaches the point of feeling as though it is no longer even there.

I rip into the wires, tearing them from me rapidly. The machine's alarm siren loudly as life is no longer detected. I pull the tube from my arm before turning to the blue coloured substance. It beeps, releasing a drop.

Don't think so! I tell myself.

The substance dribbles onto the floor. I stare at the ground. My bare feet dangle off the side of the bed. The white floor looks as though it is slippery. I lower myself gently. Resting all my weight on the bed I manage to stand. I move awkwardly, little by little releasing more weight onto my legs. They are stiff and ache but show no signs of giving way. I release the bed. The strange gown I am dressed in tangles under my feet as I shuffle along the floor. I tug at it eventually freeing it.

I must hurry; surely those alarms will alert my captor as to my escape. As I make my way to the door I try to remember how I got here. My mind is blank, not one memory of late can be accessed. Strange. I shake my head, concentrate on the door. I look for a handle but cannot find one. I examine it. The door is two times the size of me in height and stretches out much wider than me. I push on it. It is sealed tightly. I gaze at the hounds either side of me. They are enormous, their heads turned towards me. I get the strange feeling that they are watching me for some reason. I shiver at the thought. Regardless of my irrational fears, the key to opening the door must be something to do with them. I place a shaky hand over one side, pressing against it. Nothing happens. I notice a small marking on the inside of its right ankle in the shape of a tornado. I slide my hand across it, examining with my fingers. As I make contact the crystallized eyes of the hound glow green. I pull my hand away instantly frightened. What did I do? After a second or so they diminish and return to normality. The adjacent hound also bears the same marking. An idea interrupts my thought. I touch the left marking before shuffling to the right one, sweeping my hand over it. Both sets of eyes glow green. I half-smile at my achievement.

The hounds' heads rapidly break free from their holdings, bowing to my request before reaching towards the door, encasing their jaws deep into the crystal creating a large crack. The haste in which they animated, accompanied by the deafening sound of crumbling rock makes me jump from my skin. I did not expect them to come to life! My heart pounds as their heads return to position and become still once more. The cracks dispense, spiralling towards each other as if racing, they make contact as they reach the centre. The door bursts into millions of pieces revealing a brightly lit corridor. I rush through not wasting any time. I turn around wondering how to close the door, I am met with surprise when I see that it has already sealed. I press against it. Solid. How strange.

Just as I am about to make my great escape, a sickly feeling overcomes me bringing a wave of dizziness with it. Then a pain in my chest halts me in my tracks as it tears through my ribcage. After a couple of seconds, most of my ailments pass and I push forward neglecting to even spare a thought for what my body had just experienced. I do not know where I am heading but I carry on regardless. As I rush past a mirror I catch a glimpse of my reflection, I spare a moment to inspect myself. My battered torn image does not even look like *ME* anymore. The tube that sticks awkwardly to the right of my mouth which I had all but forgotten about, my right wrist is in a cast. Many bandages encase my wounds; I look like an Egyptian mummy. These coupled with all of the visible bruising and scars littered across my small frame bring tears to my eye. What has happened to me?

Ahead I hear footsteps. I manage to fumble myself into another corridor just in time. The strange people stroll past without looking down my way. I breathe a sigh of relief before peering around the corner, ensuring I will not experience any unwanted encounters. When confident I carry on down the hall.

These corridors all appear the same to me. I notice various signs strewn about but nothing I can read in my state. Just as I go to round yet another corner I hear someone shout behind me. I turn horrified. A large burly man is pointing and shouting at me.

"Wait. Stop!" I hear him shout as I vanish from sight.

I have to think quickly. I can but merely shuffle along with little progress whereas he is able-bodied and can catch up with ease. I turn a corner to my left. A couple of steps into it I see another turning to my right. I rush as quickly as possible, praying he will not take the same path. The pain in my chest returns and my vision blurs once more. I struggle onwards. I head down my new route glancing backwards regularly. A large door looms ahead similar to the first I encountered. I repeat the process animating the hounds. They crack the stone and as it spreads the door dispenses. I usher myself through.

Incredulously I have managed to find my way outside. The dark blue grass blows gently in the wind. Many large modern structures surround me. I look up; the sky above shimmers out of place as if manufactured. I shake my head; I cannot hang around out in the open with my appearance. Without glancing back I travel down the back of the building and into a shadowed street, shrouded in darkness due to the large building ahead. My bare feet scrape across the smooth ground as I trudge onwards. I concentrate on them, keeping my head down in case spotted.

An eternity passes before I emerge from the darkened street. The light makes me cringe; my eyes had adjusted to the darkness. I hear someone behind me. I search for my next route. Another door ahead. It is my only option. I initiate the process quickly. I rush through without a second thought. My jaw falls slack as I realise where I have ended up. I am back in the corridor I began my escape or at least a similar one, after all, they do all look the same. The large man is ahead of me once more. He charges, shouting, waving his hands. With my heart pounding, I rotate on the spot and exit from where I came. Unfortunately, I do not end up back on the street, I simply find myself in the original room in which I awoke. Confusion creases my features as I scratch my head. What the hell is going on?

I do not stop to ponder. I merely open the door and exit the room once more. I turn left in the corridor this time, praying I can escape via this alternate route. I manage to get to the end of the corridor without encountering anyone. The corridor comes to an end, left or right? I turn left. Two people block this corridor, they advance on my position. I swivel around and take the right turning. Just as I am about to pass the second door on my right I notice two people appear ahead of me.

I slap my head, taking my only option, I backtrack. I rush along as fast as my broken body will allow. I steal a glance as I come alongside the first door. Four people are advancing on my position. Just as I am about to open it someone grabs my shoulders. I gulp; making eye contact with my captor. It is the large man that has been following me all of this time. He is dressed all in white, with a mask covering his mouth and nose. From under it, I can see he is smiling.

My chest burns and I convulse, my vision blurs. Through impaired vision I see his eyes glow bright yellow. This image forces me into my past. I recess deeper as insanity digs its claws deep within the chambers of my mind. I see Splite standing before me. I thrash wildly. I scream out but only muffled sounds escape my tube. Splite slides behind me as I try to escape; he links his arms under my shoulders and back towards himself, restraining me.

I wriggle and writhe under his impeccable strength. My body screams out in agony as I force it beyond its pain barrier. A demon-like creature rushes in front of me. Its jagged teeth protrude from the disgusting mask it wears. Holding out my arm it produces a needle. I pull my arm free, but a second and third join forces and hold my arm in place.

"Noo," I cry, or at least try to.

The needle enters my arm, just as my captor is about to insert the black substance into my veins someone shouts from behind. I cannot hear or see who is speaking but the creature halts its action. It nods before retracting the needle. The beast backs away from me and my legs collapse. I fall to my knees, relief sweeping over me. My head falls forward. A couple of seconds pass before a finger lifts my chin. My vision clears a little as I realise who kneeling before me. Dion.

I try to throw my arms around him but I am still restrained by... I swivel my head rapidly, heart leaping into my throat. It was not Splite restraining me, yet the large man. I breathe a sigh of relief and turn back to Dion.

"What are you doing?" Dion's eyes are filled with guilt as he helps me to my feet.

All of my fears, all of my turmoil simply fades away at the sight of him, my saviour once more. All must be well if he is here with me. Dion activates the door and we enter the side room. He lifts me gently onto the bed. My body seemingly sinks into the mattress as it relaxes. Another man enters the room. I instinctively spring up. He has long black hair and looks much like Dion but is a great deal larger with a muscular build. His nose is slightly pointed with a small scar across the ridge. His eyes are only one colour; black.

This strange man pushes me onto my back gently. I try to resist but my body gives in and I have not the energy to fight.

"She is strong," the man turns to Dion.

"Indeed…" He nods before resting his gaze upon me once more. His eyes are now filled with hope yet mixed with sorrow.

"Okay, I am going to remove the tube Lexi," the odd-looking man states.

Dion places his hands on my shoulders and the man takes hold of the top of the tube. He takes a syringe and deflates something inside the tube and pulls slowly, I heave. He picks up speed and the tube vibrates, scratching the inside of my gullet. I struggle but Dion holds me in place. With a final swift movement, he removes the tube and I retch uncontrollably. Finally, I gain control of myself. My gagging ceases.

"Where am I? Who are you?" I croak painfully. My voice is deep and tender.

I cough creating an immense burning sensation within my throat. My hands wrap around my neck as if such action will assist my pain. Obviously, it does nothing to dull it.

"Slight memory loss, she does not know who I am. It will most likely return, but I do not know for sure," he ignores my question, directing his speech toward Dion.

"This is Lyca. He saved you. What is the last thing you remember?"

I strain, searching my mind for any memory. I feel as though the moment I reach out for them they simply slip further away and the only thing I can think of is one word, a word I do not even understand myself...

"Elliott..." I choke.

"Elliott?" Lyca raises an eyebrow.

"Long story which will be explained at a more appropriate time," Dion blushes with a glimmer of anger.

Lyca parts my gown, inspecting my chest. The exposure makes me feel uncomfortable but I resist the urge to bat him away and after a couple of minutes, he places it down before picking up the tube of the blue substance. Replacing the needle he grips my arm.

I tense against him, my breathing becomes shallow as I panic.

"No, get off me!" I try to shout, thrusting my arm away.

He grabs it once more, pulling it towards him. I fight but he is much stronger than me and I lose the battle instantly. Flicking my arm he finds a vein before placing the needle into it. Then he replaces the restraint. Before I can even reach over he is at my other side, fumbling with the second buckle.

The machine beeps and a large dose of the blue substance runs into my arm. The intensity of the burn increases as the duration is prolonged due to such a large volume of the liquid.

"Dion...." I shriek.

The room spins as panic attacks me. My heart pulsates, my palms become sweaty as I lose my senses to my feeling of impending doom. Dion, noticing my spiral places a finger under my chin directing my eye line to match his.

"Lexi, be still," his voice is firm as he kneels before me.

"I.....I can't. I don't have control, my hearts going to explode," I whisper.

My arms begin to glow blue. Dion frowns at me straining his handsome features in disappointment. His face only a few inches from my own.

"I know an excuse when I hear one Lexi. You are strong, do not deceive yourself into thinking you are a powerless victim to your own emotions."

Almost as soon as Dion's words penetrate a wave of relief rushes over me. I manage to calm my breathing as my palpitations begin to reduce. Although my hands still shake slightly the bulk has dissipated and my light fades.

"What was that? It felt like I was having a heart attack or something" I open my eyes to meet his gaze.

"You had a panic attack."

"Really? I've never had one before."

"Sometimes they can simply just happen even if you have never had one."

He pauses.

"Trust me when I say that we are helping you. This treatment is needed to overcome this bizarre ordeal."

He sits on the bed beside me, tucks a piece of hair that has landed over my eyes behind my ear tenderly. Emotions run wild as I think of Dion in more of a romantic way than I have ever before. The feelings confuse me and I force them back down. Not allowing my secret desires permission to surface and ruin everything.

"You were attacked by a werewolf."

A vision of teeth and a large mass of fur flashes before my eyes. I gasp.

"It tried to turn you but somehow did not manage to complete the process. Although you should have turned, remarkably you did not, but the infection was spreading."

A flash of claws rammed into my heart. I glare at my chest remembering partial fragments.

"The blackness was infesting your body and would have either killed you or turned you into one of them but we do not know which would have happened. Luckily we managed to escape and I brought you to Lyca. He tried to counteract the process which is when you blacked out. You have been unconscious for three weeks."

"Three weeks?" I exclaim.

Dion nods, "yes, we brought you to the medical facilities and prayed for the best. This substance is still countering the remaining virus, assisting your internal battle. Which still has not been won, but at least you are alive and awake."

A tear forms but he scratches his eye removing it before anyone could witness his sorrow. I lie back in silence a moment as I allow the facts to sink in.

"Are the restraints necessary?" I hear Dion ask.

"Well the process is quite painful can she be trusted to not remove it? Without this she will most certainly not win this battle, with it at least she has a slim chance."

"She understands the risks she can be trusted."

Lyca raises an eyebrow before whispering "Are you sure? We cannot afford to risk losing such attributes to something as minor as restraints."

"I am sure!" Dion states forcefully.

"As you wish."

Lyca and Dion unbuckle my arms and lean me up against the pillow.

My chest bursts into agony once more as my vision blurs. I groan, clawing at my chest.

Lyca and Dion rush to my side in a panic. Dion pries my hands from me whilst Lyca examines where I was clawing. My vision clears remarkably fast, allowing me to view what Lyca is inspecting.

The left side of my chest, encircling my heart is a large area of black skin with blue veins spread throughout. The horrific sight seemingly shocks my memories into place and my discomfort finally passes.

"I remember the attack, it stabbed my chest and I screamed. Then it fell backwards, bleeding, holding its ears. The blackness spread so quickly," I cry, running a hand over it. Recalling my image in the mirror alongside this new deformity I begin to spiral.

"Look at the state of me!" My anger flourishes. "I am disgusting. I already had enough scars and wounds."

I frantically point out my deformities; the fused fangs of the horse from our home, my missing finger from training, the scars Splite inflicted all over my body. Tears form as my emotions run rampant. I cannot contain them. I take a deep breath as my anger flourishes. My body is disfigured. How could anyone ever look at me again? I disgust even myself. Why have I been tormented this way? I feel the energy build within me. It intensifies, growing in size. My eyes begin to glow blue followed shortly by my arms. Clenching my fists and gritting my teeth a burst of pure energy erupts from my hand impacting the door with great velocity. It shatters into a thousand pieces. The shards then cease their descent and glow blue. My anger rampages as the shards pulsate. I see nothing but red.

Suddenly Dion snaps me from my downward spiral, realising what will happen if I allow this to continue I try to calm myself. I locate my anger receptacle forcing it back down. I will not allow it free reign, not this time.

I flick my other hand at the shards and they swarm around the large gaping hole I created. They smash into different shards forming a large piece of crystal. When the crystal covers the entirety of the door I encourage the edges to manipulate and fuse. The door shimmers a moment before returning to its normal state as though nothing had happened.

My energy levels die down and with it my blue glow. The last to fade are my eyes. They eventually return to a normal colour. I shut them, turning onto my side utterly ashamed of my outburst. Why can I not control myself?

"Are you okay?" Dion asks after a long silence.

I nod in reply before gaining enough courage to open my eyes. Lyca is frozen in place, staring at the door in awe.

"I'm so sorry," I stammer, my sore throat breaking up my words slightly.

Lyca wanders over to the door. He sweeps a hand over each hound and the door opens. He closes it instantly with the wave of a hand and turns back to me.

I gulp as terror engulfs me. What will he say, will he be angry? My terror soon fades as when he turns to me, he does not bare an angry scowl, but a smile.

"That was quite something," he beams.

"Huh?" I question his excitement.

He does not respond to my question.

"Are you sure you are okay?" Lyca repeats Dion's earlier question.

"Yes, anger....is an issue for me....but I'm okay."

His smile broadens. Turning to leave he lays down his orders

"You must rest. I bid you both farewell."

I turn to speak to Dion but before I even manage to make full circle my eyes begin to close and within seconds I enter the world of dreams.

BatTLe

LLexi" Dion's voice booms through the wall jolting me from
my slumber.

I erect myself, instantly awake. I stare around. I have
been moved to a different room. This one is similar to the previous yet is
laid out differently and has more contents than the very basic one in which
I first awoke.

The door shatters to the left of me. A black curtain surrounds it and
after a second or so Dion emerges from behind.

He approaches as a smile creeps across his face.

"How are you feeling?"

"Confused and weary," I croak, my throat still raw from the tube.

I fumble with the crumpled quilt surrounding me. I avoid Dion's
gaze as I try to gather my courage.

"What is it?" Dion presses, lifting my chin to meet his gaze.

"Well I was thinking about what happened and realised I don't
actually know what happened. I don't even remember anything from my
life except you and those beasts."

"More memory loss? When you awoke previously you
remembered more than you do now, how odd. It will be okay, they will
return I am sure."

He smiles comfortingly.

"The way werewolves convert their prey into their ranks is to inject Rube directly into the heart."

I interrupt "So they don't bite or scratch them?"

He chuckles "That is a stereotypical remark. The werewolves have advanced greatly. Many are very intellectual with the possession of our abilities'. They have a partially governed society in the way that they do not transform all their prey into a beast. Most chose wisely, selecting those that will positively provide for their ranks. If they turned people with a scratch their ranks would be much greater in volume but significantly diminished in every other way. Obviously, some chose not to follow these rules and rampage but most see the sense and obey."

I shiver as his words hit me with great force. All colour drains from my skin. My stomach churns inside as a sickly feeling rises. I gulp before speaking.

"S.... so I am going to turn into one of them?" I strain horrified.

I manage to push my bile back into the depths from where it had risen. I hold control over my stomach, for now.

"It is a possibility."

His words cut through me like a knife. My heart sinks as my ducts overwhelm, spilling the salty tears onto my cheeks. My whole world spins as I contemplate my fate. Life as a werewolf will not be acceptable.

"No! I refuse to become one of them. I will end myself before I let that happen!" Tears stream down my face as my temper rises once more.

"Calm down Lexi," he places a firm yet comforting hand on my shoulder, "you are still in battle but the prognosis looks promising."

I return his stare. "Promising?" I sniffle.

"As I have said they change their prey with Rube injected into the heart."

"Which is what it did to me," I cough as my throat burns.

I place my hand over it.

"Yes but it seems the beast did not have time to finish. Although the process is rapid, you must have reacted instantly and repelled the threat. The claws usually embed and cannot be removed until the process has finished. Those here have only ever seen it once before."

"What happened?"

Dion shuffles uncomfortably.

"He died."

My hands grow cold, my body numb. I begin to shake. My head droops as I allow the words to penetrate.

"There is a difference, he did not last as long as you have. He could not speak when brought here. They did not know what he was suffering from and although they tried everything, this situation was not even thought of. He died and the answers died with him."

"Why did he die? Should he not have turned?"

"Yes he should have turned and now with this knowledge we can only assume, either the poison ended him or, he somehow ended his own life, knowing what he would become and that he could not be saved from that fate."

A memory sparks into my mind as I remember the conversation between Lyca and Dion about him. A single tear forms within my eye, I allow it to fall; I sympathise with his situation.

"Formarem," I whisper confused by the memory.

"Mutator formarum," Dion corrects me.

"What does it mean?"

"The Houndori are named so as they have special abilities and that is a process. The place we reside in is their home but they are extremely powerful and many of our kind look up to the Houndori. It has become somewhat of a neutral place of admiration. Many different variations of species meet here, seeking advice, shelter amongst other things."

"They have extensive knowledge about the world and specialise in medical arts, in which we are located right now. The most imperative fact about the Houndori is that they are Therianthropes. Or a Lycan if you wish to name them something a tad more simple," he chuckles.

"What is that?" I ask eyebrows raised.

Dion thinks a moment before speaking.

"It is a different strain of lycanthropy."

My blood runs cold.

"What!" I shudder.

"Yes it is correct but although it is a form of werewolf genetics, it is nothing like it. There is a similarity in that they can shift their forms from humans into that of a wolf. Lyca is a therianthrope."

Silence befalls the room as I contemplate this new information. I think back to my encounters with the beasts that so easily demolish lives. If these genes are one and the same, how can they not have that destructive instinct?

I shake the thoughts from my head.

"They can shape shift into wolves, werewolves have permanently shifted their form into that of a more powerful disfigured wolf."

I hold my head as it aches from all the information.

"So what exactly is this Mutatum form spell then?" I ask, head still lowered.

"It is the process he carried out on you..." Dion ceases his sentence as if unfinished, holding back something.

I look up expectantly; he avoids my gaze.

"Yes I understand that, but what does it mean?"

He returns my gaze but does not speak, his features appear uncomfortable.

"I know you're hiding something, you're not good at lying. Just tell me!" my voice stern.

He sighs.

"Very well, the process is much like that of the werewolves transformation, the substance is transferred into the recipient as with you."

My heart sinks as I realise what the process is.

"I have two different genes that are essentially the same in my body?"

Dion nods in response.

My emotions swirl as fear and despair threaten to take control.

"What will happen to me?" I struggle to hold back inner feelings.

"We do not know."

"You don't know?!" I shout, "How can you do this to me not knowing?"

"As I said the Houndori are renowned for their knowledge on the medical profession. Lyca worked out that if he counteracted the Rube with their Ebur then you may have a chance. Without it, you would have been slaughtered as soon as you transformed."

"And also my selfish reasons.....I cannot lose you Lexi..." he lifts my chin, his warm smile greets me.

I return his smile with mixed emotions. I allow my body to relax, my emotions to calm as I mull over Dion's words. I did sanction this process. I do remember that surprisingly and I would rather be alive and human, or as human as I will ever be, than one of those beasts.

"Does this mean I will be able to shape shift?" I ask.

He twists his ring as he speaks "I do not know you would be better off speaking with Lyca but I doubt even he will know. As far as we know this has never been attempted before and therefore the results are unknown."

I contemplate the situation for a long time in silence.

"There is one more thing..." he trails off.

More? What more could there be? I think to myself as I stare at him awaiting his words.

He hesitates.

"Okay, I do not wish to keep this from you, so here goes, the process of changing humans, or at least human Magi into Lycans is…just a tiny bit…banned," he raises his brows and half smiles.

I crease mine in response "What do you mean, why is it banned?"

"Well it's a very dangerous process," he presses two fingers together motioning, "it can have a *small* chance of a fate worse than death…" he holds up both hands in a shrugging motion.

A sickly feeling engulfs me as the words penetrate.

"It did not happen to you of course, you certainly would not be here right now speaking to me."

I sit a while processing the information. Dion and Lyca saved my life with some dangerous act that has been banned in their society. I do not know how I feel about all this…

"What if this all goes wrong?"

Dion's head stoops, he avoids my gaze and I instantaneously know the answer. I guess I have known the answer for a long time for if the roles were reversed I would also carry out this act. I slowly twist my waist around, allowing my legs to dangle over the edge of the bed.

"What are you doing?" Dion presses, puzzled by my actions.

"I need to get out of here," I state firmly.

"You cannot leave."

"I am not about to stay in this room forever."

"Yes but…" he stares at the blue drip.

I reach over, pull the bag from its holding and tuck it against my chest tightly. I smile cheekily in response. A slither of liquid squeezes from the bag and drips along the tube. I prepare for the imminent burning sensation. As soon as it reaches my vein the discomfort increases resulting in a small cry escaping my lips.

After the worst passes, I ignore Dion's sympathetic face and concentrate on becoming mobilized. My arms shake vigorously as I distribute all my weight on them, lowering myself.

Finally, my feet impact the cold floor. I release the pressure from one arm, moving one foot forward. My other arm buckles but I manage to stabilize myself after a couple of wavering moments I steady and force my other leg forward. My legs feel as though they are made from lead, I struggle greatly to manoeuvre them but I persist, forcing my muscles to strain, then locking my knee tightly as I switch legs. My progress is agonisingly slow. I manage to make my way up to Dion before exhaustion buckles my legs and I flop. Dion catches me with ease, expectant that this action was inevitable. A slicing pain to my left breast makes me wince silently. What was that?

"I think you should get back into bed," Dion creases his features in concern.

A tinge of anger rises as I curse at all of the sympathies I am receiving. I do not wish for people to feel sorry for me; it merely angers me.

Puffing I turn to Dion "I want to carry on."

He begins to open his mouth, probably to try and convince me otherwise but he does not attempt to create a sentence as realisation forces him to halt; I am stubborn and he will not win this battle with words. He merely bows his head slightly and tucks his arm around my waist luckily avoiding the area causing me pain.

He assists me to the door I wave my hand over the symbol on its right ankle; Dion reaches over for the second symbol. The hounds creak into life, dispensing the door before us. It shatters and we cross the threshold.

As we exit I take in our surroundings, the white walls, numerous doors all the way down the corridor. Very similar to where I last was.

"Where do you want to go?" Dion asks.

"Anywhere away from here," I respond breathlessly.

Shaking his head he obeys my request. We set off turning right. After what seems like an eternity of bends to which I take no notice of, we exit the building.

A couple of odd-looking people are scattered around, each one staring at me strangely. One person has no eyebrows, which looks extremely bizarre. I look at another person, this one has blue coloured skin and does not have a nose. It giggles at me as we pass. I ponder their strange appearances and why they all seemed to be staring at me. Then as I allow my head to drop I realise why they are staring so intently. I am still dressed in a horrible gown that swings open at the back revealing all of my...hidden secrets...to everyone! I blush an intense shade of red.

"Is there anywhere I can get some decent clothes? I feel like a laughing stock."

Dion smiles, raising his brows as we turn left. We walk for about ten minutes taking different streets, my breathing becoming more rampant by the second. I pant heavily when we finally stop. I look up. Two large gates stand before us, shrouded within a forest of multi-coloured trees. The gates are similar to the other doors, two hounds twisted and cursed into the metal. We shuffle towards them. Dion touches a similar tornado symbol. I await the moment that the hounds will spark into life, opening the gate for us. To my surprise they do nothing but remain inanimate, their blackened crystal eyes staring back at me. After a couple more seconds a metallic panel emerges from the symbol. It slides from within then radiates a black light as it pulsates. Dion takes my hand, placing it on the panel. The instant I make contact the gates creak before sliding open.

"What was that?" I ask.

91

"It is like a fingerprint scanner I guess but instead it scans for specific energy. It is essentially a lock, not allowing anyone passage unless they have been programmed in."

I scratch my head, "how did I get programmed in if I haven't been here before?"

"We have our ways. Come we must get inside," he looks to the skies before hurrying me along slightly.

Pressing along the stony path, we follow as it twists around. The tall trees surround us, not allowing much light in. They have overgrown and meet in the middle creating a tunnel-like darkness.

I begin to struggle as Dion almost drags me along the path.

"Wait a second," I puff exhausted.

"We cannot wait here."

Before I could even utter another word he sweeps me from my feet and cradles me within his arms. I begin to protest but realise I am too weak even for that. I allow my muscles to relax as he extends his stride. A large house comes into sight in the distance. As we close in I realize that it is formed in the shape of a hounds head. The large eyes stare at me. I assume those are windows but I cannot be sure. I shiver as we approach the open mouth. Its sharp fangs hang above us as Dion repeats the process as with the gate. I reach up and touch the tip of its sharp teeth. They are remarkably smooth, carved from what appears to be some sort of black marble. The panel reveals itself and the process is repeated. The mouth we are stood in begins to close. I scream as small fragments fall from above. The sharp rocks close in on my position. Panic strikes me as I wriggle around in Dion's arms. He ignores my struggles and tightens his grip, staring intently at the door which strains under the pressure.

The ridge of the mouth looms before us as a tooth threatens to impale me. Just before the teeth reach us, the door cracks and breaks. Dion hurries forward. Seconds later the mouth closes, blocking the entrance once more. I punch Dion's arm as I try to soothe my rampant heart. I gulp air in as my breathing races.

He releases my legs, gently easing then to the floor. I double over, exhausted and terrified I fall to my knees. I lie back on the floor, sweat pours from me. The long warm fur surrounds me, seemingly soothing my aching muscles. The drip enters my arm once more I writhe on the floor tensing against it. After a couple of minutes, I eventually gain control of my bodily functions.

I relax on the fur; it seems to close in on me, wrapping me in its warmth. Then I realise what is happening. Panic-stricken I try to move, but I am too late. The fur has grown and now covers my chest. It pushes me down, restraining me. I cry out in pain as it applies pressure to the wound above my heart.

"Dion!" I cry.

Dion rushes forward, tries to pry the fur apart, it does not budge. Then a familiar voice floats around the room.

"What is she doing here?" Lyca asks calmly yet sternly.

Dion's eyes track the voice. He lowers his head as he meets the eyes of Lyca.

I manage to twist my head to the left, Dion is blocking my view.

"She asked to leave, I tried to persuade her but she is stubborn."

Dion moves to the side and I see Lyca for the first time. His face is emotionless as he stares from me to him.

"So what if she is stubborn, she should not have left the medical centre."

I strain to breathe; the fur tightens its hold. My lungs constrict as they struggle. It reaches the point that I can no longer breathe and I try in vain to catch their attention. I am bound too securely to even move.

"She will be okay to leave Lyca. She is strong. I could not refuse her."

Lyca stares at him, he scowls.

Dion finally turns to me as I turn white, my lips blue. His mouth hangs open as he shouts.

"Lyca!"

The strange man strides over with little haste. He waves a hand over me and the fur retracts. I gasp as the air inflates my lungs once more. My colour returns as I cough violently.

"Sorry about that," Lyca holds out a hand.

I hesitantly accept, eager to remove myself from the strange fur which surrounds me like a carpet, except this is constantly moving, as if alive, swaying in the wind.

He lifts me to my feet with ease and I cannot contain my shriek as I am thrust forward. I instantly cover my mouth, regretting allowing the noise to escape my lips.

Both men speak simultaneously

"What is wrong?"

I wave the question away as I desperately try to think of an excuse.

"You just took me by surprise, pulled my arm a little too hard" I lie.

Both men seem to breathe a sigh of relief and accept my bending of the truth. Lyca wraps an arm around me, escorts me into a different room and places me on a fluffy sofa. This is a different texture to the living carpet and does not move thankfully. I allow myself to relax, closing my eyes. I feel something brush up my leg and panic. Opening my eyes I see Lyca wave a hand in front of me and my gown begins to rise on my left side.

I grip it tightly, desperately trying to force it down. It does nothing, only my hand follows it upwards. I give in with a sigh. My wound is revealed, open and sore.

Dion's face drains as he catches sight of it.

"Why did you lie?" he asks.

"I am tired of everyone rushing around me all the time. I'm sick of all the sympathy." I huff.

Lyca's eyes burn with anger.

"I told you not to bring her out. Look at this mess."

I peer down for the first time. The claw marks, previously stitched, must have torn when I fell into Dion, opening the wound even further. Blood dribbles down onto my stomach.

"We have to get her back."

"No." I choke.

They discuss further ignoring me completely.

"I'm not going!" I shout, rage filling me.

My arms blink into life, sparks shoot from my energy as it increases. I close my eyes, take deep breaths. I gather my anger, manage to contain it. My hands colour fades and I open my eyes.

Both stare at me shocked by my outburst.

"I won't go and if you try to make me I'll fight everything you do to help and I will win," I state tearfully, "I am a person and I can make my own choices. Stop ignoring me!"

BElief

66 Please?" Dion pleads.

Lyca scratches his head. He sighs, "alright, we can do this here but it will not be as easy."

He lifts me carefully, I despise being carted around as if I am unable to walk but I hold my tongue. We cross through various rooms to which I do not take any notice. I am beaten, broken and on the verge of giving up, I do not care anymore. The hardships I have endured in such a short period are more than enough to fill up a couple of lifetimes. Why is all of this happening to me? I look up as if speaking to a god I do not believe in. I have lost so much in this world. I sigh loudly.

Dion flicks on the light as we enter what appears to be a medical room. A large bed with restraints is the haunting centre piece. Lyca slides me onto it. The blood flows more fluently from my wound from the disturbance.

"I will have to re-stitch it; this sort of wound cannot be healed."

Dion nods as Lyca searches his neatly laid out cupboards. The room is as white as the medial halls, each cabinet sits neatly against the wall. There is not a piece of equipment out of place. I think Lyca may have some sort of obsessive disorder viewing his home as I have. The floor and walls are solid white marble, although my blood soon taints the colour. It dribbles onto the bed and quickly forms a puddle on the floor. It swirls a moment before disappearing down the drain to my left.

"I fear I will not able to sedate her, merely numb the area to some extent."

"I could try?" Dion asks.

"No it will not work. We have tried. For some reason, the poison in her blood, at least temporarily, counteracts our energy to force unconsciousness, it takes a lot of effort and mostly does not work. She will be fine as you said she is strong."

Lyca produces sterilized equipment on a trolley. He picks up an enlarged needle filled with a clear substance. After flicking and releasing some liquid he turns to me.

"This will hurt."

Dion moves over behind my head, laying his hands across my shoulders tenderly. His muscular arms laid across my chest makes me feel at home, even if it is only to pin me down. Lyca injects my skin numerous times. I shriek and shy away but Dion has a firm grip and I am not able to move for very long as he tightens up more. Each injection feels like a knife gouging my skin. Tears stream down my cheeks as I tense against it.

"Relax," Lyca soothes, "I know it is difficult but you are making it worse."

I try to order my extremities to relax, my muscles to cease their contractions and lie still. With great effort, I manage to force my body to obey. I merely grit my teeth instead. After a couple of seconds, Dion removes his hands. Lyca prods my side and chest.

"Can you feel that?"

I shake my head in response. The numbness has even spread to my shoulder. Lyca returns with sutures and begins his work. I watch as the needle pierces my skin. I can feel a slight tugging sensation as he stitches it to the other side. Pulling gently, my open pieces of skin are forced together. He repeats the process all along the entirety of the wound.

"You are strong Lexi."

I roll my eyes at his attempt to make conversation.

"What is wrong?"

"I'm tired. Tired of fighting, tired of all this," I puff.

"I never asked for any of this. I don't want to be anyone special. All I ever wanted was to lead a simple life with my simple pleasures. Instead, I'm ripped from all of that and sent to hell…" A tear forms and I must stop a moment to contain it.

"And for what? To be able to have these powers? To be able to move objects with the wave of a hand? I mean what is even the point of any of this?"

"You *are* special Lexi," Lyca remarks softly, which does seem strange coming from such a stern character.

"I don't want to be *special!*" I snort.

The darkness within increases as I envision what my life has entailed, it spreads throughout my limbs. It clambers my spine, sending chills down it. I shiver as I imagine the dark strands cross over my eyes, encasing me within my empty shell once more, unable to redeem myself, to pull myself back from the grim thoughts. I roll my eyes and shiver. What would actually happen if I allowed the darkness in? I would not like to think.

"You have endured hardships, much more than most. I wish I could say everything will be okay but I cannot. You are miraculous and such bad events will most likely haunt you forever. At least you have your friends," he smiles.

A sudden flash of images forces the darkness back. The strands retract, prevented from taking hold the gaunt thoughts dispense instantly. They hiss and writhe as they are forced back into the abyss. A smile crosses my face as my eyes light up at the thought. At least I have my friends. Those who are willing to follow me and share my burdens, I fear without them I would have been taken a long time ago.

"My friends! How could I forget?" I jolt up.

Lyca's hands move swiftly, ceasing my actions

"Lie still," he forces me back down onto the bed. My smile remains as he carries out the rest of the work.

"Where are they?" I ask doing a complete circle on my darkness just moments ago.

"They are here, all in good time."

My thoughts whirl as I reminisce about our friendships. All shadowy thoughts evicted from my mind as though they were never even there.

A familiar voice echoes around me. I snap my head around, trying to locate from whom it originates. Lyca's expression changes to portray his confusion.

"What is it?"

I turn again "Who's that?"

"Who is what?"

"That voice, where's it coming from?"

Lyca quickly places a hand over my head.

"You don't have a temperature. There is no voice, only ours," he states checking my pulse.

'*Kiddo?*'

That word triggers something within, some memories rush before my eyes as though flicking rapidly through the pages of a book. Then suddenly it ceases the manic frenzy. A name now floats around in my diminished memory banks.

"Elliott?"

'*That's me.*'

I twist my head once more trying to locate the voice.

"Who's Elliott?" I ask Lyca.

His nose crunches as he mulls over the question.

'Lexi I'm part of you, within your mind. Do you remember?'

I hit the side of my head.

"I'm going insane," I hit myself once more before Lyca grabs my fist.

"I cannot help you if you do not tell me what is wrong."

"It…. It's inside my mind?"

"Dion!!" Lyca shouts.

He enters the room moments later, I did not even realise he had left. Unwilling to witness another hardship occur to a strange person he has become emotionally attached too, he vacated our presence silently.

"Who is Elliott?" Lyca raises an eyebrow.

Dion's head slumps as soon as the name is uttered.

"You do not remember him at all?" He turns to me.

I shake my head, bewildered.

"This is one of the, may I say, odd occurrences I had wished to inform you of," he pauses.

Lyca's expression forces his continuation.

"Elliott is another conscious, which has been trapped in her," he half produces a worried smile.

The room around me begins to swirl. I become dizzy and reach out, steadying myself on Lyca.

"Lexi you must remember," Dion crouches beside me, "the werewolf attack, and the magical sphere, you saving my life?"

I rack through my memories, trying desperately to rekindle with them.

"Nothing," I shake my head, "I remember nothing."

Dion presses a hand against his head before continuing.

"We have found how werewolves manipulate energy. The source of their powers, well in fact Lexi has. Elliott was a Magi before his demise of course. He was propelled into the afterworld."

"Which the werewolves command currently," Lyca interrupts.

Dion nods in response, awaiting the answers to formulate.

It takes a couple of scratches of his head, but finally, his realisation can be seen as his features alter.

"No, it cannot be!" he exclaims.

Dion nods once more.

"They are manipulating *our* energy? But how?"

"I do not know but he could not get out," Dion trails off.

Lyca's features drain as he stares at Dion in disbelief. I look from Lyca to Dion as confusion claims my mind.

"I have another consciousness inside me? Werewolves used it to gain abilities? What's going on?"

'You've lost your memory of me.'

My head twists as the voice interrupts my train of thought once more. Panic sets in as I try to piece together my shattered memories. I strain at the effort and almost break down as I am overwhelmed by grief. Head throbbing, I place a hand over it and try desperately to ignore the voice in my mind. The voice continues and my sanity strains.

"STOP!" I shout.

The room falls silent as all stare uncomfortably at me. The voice ceases conversation as I try to shake the pounding from my skull. I feel the strands of my sanity fraying, I rub my eyes. As I cradle my head Dion places a hand on my shoulder. My sanity is a very frail thing indeed. I walk a very thin line when it comes to that; I do not require voices in my mind pushing me over the wrong side of that line. I almost feel as though I am walking a tightrope, easily able to fall either way, struggling, battling to stay upright.

"I know this is difficult as you do not remember but you accepted Elliott. You insisted that he remain within you for fear of sending back into the werewolves grasp," he squeezes gently.

A single tear drops onto my cheek as I struggle with my circumstance. I shiver.

"How am I supposed to deal with someone inside my mind?"

"Like I said you agreed to this arrangement against my better judgement. I am sure if you wish we could remove him, but I would not advise such a hasty decision. You have lost your memories and when they return I believe you will regret it."

"We must remove it!" Lyca interrupts.

I stare from one man to the other, trying desperately to decide what action to take.

"You cannot make that decision for her."

"Hah! I can do what I like," he almost shouts from anger.

"No Lyca, you cannot. You may be able to call a meeting and manipulate others to see as you do but I will not allow her to be controlled. I will assist her in any way possible to escape if it comes down to that. She is powerful and her true abilities will be seen when her requirements are great, I doubt you could truly stop her. She is extremely resourceful."

Lyca creases his face as he allows Dion's words to penetrate. He scratches his head as if planning something. He shuffles up beside me.

"You must see sense; you cannot have two conscious minds within one body. I do not know what it will do to you."

I lie in silence for a while thinking about the options I am faced with. I am terrified at the thought of someone nestled within me, able to hear each thought I have, my privacy no longer existent. I shiver as I realise that it is most likely listening to my internal battle as I sit here discussing it with myself. I push all from my mind and turn to Lyca.

"I won't rush this decision; if I do I'll regret deciding so quickly without memories to sway me either way."

Lyca's features drop as anger crosses his face.

"As you wish," he forces a smile before returning to finish what he started.

Elliott does not speak again. I silently thank him for not making me feel more uncomfortable. I ignore my current situation as I try in vain to rekindle my precious memories. After failing I lie back and relax.

A short while passes before Lyca finishes his work. He collects another bag of the blue liquid, hooks it up to a portable stand before approaching me. I feel the needle exit my vein and before even one second passes he has replaced it with the full container. A sharp scratch is quickly followed by the burning sensation. I writhe as it fuses with my blood, travelling around my body, hopefully assisting my battle. Eventually, the pain diminishes and I relax.

Lyca pats my right shoulder before exiting the room.

"Thank you!" I shout after him.

He does not respond. I lower my head, lifting my blooded clothing I peer at my chest. The suturing appears professional. A small area surrounding where the claws made entry remains black, with blue veins that glow brightly. I tear myself away from yet another disturbing scar that has befallen the battered carcass I reside within. I have always been a bit strange when it comes to scars. I have one on my stomach just above my umbilicus from surgery as a child and I have always admired it. I normally take pride in my scars, proof of what my body has been through and come out of the other side, but these are so plentiful that I simply do not wish to accept them.

I inhale a couple of deep breaths before shuffling around to the edge of the bed. Lowering myself I plant my feet firmly on the ground. The effort strains my body and sweat begins to run from every pore.

Concentrate on the exit; just a few steps away. Positive I can make the distance I put weight on the bed and manoeuvre as far as possible whilst still stabilizing myself.

One more step and I will be on my own, unaided. I close my eyes and release pressure from the bed. I take hold of the stand as my feet sway unsteadily. Dizziness engulfs me. I force one leg forward. In quick succession, I follow with my other leg. A couple of times I waver, almost toppling over but I manage to complete my journey. I reach out and grasp for the door frame in desperation. My breathing is rampant. I rest against it for a while. The effort my body is consuming to complete even the simplest of actions is so extensive in my current state. I puff aloud, exhausted from not only my exertion, but exasperated with my life of late. I hold back my distress and push those thoughts down. It is not healthy to allow the dark feelings to surface. I stand in the doorway a moment, swaying, trying to contain my dizziness.

"Are you okay?"

Seconds pass, I do not respond.

"Lexi?" Dion's voice is strained with concern.

"I'm alright," I manage to utter.

Dion grips the stand that I am clutched to. He offers me his arm I accept without a second thought. Shifting my weight from the door I transfer it onto Dion. He leads me slowly to the couch I had previously resided on. A sigh of relief escapes my mouth as my exhausted body is allowed to rest once more. I take a couple of seconds to return my breathing to normal. As I distribute my weight backwards I allow myself to truly view my surroundings. The entire room is rather stunning. It is filled with various pieces of technology that I have never laid my eyes on before. I could not even assume to know what their purpose is. The carpet moves beneath my feet as if living. I shiver as it tickles my feet.

"Creepy," I shudder, pulling my feet upwards.

The large room is decorated black with various silver patterns lining the walls adding variety to the otherwise colourless room. Of course, the centerpiece of the room is the large marble fireplace formed into the shape of the hounds I see so frequently around this place. They are in a sitting position, heads pointing directly at me. Their eyes glisten black and they seem to stare at me. I realise that the hound to the right has a young baby nestled beneath it. I notice the eyes staring out from in-between its legs. The carvings are amazing and contain so much complex detail. I smile at their magnificence.

Dion has slipped from the room without me noticing. I search for him but he is nowhere in sight. I shuffle my weight around and manage to lie on the sofa. I feel so minute against the enlarged seat. I allow my eyes to close and myself to become lost in the warmth of the fluffy material. Sleep is welcomed as my battered body relaxes. I allow myself to slumber, safe in the knowledge I will come to no harm for a change…

TRanQUIliTY

Movement beneath me forces me to wake. I jolt up, panic sets in as disorientation claims my senses. I thrash my arms before I even have a chance to open them. Then Dion's voice soothes me.

"You are okay, it is only me."

I open my eyes to see him smiling down at me. I peer around. I am in his arms and we are climbing a glorified staircase.

"I am taking you to your room; you appeared so uncomfortable on that chair."

"Thank you," I yawn, "though I doubt I will be able to go back to sleep."

Dion laughs "I should think not you have been for at least a day."

"What?"

"You heard correctly."

"No. I can't have been out a full day. What's wrong with me?"

"I think you can get away with it on account of what has happened recently. Anyway sleep is great for regeneration; you are not consuming and over exhorting your body giving it time to rest."

"Yeah. I guess so," I puff.

I do not take much notice of which path we choose. I merely close my eyes and relax as he shifts through the corridors. We stop after various turns and I hear the door crumble before me. I open my eyes as we enter.

We are welcomed by the beauty of the room we now reside in. The enormous bay window catches my attention initially. We must be in one of the eyes of the hound which the house has been formed into. I smile.

The bed to the right of the enormous window is like nothing I have ever laid my eyes upon before. The sheer size of it sends a shiver down my spine. It appears to be made mainly of leather except the leather is not as I would expect. Its surface is shiny and reflects my image as we approach. There are strips of red lighting surrounding the base creating an astonishing illumination. Four large bed posts wind upwards, swirling like a DNA strand. Each has a light strip intertwined within them. They twist at the top and connect each side. A feathery wing-shaped throw elegantly flows down, creating curtains, allowing maximum privacy and exclusion.

"This is *my* room? *My* bed? I'll get lost in this!" I laugh as he places me on the bed.

I descend into the mattress as if it is swallowing me. It moulds around my body creating ultimate comfort.

"Wow!" I utter.

I stroke the white and brown fur cover beneath me.

"This is stunning."

"Yes, most things here are visually remarkable, but you have one of the best rooms," He smiles, winking.

I admire my surroundings and when I spot something to my left I become very excited.

"Is that what I think it is?"

Dion turns to where I am pointing and nods.

My smile extends as I slide down the side of the bed. My feet pad softly on the white fur carpet. I falter a little. Dion dives forward dramatically, places his hands around my waste. I shuffle along slowly but I do not care. My vision fixated on one spot.

As we approach the large mirrors I realise they are of an odd design. Each mirror appears as though it has been shattered into large pieces and reassembled in different locations. Pieces overlap and twist in all directions leaving small gaps in between creating a stylish modern appearance. The mirrors stretch over the full length of the wall and look magnificent. My reflection distorts as I close in.

Dion waves a hand in front of me. Every other mirror lurches forward, slowly rotating. When the full cycle has completed, a rack appears from nowhere. The clothes are still in motion from the sheer force. My eyes light up as I am presented with the largest variety of t-shirts I have ever seen. As I scan the remainder of the wall I notice the different mirror sections contain different items of clothing: jeans, skirts, jumpers, shoes and many more.

"Wow," I utter once more.

I select a lilac low cut t-shirt with a slightly gothic style. The pattern in the form of a large slash down the left half of the top with stitching to mimic the effect of a repair. The snug-fitting top also has holes down each side, revealing the skin through the mesh. I move along to the jeans section, Dion assisting me gently. I select a pair of dark hipster jeans with a splash of red colouring dripped down the back and one side of the pant leg. Pleased with my choice I grab some socks and underwear before approaching the shoes. They line the shelves and the variety is endless. After a couple of bad choices, I finally pick a pair of black long-furred boots.

Dion assists me over to the white fluffy sofa to the right of the bed where I ease down on the seat. A large fireplace much like the one downstairs is directly in front of me.

"Are you okay now?" Dion drags me from my trans.

I shake the glaze from my eyes.

"Yes," I smile.

He nods his head in response before turning to exit.

"Dion," I shout.

He turns.

"Thank you."

He smiles before spinning on the spot and exiting my room.

I glance around once more. Nothing much more is contained in my room. A strange feeling overwhelms me as I think about this being my own space. I shake my head, dragging myself from my imagination I concentrate on my clothing. I can finally have some decent attire for once.

The gown I now wear is blood-stained and disgusting. Turning around I notice a large jagged ovular object close to the bed. It has the appearance of a mirror. Taking a deep breath I push from my seat. My legs wobble unsteadily but I manage to lock them in place as I steady myself. I shuffle towards the mirror, leaning my weight on the portable stand attached to me. With the contraptions assistance, I make the distance. Sweat drenches me.

I stand before the misshaped oval. Scratching my head I ponder what action I should take. Reaching up I pull the top towards me. It swings around, revealing another black surface.

"Hmm…"

Running a hand over the surface, it ripples. I drag my hand back, jumping from my skin.

"What on earth?"

My reflection now ripples across it. I stand a moment. As the ripples spread they become less frequent and eventually cease and lie still. My reflection disappears and the dull complexion returns. Scratching my head I hold out a finger. Pointing I press the middle of the slab. My finger becomes immersed. The pinkness of my skin seems to spread across the surface. In a panic, I try to remove my finger. The now springy surface merely follows me, still attached.

As the whole surface turns pink, it releases my finger and springs back into place. The colouring disappears as the blackness returns. This time it is reflective and I now stare at myself.

"How strange. What kind of mirror would do that?" I rant aloud.

I chuckle, relaxing my frayed nerves. I examine my face. My appearance haunts me; skin blackened from grime and stained with blood. My blonde hair is now very long and completely wild from neglect. Although I do quite admire the length. I shiver as I notice something nestled deep within my eyes. For the first time in my life, they have the same darkness which I witnessed every day in my best friends eyes. That seems like a lifetime ago now. Ellies' eyes had always given away her grief and turmoil to which I seem to have gained that very same trait. Even with the passing of my father, the worst part of my life (or so I thought) I never seemed to lose hope as I have now. A tear streaks down my face. I wipe it away creating a small clean section.

I shake myself taking a hold of reality. I must not dwell on what has happened otherwise it will destroy me.

"I need a shower," I grunt.

As I speak the words a door appears out of nowhere to my left. I catch a glimpse from the corner of my eye and snap my head around. The door shatters as I approach without command. I shiver as I peer inside. The whole room is tiled with the black marble. The room has a toilet, sink and a bath behind a blue-tinted glass window. As I enter I notice a drain in the centre. The door behind me seals itself with a loud crash that makes me jump. This is a shower I realise. Peering upwards I notice small holes dotted around the ceiling.

I examine the surrounding glass. Running my hand over every possible inch of it I realise that the toilet, bath and sink are inaccessible.

"What's the point of that?" I ask myself.

I scratch my head before leaving my question behind and concentrating on the shower. At the top of the door is a large section to hang clothes from. I undress and hang my up my grubby gown. If I can rest against the glass I will be able to bathe myself. I hope. Searching my surroundings I try desperately to locate some sort of switch to turn the shower on. As previously examined, the glass disguises no secret devices. I puff aloud.

"How does this stupid shower work!" I shout angrily.

I scream as scalding water sprays down on me.

"Ouch too hot," I shy away.

The water instantly cools obeying my verbal command.

"That's okay," I smile at my accomplishment.

The temperature is maintained and I relax. Sliding down the side of the glass I sit on the tiled floor. Gathering my legs in front of me I wrap my arms around my shins and rest my head on them. The water caresses my body gently. I sigh with delight. The colour of the liquid around me blackens as all the grime of the past few months is chipped away. I take a stab in the dark.

"Soap?" I question.

Nothing changes.

"Hmm."

I shrug, what more can I do. The dirt seems to embed itself into my pale skin, staining me.

Suddenly the texture landing on my back alters and the liquid seems to thicken. I run my hand over it and the liquid foams. The water has turned into liquid soap. Once I have rubbed it into my whole body, as if reading my mind, it transforms back to water. The red soap forms a puddle around me as it is washed away. I shiver as it reminds me of blood, the colour mimics it perfectly.

My heart rate increases as I imagine a pool of blood surrounding me, my blood. I begin to shake as the panic sets in. I rock myself back and forth trying to calm my palpitations. Dion is not here to pull me from what I now know to be a panic attack. I eventually manage to calm my racing heart when the water runs clear once more. Sustaining my weight against the glass I slide up onto my feet shakily. I do not like this new affliction I have suddenly gained. I try to remove it from my mind as I look at myself. My skin seems to shine from cleanliness. Closing my eyes I tilt my head backwards. My face gently embraces the warmth. I shake the water from my head and shuffle towards the door leaning one side against the wall with the other holstered by the portable drip stand.

Finally, I reach the door. I smack my head with my palm as I realise something.

"How am I going to dry myself?" I look around for some sort of towel.

I reside that the towels must be in the wardrobe and touch the symbols to open the door. As I make contact nothing occurs.

Creasing my face I try again. Still nothing. Then I sense something. The walls at either side of me are glowing red. Heat radiates from them. My body dries rapidly and the elevated warmth dies instantaneously, returning the room to normal temperature. I step onto the white fluffy carpet feeling lighter, as though a great weight has been lifted from my shoulders. I smile as slow progress is made toward my selected attire. My legs becoming stronger with each stiff movement. Although I still rely on the stand to assist me.

A burning sensation forces me to look at the substance. It is almost empty. It will need to be changed soon I realise. Ignoring the burning I continue my journey. Eventually, I reach the sofa. With a struggle, I pull on my underwear. In quick succession, I pull on my new clothes, not wishing to view my body for fear of what I may find. I struggle to move the drip around. I do not wish to remove it and replace it as I do not know what I am doing. I think a moment then twist it back up my arm and down my side. It is twisted but I can do nothing else. The clean clothes fill me with a buzzing feeling. I am so ecstatic to finally be clean and in clothes of my choosing.

I shuffle along to the mirror once more. The reflective surface has disappeared once more so I repeat the previous process. The surface bubbles and my reflection stares back at me. My smile enlarges as I approve of my appearance.

I walk around the room, trying to strengthen my legs since they have been out of commission for weeks. After a few circles, I tire and decide to sit on the seat in the large bay window. I shuffle around for a while trying to get as close to it as possible. I relax, staring from it. Trees seem to curve inwards as if trying to encase the house, obstructing its view from the world. Birds sing gently in the large garden to the left which stretches further than I can see. The enormous grounds flourish with varied species of wildlife and a couple of people rush around busily working the beautiful grounds. I close my eyes and relax in the peaceful place I now reside in.

After an unaccounted period of time passes, a loud bang startles me. I jump out of my skin, falling from my seating. I thud on the floor landing awkwardly on my left shoulder. A sharp pain creases me and I quickly flip onto my back releasing the pressure on my shoulder. It still aches agonisingly. I shake my head.

I doubt my legs are strong enough to lift my weight from the floor unaided. I tense them; they shake and fail beneath me. I grasp the seat with my right arm. This is the weaker of the two since the fracture and as expected it also fails me. I slump back to the floor.

"Great," I puff.

I can do nothing but sit here. I look to my shoulder. It is twisted disgustingly and hangs loosely beside me. Have I dislocated my shoulder? Seriously? I shake my head once more and blocking most of the pain I lay backwards. I can do nothing without assistance so I decide to try and sleep until someone comes to check on me. I open my eyes. If someone ever comes to check that is. Allowing them to close once more I manage to drift into a light sleep.

"Lexi?" Dion startles me awake. "Why are you laid on the floor?"

Yawning I stare at him as he kneels beside me.

"Something frightened me," I yawn once more. "I fell and couldn't get back up. So I waited," I smile.

"Oh no! I am sorry I was not here," Dion panics.

"Stop beating yourself up. It's not your fault." I smile.

He assists me up onto the seat once more.

"Wow Lexi, you look…beau…lovely," he blushes. "I see you found the shower," he smiles.

"Thank you and yeah, very strange this place…Ermm also, do you think you could help me with this?" I point to my shoulder.

Dion's colour drains as he notices my arm for the first time.

"How did that happen?"

"I fell onto it. I think it is dislocated. I can't move it. And before you start it wasn't your fault. You can't be by my side all the time. I wouldn't want you to be" I smile.

He gives me an evil look in jest but I notice a small glimmer of a smile as he rolls his eyes.

Assisting me to my feet he remarks

"You are going to be the death of me with your clumsiness."

I grin and laugh.

"Come on let us take you to Lyca, he can deal with that better than me."

"He won't be happy," I grunt

A sigh escapes Dion's lips as he realises the grief he will have to endure.

"Yes but still he is the best person for it," he half-smiles. "It will be fine."

He tries to reassure himself more than me. I laugh. I am lifted into his arms and we exit my abode and descend the staircase. We search many rooms before Lyca is finally located. He resides in a large room filled with a seemingly endless supply of books. They stack the walls and numerous bookshelves are spread throughout if wandering through a maze. In the centre is a collection of bean bag seats along with three black fluffy sofas formed into the shape of a letter c. Lyca is sitting on the centre sofa, his back facing us. A large collection of books are spread before him on an enormous black glass table. A couple are open and he flicks between them. It looks as though he is trying to locate some piece of information.

I cough quietly to make him aware of our presence. He does not turn. I look to Dion. He smiles and shrugs his shoulders. Placing me on my feet I step towards him.

"Lyca?" I question him.

He remains unaware of our presence. I scratch my head as I shuffle around the front of him. As his eyes come into view I scream and fall backwards. I land softly on a bean bag but my terror remains.

I try to scuttle away but I cannot stand. I look to Dion.

"What's that?"

He approaches, standing beside me he stares at Lyca.

"He is reading."

"Huh?" I stutter.

Dion laughs. This is the first time in what feels like an eternity that I have heard him laugh, seen him this happy. I smile at the sight.

"That is how he reads material. He can do this at a much more rapid pace than if he did it normally."

"But his face, it's not his…"

"The face you see is Lyca's but he is partially transformed. He has some human features but his wolf features are more dominant giving the impression of his large dog-like snout and head yet very human-looking eyes."

"That looks horrible," I shiver. "Does he know we are here?"

"No. Usually, when this is done he sets a goal most likely until he locates what he is searching for or until a certain time limit has passed."

"So we have to wait?"

Dion shakes his head, "watch."

He closes each book. Lyca's trans breaks instantaneously and he shakes his head. When he turns to us his face has returned to normal.

His eyes narrow at Dion as he tries to work out why he was disturbed.

"What is wrong?" He eventually asks.

"Why do you presume something is wrong?" Dion half-smiles.

Lyca just stares, an eyebrow rose awaiting his confession.

Dion's shoulders slump as he opens his mouth.

I cut him off "I fell; I think I dislocated my arm. I was hoping you could help me."

He approaches me; lifting my left arm he examines it.

"Yes it is." Lyca's temper flourishes, "how could you let this happen?"

Dion's eyes sink to the floor like a naughty child being scolded.

"Stop it. Dion isn't my bodyguard. He can't be by my side all the time and I wouldn't want him to be. Just stop shouting at him all the time over me. I'm not a child" I shout.

"I disagree," Lyca states

"What do you disagree with?" I quiz him.

"Dion should protect you. You are young and feeble and too valuable to lose."

My jaw slackens as his works penetrate. I sink to the floor my head lowered. Anger rises from within as I speak.

"Why does my life suddenly have a purpose? Why should I leave everything I know and love to come here and live such a miserable life?" I pause, anger flourishing.

"Don't you see all I do lately is suffer? And for what? To be 'too valuable to lose'? I'm not someone's property. I am a human being and I have feelings which you just destroy so easily. So thank you Lyca!"

I exit the room swiftly leaving them with my angered words. I push through the maze rapidly and find a door. Peering around I realise I do not even know how I got here, therefore, do not know the way back. Turning around I peer up the corridor.

"Should I stay here or explore? It would give them something to think about. Hmm....." I ponder the question.

A wicked smile forms and my facial expression gives away my decision. I turn right, head up the corridor I know I have never been up before. Odd paintings are set at different heights across the wall. I do not take the time to study them. I want them to squirm after what Lyca has just said to me so I hurry out of sight. This place is enormous I realise. There are endless corridors which look identical. One who was more accustomed

117

to the halls most likely would be able to differentiate but I, for now, cannot and I soon find that I am completely lost.

I smile as I continue my journey into the unknown. To my left, another corridor filled with many doors as like most corridors here, to my right, an enormous staircase. I scratch my head. Which will they assume I would not take? The stairs, I gulp.

I will struggle greatly ascending those. I think a moment, turn to my left to avoid the gruelling stairs then Lyca's words surface once more and they rile my temper. I turn Right.

Gripping my portable stand I shuffle towards the bannister. Looking up I begin to count the stairs. I gulp when I get to fourty and they merely curve around to each side, rendering my count unfinished; I cannot see the remainder. I ignore my reservations. I approach the intimidating staircase.

"How should I do this? I have one arm and need two with this stand," I scratch my head. Then an idea comes to mind.

I turn around, sitting on the first step. I push from my legs planting my bottom on the next step whilst using my free hand to drag the portable stand up with me.

"That wasn't so bad" I chuckle at myself, "39 to go."

I continue to climb; I manage around thirty eight stairs with no problems. As fatigue grips me, my legs begin to struggle under the strain. They shake but finally I reach the 39th step. I am leant forwards as the stand is still on number thirty eight. Breathing rampant, I begin to sweat. I rest a moment but my back begins to ache from the position I am forced to take. This stand needs to be on the same step as I am. Gripping tightly I drag it towards me. It has almost cleared the step when I lose my hold. The moisture on my hands make it extremely difficult to maintain a solid grip. My fingers slip and the stand begins to fall. It seems to plummet in slow motion but I conduct a plan rapidly. I push from the step, allow myself to slide down, reaching out my feet, I manage to wrap my legs around it, halting its descent. With my free hand, I turn and grip the banister to halt my slide.

I cry out in pain as all of my body weight now rests on my dislocated shoulder. The moment my body ceases to slide I turn back over and plant my bottom firmly on the step. Tears of pain run down each cheek. I tap into my energy, allow it to flow over my arm, dulling most of it once more. I am surprised that the force did not re locate my shoulder but the angle must have not been correct. I sit on the step for an eternity with my legs wrapped around the pole of the stand, trying desperately to return my breathing to normal.

Eventually, my body calms down and I think for a moment. I shuffle backwards, ensuring I am at the very back of the step. Reaching forward and pulling my legs in, I can almost grasp the pole. Just a little more….I lean forwards and slide slightly. Ignoring it I stretch out. Just as I am about to slip from my seating once more I grasp the stand and plant my feet firmly on the step below. Placing the stand on my step I sigh in relief. Lying backwards I rest a moment, thankful I did not detach the essential drip from my arm. Who knows what could happen? Sharp teeth, red eyes flash before me. I jolt up, terrified. I shiver.

Shaking myself off I continue with my previous method, this time placing the stand on the upper step before myself. This will also allow my legs some reprieve as I can drag myself up with my arm to assist me even more. I climb eight steps before reaching the 39th once more. Slightly hesitant I move past this one rapidly in fear of a repeat occurrence. I continue to the next step and peer to both of my sides. The stairs split into two. They curve from the main set and lead to two landings above me. I decide on the left side as I am in closer proximity. It would be beyond idiotic to choose the furthest away.

"What like how idiotic it was to climb the stairs in the first place?" I chuckle to myself.

Twelve more steps and I finally reach their end. I allow my body to fall backwards, once I am a little way from the edge of course. My breathing is rapid and my body temperature has risen greatly.

"I made it!" I smile at my accomplishment.

I stay where I am for at least ten minutes. Finally reaching up I grip the banister, drag myself to my feet. I steady myself and peer over the edge. I had not noticed before but the actual steps on the stairs are enormous. The height and depth enlarged so much more than normal.

"No wonder I struggled so much," I puff.

Switching my grip I allow the portable stand to sustain most of my weight, rolling it forward I drag my worn body behind it. I enter the door directly ahead of me.

I am greeted with another corridor, more paintings are strewn around but there are no other doors. A large archway ahead catches my attention. As I close in I realise that it is made from a statue of a hound leaping, thus creating the arch shape. This image is everywhere in this place. I pass through the arch to another choice of direction, left or two different right turns. I chose the second right turn. I make my way through a couple more corridors before I reach a final door. I can go no other way. There are no turn-offs, no other options. I can either turn back or go through this one.

I turn around, prepared to head back; I do not wish to intrude. Then something within entices me to glance at the door once more. I do not know why but I take a step forward. It seems to be dragging me, forcing me to enter the room. I give in to its power and follow willingly. Curiosity taking hold.

I touch the door, as I make contact a green light surrounds it. I take a step back puzzled. I opt once more to turn around but the green energy surrounds me. It seems to be ordering me to enter. As if against my will I touch one symbol then the other. The door smashes and I enter.

REtuRn of thE Lost

The green energy dispenses the instant I open the door. I scratch my head. What a strange feeling. This room is full of boxes higher than I can see. They appear to be made from the same marble as with everything else but seem to be nothing more than storage boxes. I crease my face in confusion.

"Why was the feeling to come here so strong when it's only filled with boxes?"

I shake my head before turning to exit. A light catches my eye. I twist my head rapidly. Eyes narrowed. The green light disappears as soon as I turn but not quite fast enough for me to not notice which box it was emitting from. The box now directly in front of me blends in with the others. There must be something in it. I shuffle forwards. As I grip the sides of the enormous box I almost fall into the blackness but I manage to hold firm. Then all of a sudden a green light shoots from within, encircling me it drags me forward. I lose balance and fall into it. I yelp but there is nothing I can do.

Opening my eyes I find myself back in the torture room. I remember the events as some of my memory returns; it is the night of our escape. I am looking through my eyes but I cannot control myself. Splite is ahead of me. He battles with me furiously. Splite knocks me with a blow and grips me tightly breaking my arm. Then as my head turns I notice something that confuses me. I am not the one battling Splite; *I* am on Leos back, struggling against him. As the eyes I am looking through cock to the side I finally realise who I am peering through. Amahté. We exit the room and his head sinks.

Amahté goes sprawling across the floor, Splite must have tossed him aside. My eyes remain fixated on the floor. I can only see Splits feet as he approaches. Kicking Amahté onto his side he stares into his eyes. It sends a shiver down my spine, seeing my tormentor up so close once more. It unnerves me. Satisfied he turns to leave. I am guessing Amahté's life has ended. Why do I have to see this? I cry.

Then just as he is about to leave Amahté moves. He leaps up and glows the darkest green I have ever seen. It has black patches in the ball of energy he is forming. It hisses and burns Amahté skins as he enlarges it. One, two times the size of Splite, Amahté launches it. He turns just before the ball makes contact. Splite yelps and his face cannot hide his shock. The ball engulfs him and then shoots earthwards. It pounds the ground until it gives way and Splite disappears. Amahté's chain falls from his wrist and he leaps out of the window. The sun burns his skin but he erects a protective barrier and scurries off. I reach out to him.

Before I know what is happening I am thrust back into the room full of boxes. The force launches me across the room and I smash my head on a corner of the marble. My vision blurs and I am knocked unconscious.

My eyes flutter open, I move slightly and my head flares with agony. I put my hand on it, creating more pain. When I remove my hand I realise I am bleeding. I shuffle into a sitting position. No one has found me yet. The headache is fierce as my senses tingle. I do not know how long unconsciousness has claimed me but as I try to stand dizziness sweeps over me. I push onwards forcing myself up. My vision blurred, I compel my body to move from the room. I kick something on my way. Glancing down I see a figure curled on the floor. What is that?

I cannot decipher anything through my vision impairment apart from the fact it is small. There was nothing here when I entered so I decide that, even though I have no idea what it is, I will bring it with me. I haul it over my shoulder and head down the corridor. I manoeuvre my way blindly, not knowing the way I came from. Miraculously I find my way to the arch. I make it as far one step from under the arch before my body gives in. I fall to my knees. I shuffle around into a sitting position and rest against the wall. The door to the staircase is just ahead of me. Swarms of dizziness cloud my mind as I try to fight to stay awake. If I fall asleep will I ever wake up again? Head injuries can be so dangerous I think to myself. Would that be a bad thing? I consider the thought of not waking up ever again much more than a sane person would. I shake the thoughts from my mind.

"I wouldn't make it down the stairs anyway," I state to myself aloud.

The small figure slides from my shoulder. I grip it and place it on the floor to the right of me. My vision does not clear; I still cannot make it out. I place a hand on it and allow my body to relax.

"I hope someone finds us soon," I chuckle dryly patting the figure. "I have no idea how long I can stay awake."

Time seems to pass in slow motion. It seems like an eternity before a figure appears at the door. Narrowing my eyes I try to focus on it. I cannot make it out. The figure rushes over and I notice the black eyes.

"Lyca?" I question.

"Yes," Lyca's voice is strained and panic-stricken.

He checks me over as I try to focus. My eyes feel so heavy; I have battled so fiercely to stay awake. One second won't harm, surely. I allow them to close.

"Lexi!" Lyca roars, terrifying me.

I open them. He is more blurry than before.

"What?"

"You must stay awake; you hit your head hard; if you don't stay awake I cannot tell if you have any impairment issues."

He lifts me. I grasp for the small figure beside me, I manage to pull it in towards me before we leave.

"That might not be a bad thing," I say aloud this time as my eyes lose focus.

They begin to close, I force them open but they are so heavy, they drag down once more.

Lyca begins to panic as we descend the stairs at such a rapid pace. "Lexi try and stay with me! Erm... who is your little friend?" He tries to maintain a conversation.

I shake my head, force them open.

"I don't know. I can't even see what he looks like. I just found him."

"Well he is green....he.....a.......large....... LEXI!" He shakes me once more as I lose consciousness between his words.

"That's nice," I mumble confused.

"What's your name, Lexi?"

"It's.......erm......" A searing pain in my head disrupts my thoughts. I groan.

"We are almost there, please just hang in there."

"Hang in where?" I mumble insanely.

I stare at my hand and notice the blood. I scream at the sight.

"Help me, I have blood," I screech.

"Yes you do have blood. Do not worry I will help you."

I calm down instantly, "thank you."

My eyes close. Sleep beckons me. Sharp pain in my shoulder regains my senses slightly and I open my eyes once more. Lyca is in front of me, I am back in his medical room. Dion enters and his face drains, his skin turns grey. He rushes to Lyca's aid.

"What happened?"

"I do not know."

"How can I help?"

"Keep her awake and I will sort out her head wound."

Dion turns to me. My arms are cradling the small figure.

"Hey Lexi. I see you have found something?"

I look from Dion to the blurry mess cradled in my arm.

"Who is he?"

"Erm…"

"Here I can tell you, move your hand so I can….." He trails off.

"No, that is impossible."

"What is the matter?" Lyca asks.

"The creature she is holding, it is impossible," Dion stutters.

"Why is it?"

"He died, or even if he managed to survive, he would not have been able to find us, not in a million years."

My eyelids grow heavy.

"Dion talk to her."

Dion shakes his head. "Lexi, you must stay here, for Amahté sake at least."

My eyes shoot open, focusing instantly. That name seemed to bring back my senses.

"What do you mean?" I ask.

"That little creature in your lap, it is Amahté."

"No. That's…"

"Impossible?" Dion finishes my sentence. "He is not conscious but he is here and he will need you."

My battle suddenly becomes fiercer. A spark of hope flickers within. I must fight for him, I must help him the way he helped me, I cannot abandon him again. I *will* not abandon him again.

I stare at his figure through blurred vision, I stroke him gently. This time every instance sleep threatens to take me I manage to force it backwards, each time prevailing.

Lyca manages to tend to my wound. Once the bleeding has ceased my vision clears slightly. I see Amahté for the first time in a long time. He is a sight for sore eyes; his overly large head falls to the side and almost drags him from my lap. Dion's reactions are quicker than mine and he catches him easily. He has various wounds and slight scarring on the side of his face but other than that appears unscathed on the outside at least.

"I have stopped the bleeding but we have to watch out for brain swelling and damage. We will not know unless the symptoms arise. At least one of us must accompany her at all times for the next few days or so just to be on the safe side, that way we can treat anything that may arise," Lyca interrupts my thoughts.

"I have also fixed your shoulder. I am going to put this on to keep your arm in place."

He produces what appears to be an adapted belt. He straps it around my chest. My arm is carefully lifted into the attached sling which is then fastened around my neck. The moment the last strap has fallen into its buckle the strange sling bounds my arm tightly to my chest. It is as if all the air has been vacated as it moulds to my arm and forces it into me. I groan as my shoulder aches from the pressure. I try to manoeuvre it. I cannot move it all. I reach over to try and loosen it but Lyca stops me.

"It will keep it in place. It will hurt because of the pressure but it will help you. Plus I do not trust you to not move it. You are so active."

I shoot him an offended look "But…"

"No. No, but. I will give you something for the pain so you do not have to constantly use your energy. You can relax."

Lyca turns and enters a side room. I look to Dion once more who is examining Amahté.

"Is he okay?"

Dion looks up startled. "Well, I think so. I think he is just unconscious but I cannot be sure. He is an odd species that I am not accustomed to."

I smile, confident my little friend will return to us. He obviously fought to get here.

Lyca returns with a new bag of blue substance and replaces the almost empty drip. The burning sensation returns but I do not allow it to bother me, I have become more accustomed to it now. He also holds another needle.

"Your pain killers and something to help protect against swelling."

He holds it up.

"A needle? Can I just take a pill or something?"

"No, this will also help us notice symptoms of swelling more rapidly, plus it will get to work on your pain much faster than a tablet anyway."

I sigh. I despise needles. Closing my eyes I hold out my arm. A sharp scratch in my neck makes me open them once more. He has injected my neck. As he pushes the milky substance into my vein the pain increases. A couple of seconds later he removes the now empty vile.

"Ouch," I rub my neck.

He removes my hand and massages my neck, encouraging the substance to dispense more rapidly.

"Yes okay it does hurt but it is only for a couple of seconds and it relieves your pain so it is worth it."

Lyca massages a couple more minutes.

"How does that feel?"

I look at my arm.

"Wow, I can't feel anything."

Lyca smiles before retrieving a small torch. He shines the bright red light in each eye, flicking it into and away from my vision.

"Okay. You might be concussed but you should be fine hopefully. I would prefer if you tried not sleep for a day."

I shuffle towards the end of the bed. Lyca presses a hand on my chest.

"Whoa wait what are you doing?"

"I was just getting up…"

Lyca stands in front of me, offering out his arms.

"No, not again."

"Yes. You have hit you head extremely hard if you mobilise you will most likely go dizzy and fall."

"Fine," I puff "Although I feel like some sort of child's doll."

I lie back once more and he slides an arm around my back and my legs. He lifts me.

"Where would you like to go?" He smirks cockily.

I squint towards him as I shake my head, rolling my eyes.

"Well somewhere I won't get bored would be great on the account of me not being able to sleep and all," I puff.

"I have the perfect place. I wish to know how this happened, but you have been through enough today so I will leave it until tomorrow if that is okay?"

"Yes."

I am silently thankful that I am spared the third degree for another day. We walk in silence. Lyca carrying me, Dion following closely behind, Amahté cradled tight within his arms.

We exit a door and head outside. As we weave through the paths I admire the beauty of the garden. Purple spotlights pave the path and a small section of the grounds. The trees stretch over and touch in the middle, preventing most of the light from entering. My head aches profusely but I try my best to ignore it.

The moon is high in the night's sky ahead of us. It is purple with odd markings down the middle. I narrow my eyes. They appear to be enormous claw marks. I shiver at the sight. Then as if it was hiding, another moon suddenly appears to the right of the other. This one is blue with an enormous indentation that has the appearance of a paw print.

A large building appears before us. This one is made from the same material as Lyca's house but is in the shape of a normal house. The roof, however, seems to be made of a clear material, thus creating one large window above.

We enter. The floor is not carpeted but created from white marble. Large corner sofas are situated in the centre of the room, a table and chairs lay just behind, and beyond that an extremely large kitchen. A whole wall is dedicated to books and has numerous shelves filled with them. It also has a bed to my right. Lyca walks over to the only other door in this house. He opens it and inside is an enormous group of empty stables. He waves a hand over the door as we enter the house once more and to my surprise it does not close behind us. Lyca places me next to Dion. He retrieves a small pet bed and offers it to Dion. He is reluctant to release Amahté for some reason but eventually gently places him inside and covers him up.

Lyca places him on a stand so he is off the ground. He checks once more on me before turning to depart. He reaches the door, turns around.

"Oh and one more thing, I am sorry for what I said before. I did not mean it. You are not anyone's property and I was just being naive and selfish"

Before I can reply he has departed our company. I turn to Dion who has not stopped staring at Amahté.

"Are you okay?" I ask.

He drags his gaze to me, forces a smile. "You are the one who is battered and in pain and you are asking if I am okay?"

I chuckle "Yes."

"Thank you I am. It is just Amahté. He saved us, risked his for all of us. I thought he must have perished and yet here he is. I could not live with myself if I did not do everything I could for him now as he risked so much for us."

I squeeze his shoulder with my free arm. "He is strong, he will pull through. We just have to believe."

He places his hand on top of mine and smiles.

"Anyway, why did Lyca bring us here?" I look around "What is so special about this place?"

Dion's smile increases as something touches my shoulder.

"That," he points.

ReUNioN

I twist my head around as I feel the wet tongue caress my neck. He leaps from sight and appears in front of me. I lock gazes with him and my smile broadens.

"Leo!!" I almost burst into tears at the sight of him.

'I have missed you so much,' Leo bows his head.

"Come here," I choke up.

"Be careful," Dion warns.

Leo gently places his enormous head on my lap. I bend over slowly; I hug him so tightly my arm aches. Tears of joy flow freely. He backs off and leaps up with excitement. Spreading his wings he takes to the air. The roof of this house is elevated enormously high, allowing Leo to fly around freely. He swirls around a couple of times before landing and approaching me carefully. He licks my arm gently and I stroke him.

Sparkie is beside Dion, he hugs her affectionately.

"Hello Sparkie."

She bows her head in response. I hear a clatter of hooves and Leo leaps onto the chair beside me, making room for the others to greet me.

Sure enough Lunar and Sapphire rush over too, each celebrating my return. They push each other, both eager to gain my attention. I hug them in turn. I look around.

"Where is Titan?"

132

Lunar bows his head.

My heart sinks as I realise what must have happened. My throat bulges as I try to contain my grief.

"He didn't make it?"

I lower my head, closing my eyes, trying to take in the horrific news. My heart aches from grief. Then I feel something on my knee. Opening my eyes I see Titan in his miniature form. Lunar had bowed his head to allow Titan passage onto my knee, not because he did not make it. My heart skips a beat as I kiss his tiny head. I toss him into the air allowing him to grow to full form. He increases in size before landing ahead of me.

Lunar and Sapphire take to the skies, playing with one and other. Titan approaches slowly. I throw my arm around his slender neck. He nuzzles me.

"I thought you....." I trail off not wishing to finish the sentence.

"He is fine. It was a tough time as he ended up with a serious infection and I did not think he would make it but then suddenly he turned things around and recovered amazingly."

I stroke him gently, thankful he is okay and that everyone survived. Finally, Manara takes her position on Dion's shoulder.

"You guys are a sight for sore eyes," I laugh.

Leo pushes his head into my side lovingly and lies beside me. Dion plays with Sparkie and Manara whilst the horses entertain themselves. I look to where Amahté is laid. He still shows no signs of movement. I pray with all of my will that he will pull through, he deserves that at least after acting like such a hero. I think back to what happened before my accident. My memory is hazy and the effort only concedes in a severe headache. I leave the thoughts for now and put them to the back of my mind. I lay my hand on Leo's back, it sinks deep into his long fur and within a couple of seconds, it is no longer visible. I stroke him gently.

"I have missed you all so much."

Leo's tongue caresses my arm before he rolls onto his back. I smile. The sofa is large and I appear minute against it but Leo's large stature is still too large for even this sofa. His head hangs over the edge as he shows me his stomach. I chuckle aloud.

"Something amusing you?" Dion breaks the silence.

"Oh nothing, just Leo makes me laugh."

With the sound of his name, he twists around rapidly and now stares directly into my eyes. Lowering his head I cup both sides of his jaw. I kiss between the bridge of his nose at the centre of both eyes.

"I don't know what I would do without you."

He licks my face before sitting upright, on guard.

I shake my head smiling at his seating, how erect his body has become as he keeps a watchful eye on me.

A burning sensation in my arm entices a moan to escape. Leo's attention darts to me as he examines the source. Opening his mouth he locks it around the tube ready to remove it.

"No. Leave it."

He stares at me.

"I need it."

'What is it?' Leo asks, relinquishing his hold over the drip.

I lower my head almost in shame. "I was attacked. This is hopefully helping me to overcome the venom."

'I am sorry I failed you but it will not happen again, I promise.'

"It wasn't your fault Leo, please don't blame yourself."

He does not reply as my words sink in, he stiffens his back, pins his ears vertically whilst by my side, eternally on guard. I run my hand over his enormous back, expecting him to push into it, returning to his relaxed form. However, this does not happen, he merely ignores my gesture and stands firm. I sigh. What have I done? He should not constantly stand watch over me; I did not create him for that purpose. He should carry out his own desires. I slump down on the sofa, saddened by his actions. Dion opens his mouth, thinks better of it before looking away once more.

Eventually, the fuss settles down and everyone around me now snoozes. Dion is the most amusing to witness. His requirement for sleep and his conscious need to ensure he keeps an eye on me are battling furiously within. His head dozes as his eyes slump once more. He forces them open yet again but no sooner are they open, does the weariness return with vengeance, forcing his eyelids to gain weight, closing once more. I notice them twitch a couple of times as if trying to pull them apart but he does not manage to this time and he finally falls asleep.

Leo has yet to fall prey to such matters and sits beside me on guard. I move closer to him, wrapping my arm around his enormous front leg. His stature softens slightly with my touch. Time passes in slow motion as the night drags its nonexistent feet. Leo has slowly begun to slump beside me. Even this tough exterior of the supreme guardian requires sleep at some point. He has managed to hold it off for many hours but I notice that it is affecting him. His eyes have glazed with his weariness and are red from lack of sleep. I decide to make sure he joins the others with a trick I figured out. I gently massage his ear, smoothly rubbing it. His head slides on its side as he lies down. His eyes close momentarily and after a couple of seconds show no sign of re-opening, I smile and pat his head. Sleep has tried to claim me on a couple of occasions but I have managed to work with my energy to hold it back. In the event, it becomes too much and I begin to drift off it jolts me to ensure I remain awake.

More hours pass and boredom claims me. I cannot move. I have nothing to entertain my mind in any way, so I decide to try to manipulate my energy to my will. At first, I begin the creation of an energy ball. It grows in the palm of my hand before I flick it upwards and lean back to watch it. The sphere spirals towards the roof. It reaches maximum height for the strength of my throw and begins its rapid descent. Palm flat I reach upwards. The ball stops suddenly. I crease my face in confusion. Why has gravity not taken control and returned it to me? I move my hand as it cramps. I contract and release my muscles trying to ease the discomfort when something thumps my shoulder. Twisting my head around I do not notice anything on the floor or in my surrounding area that could have been the foreign object. I scratch my head before a thought clicks into my mind. Slowly leaning back I stare above me. The ball of energy I created no longer floats above me.

"How strange it took a long time to fall."

Shaking the thought I return to my previous activity. I form the energy in my palm again. This time I do not throw it up. I think of an image. I picture a basic square and try to force the energy to take its shape. However, I do not know how to manipulate it to that extent and I only manage to force it to bubble before exploding in my palm. I sigh aloud. This does not deter me and I carry on through the night. About two and a half hours later I manage a shape that has four sides like my desired object. Although this one is most defiantly not a square; each side is a different length to the others and bulges disgustingly in the middle. I smile.

"Well, its close enough I guess," I chuckle dryly, thankful no one is conscious to witness my failure.

I decide to go back and form a sphere. I launch it up in the air once more. It reaches maximum height before plummeting. Holding out my palm I reach up once more and expectantly the ball stops mid-air. With a theory in mind, I close my hand. The ball does not move.

"Hmm."

Recalling the previous attempt I remove my whole hand from its path. The ball begins to plummet earthwards. I replace my hand swiftly and once again it ceases its fall.

"Hah!" I shout a little too loud.

Leo stirs a moment before lying still once more. I breathe a sigh of relief before returning my gaze. Holding my concentration on the sphere I order it to move. It shakes violently as if battling to obey or disobey my command. Concentrating hard I start to shake as I use all of my force to budge the Sphere. It inches to the left slightly. The more I concentrate the more the sphere is in motion. After an hour or so of grueling practice, I am now able to order the energy around to where I wish, although its progress is extremely slow and crippling. As I lie back psychologically exhausted I notice the light beaming through the roof for the first time. My head pounds from all the strain and I close my eyes to try to relieve some of the pressure.

Then I feel movement beside me. Dion is awakening. An evil thought crosses my mind. Opening one eye slightly I peer over at Dion. He has rolled over but is moving slightly. A twisted evil grin flashes across my face which I quickly dispense in light of my plan. Relaxing I allow my body to slump. My eyes tightly shut. I idiotically pretend to be asleep. Initially, I hear Dion gasp; he had fallen asleep.

Then he speaks, "Lexi?" he touches my shoulder.

After a couple of moments of me not moving his tone changes to fear.

"Please wake up Lexi," he gently shakes me.

I am just about to open my eyes, providing his relief when he places a hand on either side of my head, twisting my face in the opposite direction to his. Some of my memories return, blurring past my vision causing a more severe headache than I had previously. After a couple of minutes, his hands glow yellow. What is he doing? The energy enters my mind, seemingly searching around. I ponder about his actions a while, is he trying to sense any damage? I do not know but I decide to speak, allowing his fear to dissipate, "Dion?"

"Are you okay?" He presses, concerned.

I manage a nod before he releases me.

My head pounds, a searing pain throbs within. I place my hand on it.

"Oh my head."

"You fell asleep. I had to check you were okay when I could not wake you."

I sit a moment, what would he do if he knew I was playing a trick on him? I decide it would be unwise to confess so I merely keep my mouth closed. I bury my idiotic action deep within, never to be heard of again.

Dion looks at me, embarrassed.

"Can we keep this to ourselves? I do not wish for Lyca to find out, I should not have fallen asleep."

"Yeah, we shouldn't tell anyone," I blush.

Relief sweeps over his face.

"Thank you," he smiles.

Leo stirs beside me. I stroke him gently. His eyes open as he thumps the sofa with his back leg in enjoyment. After a couple of seconds, his face alters. He rolls over and sits bolt upright, continuing his guard once more. I puff at his actions and relax. My head throbs as I lie backwards.

I allow my newly reformed memories to surround me, my family and friends united for the first time. Although my new acquaintances have varied appearances to which my family would think odd and most likely be terrified of, they do not even flinch. They greet them as any normal person and accept them into their presence. We are welcomed into my home, just as I am about to enter I hear someone shout my name. I turn around, searching the area. I shrug when I see nothing and place my hand on the now-closed door. The name is spoken again. Twisting my head I finally see who is calling me. Jacob.

His hair spiked up in his usual style with his muscular arms protruding from his short-sleeved top he rushes over to me. My heart summersaults as the butterflies enter my stomach. A smile stretches seemingly across my whole face as I run into his arms. Lifting me he spins me around in a circle. His blue eyes twinkle as I stare into them. Jacob smiles at me.

"Oh, I've missed you," I almost break down.

He hugs me tight before carrying me to the door. Placing a hand on it he pushes it open. I crease my face as I stare into the unfamiliar room. This is not my house. I peer around, no one in sight. Numerous fluffy sofas are spread before me. Placing a hand on my head I close my eyes. Then a thought comes to mind.

"Jacob!" I shout, turning my head.

A man is holding me. This man is not my boyfriend. I scream as the door we entered through disintegrates before my eyes.

"Lexi calm down," speaks the man.

Through teary vision, I look at him.

"Who are you?"

"Lyca."

The moment the name is uttered my sanity returns, my haze seems to clear as the man before me reconnects with my memory. Once located it clicks into place and instantaneously I know who he is.

"Are you okay?" He asks.

Creasing my forehead I try to sort through reality and my world of dreams. He squeezes my arm gently. I shake the mist and doubt from my mind trying to concentrate.

"Erm…yes I'm fine," I shake my head.

"Who is Jacob if you do not mind my prying?"

My heart leaps into my throat forming a painful lump. Its mass increases as I think of him. Tears begin to form; I blink them away and try to sustain my voice as I answer.

"He is, was my boyfriend…" I stammer, "we've known each other since being kids and one day admitted we liked each other more than friends and decided to go from there. We were inseparable," I sigh as my heartaches.

"I am sorry," he squeezes my arm. "Maybe one day you will find each other again? You never know where love can lead a heart."

What a pleasant thought that would be. Seeing Jacob once more confuses my emotions. I loved him with all of my heart. But is that really the truth? Loved? Do I no longer hold him in such high regard? I guess it is difficult when you have not been able to see them in such a prolonged period. I may never see him again. Then there is Dion. I found him attractive from the very moment I laid eyes upon him. He has been with me throughout everything and I fear I may be falling for a man that I should not be. I also fear he may reciprocate these feelings. I shake my head trying to rid myself of the thoughts Lyca's remark sparked.

"Where are we going?"

"I am taking you to the Library where we can talk without interruption."

The rest of the journey is filled with silence as my mind drifts away with thoughts of my family and friends. Thoughts of Dion and Jacob. How could my heart betray Jacob so? I must not allow my heart its rule. I cannot fall for Dion. I will not fall for him. I must stay strong for Jacob. I am hopeful I will be reunited with him.

A lump gathers in my throat making it ache terribly. Tears well up as I try to dispense the dread within my heart. I long so deeply to be reunited with my family back home; alas I cannot be with them, at least for now, my purpose has been forcibly altered and I am needed elsewhere.

One day I hope I will be able to return but for now, I can rely on my fond memories. A single tear escapes as we come to a halt. I quickly wipe my cheek and compose myself as Lyca approaches the Library.

INteRcEPtIOn

Lyca lowers me onto the seat and sits beside me. He stares at me as if looking directly through me. His features remain stern, confusion clear within his eyes. Then before I can ask what is the matter he shakes his head, softening once more.

"How are you feeling?"

"A little sore," I grimace.

He cocks an eyebrow, "it is to be expected."

"So do you remember anything?"

I search my mind, apart from the small fragments of memories I gained about my family and friends I cannot find much of anything else. My eyes wander to the left as I desperately try to claw something, anything from my memory banks. I draw a blank and shake my head before lowering it in shame. Tears escape once more. It runs halfway down my cheek before slowing to a halt.

Lyca places a finger under my chin, slowly brings my head upwards. He wipes my cheeks before smiling gently.

"There is no need to be upset. I did not expect you to be able to. You are a Magi that has been through such great trauma. Your mind has isolated the painful memories and blocked their access, protecting you."

I sigh louder than necessary.

"How will I be able to tell you what happened if I can't remember?"

He smiles, places a hand on my shoulder.

"I have a way, but will not do it without your permission."

"What is it?"

"I can access your mind for you. I will not have control of the memories, however; I will see every aspect of your life."

I think a moment before nodding.

"Also I must tell you that when I am finished you will remember everything, your mind will be overwhelmed with them all at once, it could cause you to…"

I hold up a hand stopping him mid-sentence.

"Just do it."

"Are you sure?"

I nod once more.

Turning me to face him, he places his hands at either side of my head. He closes my eyes.

"This will sting a little."

My body convulses thrusting me into my mind. I am in a room. It is filled with countless squares all lined up horizontally in front of me. They are packed together so tightly that only the left edge of the square is visible. One square slides upwards. It increases in size rapidly filling the whole room. I am looking up at my father, he leans over my cot. I am a baby I realise. Suddenly the memories speed increases its pace, we are fast-forwarding through my life I realise. Within seconds we are at my father's funeral. I scream out in pain as the memory tears me apart once more.

Lyca quickly moves along. I am on my knees, sobbing my heart out. Trough blurred vision I see we have skipped far ahead. I am riding Fox. I see the strange creature in the woods once more. A shiver runs down my spine as I now know what that shadow was. Myself and Ellie are searching the house, my mother's torn body lies sprawled on the floor, my life slips away from me. The orb, the fields they all pass by rapidly. Dion showing me the way out. Creating Leo, escaping. We find Amahté, Splite finds us. The memories crease me once more. My broken leg, the return of Dion. The cabin, Elliott's presence forces me from control. We stop a while on my heart as I am trying to stop the poison from entering it. The strange symbol and the blue crystal. We skip forward for a long time. My memories flashing before me to rapidly to follow any longer.

Suddenly it stops dead. We are at the moment I reach the stairs, after a lifetime I clamber up them. I enter the strange room. Green energy entices me to touch the box and my body is engulfed the moment I make contact. I watch in awe as I revisit the battle between Splite and Amahté. Then he turns the tables and defeats Splite. As he leaps through the window I reach for him. Then my body is forced backwards and I am thrown from the room, along with Amahté. The memories skip forward once more until we reach the present moment.

Lyca releases my head and we are both thrown backwards. I land on top of a bookshelf. The blunt force impacts my shoulder and entices a loud scream. I roll over in agony and fall from the top of the shelf. I land hard on the ground. After a couple of seconds, my memories all rush back into my head at the same time. My mind screams from all the terror and pain that has just returned in full force. It throbs as I cradle it with one hand.

The agony worsens and I scream. It seems to throb and bulge as I roll around. My senses begin to fray and I feel my sanity breaking down. After a couple of seconds, Lyca is in front of me. He sits on my chest, pinning me down. I cry aloud as the pressure on my injured shoulder creases me once more.

My emotions explode as my arms begin to glow blue. Splite appears in my mind fresh, disgusting, smiling at me. My sanity turns Lyca into him. I force my energy into my chest as my eyes begin to emit their blue aura. My chest is thrust forward as an enormous stream of energy erupts from me. Lyca is thrown completely across the room and disappears. The pain in my head doubles the power of my energy. The room begins to literally spin as it grows out of my control. Books fly around before me ripping to shreds. Shelves crumble as the room is destroyed. Chips of marble flake away and join the chaos.

I hear something to my left. Dion is beside me, he tries desperately to calm me, but to no avail. I look to him in desperation, praying he can assist me, cease this madness. I cannot hear what he is saying. Just as I think I hear a word, another memory bursts through my conscious. The pain is unbearable and I lose myself once more. I laugh hysterically, mixed with small interruptions of crying. He shakes his head beside me, disappears from my sight. Hope fades within me.

Suddenly he reappears with Lyca. He is bleeding, his clothes and skin torn badly. Dazed he tries to concentrate. Red and yellow auras connect as they twist around each other intertwining, morphing into one.

"Help me," I manage to scream through the insanity.

They link hands. The red and yellow energy shoots upwards, it extends, wrapping around my swirling burst of energy. As I watch, the blanket seals me within. It closes in forcing my energy to decrease in size. I regain enough of my senses to halt it from forcing its way out of the bubble. It merely dwindles with some feeble attempts to escape. As the energy dies down, the contents of the room plummet earthwards. The source is now directly on top of me. I gulp as terror claims me. My aura tries to battle but I do not allow it and within seconds all energy drains from me.

My body returns to a normal colour, my blue glow diminishing with my emotions. Their energy still hovers above me. My head falls to the side as the world goes dark. I fall unconscious. Seconds later a jolt shoots through my limbs, bringing me back to the world of the living.

I gasp sitting up rapidly. Dizziness makes the room spin. After a couple of seconds, it passes and I re-open my eyes. My body is drained. I look to my side. Lyca and Dion unclasp their hands, both slump beside me. Their breathing rampant they rest a moment. I see that Lyca is severely injured, his blood drips onto the floor. I cry out standing up shakily.

"No wait Lexi, stay down," Dion manages to choke.

Ignoring him I manage to hobble away from them. They do not have the energy to follow. I do not have the energy either. Dion tries to stand, he fails. Utilising my dwindling energy resources I manage to make it to the door before a hand stops me. I collapse. I am steadied and slowly helped to the floor. Lyca kneels before me. He smiles.

His injuries no longer exist; he has healed them. I cannot control my tears and they stream down my face. I allow them to flow freely.

"Please just let me go," I cry.

Dion crawls to my other side. He places a hand on my shoulder.

"I'm sick of all this, I'm not safe, please just let me go, I shouldn't exist. I don't want to anymore. All I seem to do it hurt the ones around me. I'm out of control."

"Do not say that," Dion replies, tucking a piece of my blond hair behind my ear.

I turn to the wreck of a library.

"But look what I've done. It is unnatural, destructive, it's evil," I gulp and lower my head in shame.

"Please let me go."

Lyca takes my hand, he is still smiling.

"Please do not do this Lexi. We would like you to stay."

146

My anger erupts. My voice morphs deeper as my emotions course through my body.

"I almost killed you both, stop acting like it's all okay!" I scream.

"Because it's not," I sob.

My voice softens, returning to normal.

"Let us at least help you leave then?"

I peer to Dion. His features crease as he shoots Lyca an angered expression.

"Lyca I will not let her go. Not in this state."

"Dion we must obey her wishes. Elocin!"

He nods in return, "okay."

They help me to my feet; the three of us hobble towards the head of the house. Just as we reach the first room they force me into the seat. It all happens so swiftly. My arm is pushed into the chair; a second later the material has stretched and formed a band. It wraps around my wrist, bounding me to the chair. Another wraps around my chest and my feet. I cannot move.

"What are you doing?" I ask.

"You are not leaving," Lyca replies

I struggle to no avail.

"You can't keep me here!" I shout.

"Oh I can," he smiles softly.

"Dion, please help me."

He simply replies with, I am, before sitting next to me.

Lyca disappears.

"Fine! I will help myself."

I tap into my energy, my arms glow blue. Just as I am about to force myself from my bounds a sharp pain in my neck catches my attention. Lyca is injecting me with a purple substance.

Just as the last of the substance enters my bloodstream my energy vanishes. My arms blink out. My body suddenly feels as though it has been hit by a train. I scream in agony. Lyca rapidly injects me with something else and the pain dulls incredibly.

I relax instantly. Glaring at Lyca I try to access my energy. It does not work, nothing happens. It is almost as though it has disappeared. Lyca then replaces the blue drip I managed to destroy previously.

Confused I try once more. Nothing.

"What have you done?"

Lyca kneels in front of me. "Disabled you energy sources."

"What?! Why?" I struggle once more.

"It is the only way to stop you from self-destructing."

"No. You can't do this," I tug my arm.

"We can."

He gently places a hand on my opposite shoulder.

I gasp at his touch. He examines it upon my reaction.

"It has dislodged again."

"Get off me!" I want so desperately to remove his hand from me but I cannot move.

"You want me to leave it?" He asks.

"YES! I don't care anymore. Just leave me alone."

'Lexi listen to them,' Elliott breaks his silence.

"Shut up Elliott, stay out of this."

Lyca shakes his head.

"Very strange. Never the less if I leave your arm you will not be able to use it again."

I merely roll my eyes in response.

"Dion put weight on her chest."

I resist to no avail. He grips my chest, forces me back even more, slightly restricting my breathing.

"Sorry Lexi but I cannot just leave it," Lyca remarks.

Pushing my arm he clicks it back into place. I tense my face; I do not feel much pain and manage to contain my cries. Lyca leaves the room and returns with another strange sling.

With a wave of his hand, my bounds fall loose, freeing me. I immediately launch forward. I manage to get a couple of feet away before hands wrap around my waist. Lifting me sharply I thrash my legs around. Dion turns around to face Lyca.

"Can we not just make her sleep until we figure this out?" Dion asks.

"No, we need to be careful."

Lyca wraps the sling around my chest and my neck. I resist as much as possible but Dion has a firm grip and I am exhausted. After a second all air deflates and my arm is forced into position once again. I gasp at the pain. After a short amount of time it passes.

Dion replaces me on the seat and the restraints re-form, trapping me once more. An idea forms. I shut myself off to their discussions. I allow the darkness to roam freely. It gags me to do this but what other choice do I have? I am too dangerous, I almost ended Lyca's life and I could not control myself. I need to end my life. The venomous creature claws up my back, taking a position on my shoulder, it lingers a moment before leaping inside my head. I allow it to fill me completely. I force myself from the control of my body. It stiffens as I depart.

I am within my mind once more. The brightly lit room I envisioned suddenly turns black. It melts the beautiful walls, leaving only destruction. I rock back and forth in a corner.

'Lexi.'

Shocked I peer around. Elliott's image is stood before me.

'Hi.'

'What are you doing?' He asks me.

'You saw what happened.'

'I did but it wasn't your fault. You couldn't control it.'

'Exactly my point!'

He sits beside me.

'I know I have no place but I know you, you're such a kind-hearted person. You wouldn't hurt anyone intentionally.'

'I don't want to but why do I keep doing it? I think something inside me does want to cause pain, if not why does it keep happening?'

'I can't answer that but I think it is only because you can't control it. So because you are powerful it gets out of control and ends up hurting those around you.'

I shake my head, not allowing his words to penetrate. I do not wish to believe them. This way is better. I can do no harm.

Suddenly I feel my mind being pulled towards reconnecting with my body.

'What's happening?'

'I don't know' Elliott replies.

I feel the connection establish control. My once stiff carcass comes back to life as I am forced back to reality.

Lyca removes his hand from my head.

"I do not think so Lexi," he smiles sadly.

"Oh thank heavens," Dion sighs with relief.

My face creases as I stare around the room.

"What?" I stammer.

"I brought you back. When I relived your life I learned much about you. I connected with how you can remove yourself from the world and figured out how to pull you back."

"No!" I cry.

"Lexi, please stop this," Dion pleads.

"Sorry Dion, the world is better off without me, or at the very least those around me that I care about are," I sigh.

"You are so incorrect. I am begging you."

He goes down on one knee. I turn my head away from him, tears welling. I shut out my captors.

******

I am unsure of the amount of time that has passed since my intervention. Lyca and Dion discuss many things to which I do not pay attention.

"I have learned so much from her. The source of our energy appears to come from a growth on our heart."

"How do you know?" Dion replies.

"When the venom was travelling through her veins she managed to stop it. That is where she saw it. It was magnificent."

"Amazing."

"Yes, all these years we have existed and mastered many skills we have never known from where it originates. It is marvellous."

I zone out once more. Uninterested in what they have to say.

Hours pass by when the mention of Amahté catches my attention. I turn instantly.

"So this Amahté creature, she somehow removed him from the occurrence box."

"What?! How is that possible?"

"That is what I am wondering. I have examined him and he is not a creation, he is perfectly real. I cannot understand it."

"Will he be okay?" I interrupt accidentally.

Both stare at me smiling.

I puff aloud.

"So you are still with us then?"

"I wish I wasn't," I snap.

Dion's smile fades.

"To answer your question I think he will come round but will need to be looked after intensely. From my examination, he has broken an arm and leg."

My heart skips a beat at the good news. I manage a smile.

"Look after him well won't you, he saved us."

"Well, I was thinking you could take care of him. He knows you."

"Sorry but no, I too busy self-destructing," I smile cynically.

"I cannot take this."

Dion storms out of the room.

Lyca remains. Keeping a watchful eye on me.

More hours pass in silence. Dion does not return. I have been working on my restrains for hours now, trying to loosen them.

"You will not free yourself," Lyca breaks the silence.

Startled I jump out of my skin. Glaring at him I speak.

"Why are you doing this?"

"As much as you would like I will not let you end your life."

"Why not?" I plead

He stands, sits beside me.

"You do not deserve to die."

"How can you say that? I almost killed you!" I snap.

"I tried to tell you before I started that something like this could happen. It usually does. Well not as extreme but still I was expecting it."

"That doesn't make it right. What I did was wrong."

"You was not in control, it is not your fault."

"What about the next time I lose control? I could kill someone. I'm not prepared to take that risk."

"We could teach you control."

"No, I'm too unpredictable."

And with that I turn my head away from him, disgusted by his actions. He sighs then I hear him leave. I do not turn around. After half an hour or so he returns with Dion.

"What are we going to do with her?" Dion sighs.

"Well I can keep her energy disabled with a daily injection but apart from that, I am not sure. We could keep her locked in her room until she sees sense."

"We cannot keep her locked up."

"What other choice do we have? If we allow her freedom she will do something incredibly idiotic, and that is a fact."

Dion sighs, thinks a moment.

"Lock her in her room then."

"As you wish," Lyca approaches me.

He releases my bounds and once more I try to run. I dodge Dion's advance and slide through his legs. That pain injection is wonderful I find energy from nowhere.

I rush out of the door, run down the corridor. I pass a couple of doors and enter the next. Closing it quickly I sink to the floor. Then a sound makes me look up. I am back in the main room, with Dion and Lyca stood before me.

"Huh?" I mumble.

I turn swiftly to exit the door I entered and collide with a solid wall. Hands grip me firmly, they wrap around me. I do not fight, I merely slump. I give up, I cannot escape. My attempts are futile without the use of the vile reason I am in this mess. I relax as I am carted off to my room. I can do nothing more. They place me on the bed before exiting swiftly. The door closing firmly behind them.

EnTRapMEnt

I am that of a wild animal in captivity; torn from my own free will and forced to do as others wish. Bending me to their will as they deem fit. Encased in a room with no escape. Elliott has tried numerous things to assist me, pull me from this darkness but nothing works and I have not heard from him since. I search the room for any signs of weakness to which I can utilise and burst from this cage. The only viable option is the window. Although I am unsure exactly how I could escape via the window in this jacket restricting my movement. I look down at it once more. It is much like a straight jacket used in severe cases of mental illness where self-harm occurs. The straps prevent movement of the arms thus preventing serious harm one could cause. I allow my head to sink. This is useless.

Of course, this is entirely my fault. In my bid of self-destruction, I was idiotic enough to smash the mirror in my room in anger. I then realised I could attempt to use the shards as leverage on the window to jar it open. Upon hearing the chaos they returned to my room with haste only to find me sitting in the middle of large glass shards, bleeding from my fist and hand where I was grasping the largest piece. Their expressions as they walked in almost broke me from my depression.

I struggled to contain my laughter, which soon changed to anger as they pounced upon me simultaneously. I had not spoken to them in quite a long period at that point and I did not intend to break my silence. So I did not explain my actions. That said they would have probably not believed me. Instead, Dion restrained me whilst Lyca removed the glass. He manoeuvred me to the bed, forced me in place as I struggled against him. I looked longingly at the open door. This fuelled my anger and I miraculously managed to wriggle free. Charging full speed I almost reached the door. Lyca lunged for me; making contact with my waist he tackled me to the ground. Before I had a chance to move Dion was also upon me.

I screamed foul words at them of course but it was to no avail. Dion merely gripped me tighter and held me against the wall while Lyca left the room. My head slumped as the realisation of not escaping hit me. Moments later Lyca returned with a black leather jacket. It was forced upon me with little resistance. I had no current cares for my attire. What a large mistake that was. I shake my head before returning to my recollection. The moment the zip reached the top of the runners and the bottom button clicked into place it began to move. I remember my heart racing beneath my chest as the strange jacket pulled my arms down to my waist. The sleeves began to lengthen before wrapping around my waist and up my back. I heard the metal of a buckle fasten before the material lay still. I tried to move my arms but could budge them not even an inch. I tugged in a panic tried desperately to thrash around. I only succeeded in tiring myself and inflicting pain on my arms. They ached from their uncomfortable position and with my futile attempts at its removal.

Glaring at the jacket it entices my anger. Protected by energy, I have attempted many imaginative means of removal but nothing has worked. If only my energy was a viable option. This thing would not stand a chance. I have been trapped for six months or so now, without any progress. My depression has not lifted and I still fear for everyone's life around me. Even though I am currently indisposed when my energy returns

I am sure I would end up harming someone once more. With all of my attempts failing, I feel it is time for a different approach to my situation. After a couple of hours, Lyca returns with my daily injection. I am perched in the corner, hunched up, my head down. He approaches cautiously.

I do not move my gaze, completely ignoring him. He brushes my wild hair from my shoulder before injecting me with that poison. He checks the contents of the blue drip. A confused expression crosses his face; he is shocked at my lack of a reaction. I have battled them enforcing them to restrain me, ensuring I cannot move. Not once have I willingly allowed them near until now. He wearily sits beside me, edging his arm across both of my shoulders. I do not shy away from his touch. In fact, I enjoy human touch once more. After a couple of seconds, he raises my head, examining me. I speak to him for the first time in over half a year.

"Please can I have a drink?"

His jaw falls slack. He rushes from my side; disappearing out of sight he leaves the room, returning moments later with a jug of water and a cup. It sloshes around so violently due to his swift movement that half of the liquid ends up on the floor. He empties a little into the glass before holding it to my lips. I slurp it down eagerly before replacing my head on my knees. Then I lift it back up and with a warm smile, I thank him. I force the dull glaze from my eyes enticing the bright colour to return. I then replace my head to its original position.

After a few moments, Lyca takes his leave rather quickly. Eager to tell Dion of my improvement I suspect. As soon as the door closes I lift my head, a dark grin creeps across my face as my plan falls into place.

Each day that passes I force myself to be polite and more responsive to my captors. The glee that Dion cannot hide makes me feel guilty for the outcome of my plan but I force those thoughts away. It is for his well being, for everyone's.

I keep up the pretence that I am a bright jolly person once more, and after a couple of months carrying out this farce, they finally decide to remove the jacket. Unbuttoning it the zip reappears. He simply unzips it and they slowly remove it.

"Oh wow that feels amazing."

I stretch my cramped muscles. They have been protected by energy and are not deformed in any way but merely stiff and tender. Although they have removed my jacked they still search the room for potentially harmful objects. I do not push for anything, although I desperately desire for the cease of the injections to fulfil my plan. I play along. Both of them visit me regularly and I chat heartily away as though back to my normal self.

Lyca checks my blue drip, it is empty.

"That is the last of it."

"What?" I ask shocked.

He removes the needle.

"I think that is all you require. I will have to bring some equipment to test you but I am sure of it."

Terror grips me.

"No. Wait, what if I turn into one of those monsters?"

"I will gather the equipment, it may take me a day or so to program it all but I will return tomorrow."

He turns to leave.

I begin to perspire as my body shakes with panic.

"Could I change in the time it takes you to return?" I stammer.

He does not stop, as he reaches the door he turns, smiles and just before exiting he states that it is a possibility. Then he vanishes, bolting the door firmly behind him.

I sink to my knees as I revel in the madness which threatens to consume me. The room begins to spin. Bile forms in my stomach as I wretch, what can I do? I want to end my life not become more of a monster than I already am…

I shake my head, gain partial control of my body. Every muscle in my body screams at me to do something before I become one of those things. Wracking my partially functioning brain, straining, I realise I cannot wait until they stop my injections. I must escape now to end myself before I transform into the creature I despise the most. My hands shake violently as I search the room. I cannot allow myself to turn into one of those...those beasts! They tore the flesh from my own mother's body if I turn into one of them I will be the same as the one that ruined my life.

Then I see it, my only chance. The window! I tried to lever it open but I have never tried to go through it. It is the only possible weak point of this impenetrable room. Am I that desperate to jump through this window without properly knowing how high up I actually am? Yes! Emotions overwhelm me as I stand too quickly. Dizziness sweeps over me and before I can take my first step I faint.

My eyes flutter open a couple of times before I realise what had happened. Cursing myself I slide into a sitting position.

"How long have I been unconscious?" I ask myself scratching my head.

I manage to stand.

"A couple of hours," Dion states.

My heart leaps into my throat as I jump out of my skin. My legs shake as I hold my chest trying to steady my blazing heart. I breathe deeply.

"You scared me half to death th..."

I do not finish my sentence as I realise I am out of time. Dion must have foiled my plan. Paranoia sets in. I search for him; he is sat on the bed. He smiles.

"I apologise. I did not mean to frighten you."

My heartbeat pumps through my chest as I panic. What can I do? I look to Dion, then to the window. I am not that far away from it. Maybe if I dash for it I could…

Without thinking about it anymore I scramble towards the window faster than my legs can carry me. I hear Dion shriek from behind. I feel the energy in the room. He directs it towards me. At the last second, I dodge his blast. It smashes into the window, cracking it. I dodge his second attempt and lunge through the window.

Glass shards pierce my skin as we travel together, earthwards. I spiral down. The drop is not life-threatening. I land with a large thump. My rib cracks with the blunt force and the wind is thrown from me. I do my best to ignore the burning pain as I scramble out of sight. Taking cover behind a large shrub I grimace. I hear the crunch of glass and peer through the branches.

Dion desperately searches the area. How did he make it down here so quickly? Never mind that, get moving before you are discovered. I think to myself. Oh, how insane I must sound I shake my head.

Gathering all of my strength, applying gentle support to my wound I travel as fast as I possibly can in the opposite direction of the house. Ducking for cover at every sound I struggle onwards. Sweat drenches me. After around twenty minutes or so a fence suddenly appears before me, I almost run directly into it. Applying the brakes rapidly I skid towards it. I stop my approach just before I impact it. I scuttle behind a tree. My breathing is so rapid, I must rest a while.

I desperately try to calm my breathing. I am exhausted. I notice blood on my hand for the first time. Confused I remove it from my ribs. Dread claims me as I see a shard of glass protrudes from my skin, I am not sure how deep it has pierced but I am struggling to breathe freely.

"Well, I'm not going to make it very far with that am I?" I laugh.

I await a response from someone. When none is returned I hit myself in the head. I am delusional. I must move far enough away and hide to prevent them from finding me.

I force myself to stand.

"Ahhh," I cry aloud.

Grimacing I follow the fence line, the multicoloured trees shrouding me from sight. Stumbling and gasping from the agony I struggle onwards, following the fence line I desperately desire to cross. After an eternity I finally give weigh and my legs collapse beneath me.

"That's it, I'm finished!" I manage to choke.

Rolling onto my back I scream, opening my eyes, I see it. My whole body becomes numb as adrenaline rushes through my veins. I push myself up, waver a moment before regaining my balance I behold the threshold.

Two large gates stand before me; the familiar hounds greet me with silence. Their blackened crystal eyes seem to stare through my soul. Shaking my head I concentrate and touch the tornado symbol instinctively, nothing happens. Searching through my memories I try to remember how Dion enticed the inanimate hounds to complete their task. Seconds pass and I cannot recall anything. Suddenly something moves. A metallic panel protrudes from the symbol emitting a black light. I do not know what action to take. Scratching my head I look to my hand. Will I still be encoded after all of this madness?

"I wonder."

I cease my actions and touch the panel with a finger. It does nothing so I begin to pull away. My hand does not follow my command. The more I retract the more a force pulls me closer. Eventually, my whole hand lies flat on the panel. The gates creak open and my hand is released from its bond. I rub it tenderly before exiting swiftly.

In a blind panic, I travel at a high-speed, as fast as my failing body will allow, desperately searching for my final resting place, after all I have been through, I deserve to perish in peace at least.

My lungs gasp desperately for air; my chest begins to hurt from the strain. I must stop. I have no other option. Peering back I see have put quite a distance between us. I allow my body to cease its crazed actions. I drop to the floor with enormous force. I begin my final crawl to the shrubbery beside me. With my last effort, I manage to conceal most of my body inside the rainbow coloured leaves. I allow myself to relax. I feel pain no longer. It will not be a lengthy process; I look to my blood-stained clothing and the puddle that has already begun to gather. That shard may have hit something vital, either that or internal trauma.

My body begins to seize violently so I close my eyes. After a couple of minutes, I lie still once more. I engulf myself in my surroundings, the sounds of the obscure animals that live around here. The footsteps, they appear so close, the singing of… my eyes jolt open. Footsteps! Fear grips me as my senses temporally return. I cannot move, I can merely pray I am not discovered. My failing heart still manages to pound in my chest with the terror of being discovered.

The footsteps distant themselves from me, their sound fading as they travel further away. Something inside me crunches against my heart. It feels as though claws are crushing it, piercing it with the pressure. I cannot hold back my cries of agony. I scream as the top of my lungs before the world goes black and I fall unconscious.

Eyes flicker open, a blurred stream of rainbow colours, they close once more. I regain and slip in and out of consciousness at will. Each time remaining in the same place, at least they have not located me.

My eyes flicker open once more. I am greeted by the amazing array of colours and as they begin to blur I expect to lose consciousness for the final time. However, I am not so lucky. The leaves were not blurring due to this fact, but due to my body being swiftly pulled from where it was residing. Dion is the first face I see. He waves a hand before my eyes, I am too out of it to even react, and my eyes grow heavy.

Then warmth gathers around my rib cage. I force my eyes open once more to view what is happening. Yellow energy begins to knit my broken ribs and blood vessels back together. I feel my life returning to me.

"NOO!" I scream, feebly attempting to remove him.

I have not the energy to dislodge him but I realise a red light surrounds me anyway, pinning me to the ground. I glare towards its source. Lyca stands behind me a sorrowful expression with a tinge of anger. Within moments my rib and tissues have been healed. The energy is removed and I am assisted to my feet. The bruising and pain has lessened but has not disappeared.

I grimace as the full force impacts me. Tears roll from my cheek as I begin to cry. I cannot be strong any longer I merely give up. They assist me to a seat nearby. Once perched, Dion kneels in front as Lyca supports me. At least I assume this is the case, but thinking more clearly he is most likely preventing me from running.

"Why would you do such a thing?"

My head is lifted as he guides it up with a finger, replacing hair behind my ears he stares at me, awaiting a response. He is almost in tears. He tries to hide it but I witness his sorrow. It truly destroys me seeing him like this, guilt consumes me.

"I don't want to live anymore. Why can't you just let me go?" I mumble through chocked tears.

Dion's eyes begin to fill up, and a stab of guilt pierces my heart.

He shakes them away before smiling sadly.

"I care for you, would you allow someone you cared for to take their life without fighting for them?"

I stare in response.

"Would you?" Dion pries.

"No," I whisper.

"Then you can understand my actions. Why do you feel the need to do this?"

I sniff, wipe my tears away and stare at him sternly.

"I am a menace, I am unpredictable and the world will be a better place without me. All I do is hurt, people. My sanity can't take it. I am tired of fighting my destiny, this is my choice and you should respect it!"

"Then why are you?"

"Huh?"

"Why are you fighting your destiny?"

"I'm not, I'm giving in to it!" I snap.

Dion grasps my head forcefully. I glare into his eyes, deeper and deeper. A cloud begins to form, engulfing his hazel eyes, turning them grey. Then I see it. A memory shared with Dion an eternity ago, I watch the scene play out before me; I am sat in a crystal throne, watching myself perish at the hands of the despicable horned creature. It reaches for me and I scream, losing connection to Dion.

I shy away from him as he releases me, slightly dazed he rubs his head. My heart pounds beneath my chest as I try to escape those images, I flail around but Lyca is not fazed and merely hangs on to me tightly. Dion recovers rapidly.

"That is your destiny."

Confused I stare at him "If that's my destiny, you would rather me be crushed by that monster than die peacefully now?!" My anger flourishes.

As my rage travels through my body I notice my finger is blinking blue. Hope gathers inside as I pull my arm close, hiding it from sight.

"No, that is not what I mean. The future is volatile, it can be changed. An example if you had perished here today that future would not have taken place. I mean the powerful, brave woman you witnessed. That is who you are destined to become."

I peer backwards; my energy is travelling up through my body. Just a couple more seconds.

My body erupts with a throbbing blue energy; my eyes turn blue as I become stronger.

"No!" I shout, my voice morphed deep and inhuman.

With the flick of my wrist, I remove Lyca from my side and pin him to the ground. I begin to levitate. Turning to Dion I notice a single tear falls down his cheek as he lowers his head.

"You won't stop me," I screech.

He rises from his knee, his head still lowered.

"I will not."

"WHAT?" Lyca exclaims. "What do you think you are doing?"

Dion turns to him.

"She is correct; this is her life, her decision. We will no longer force her. It will not work. She must choose to live herself; otherwise, we will be sleeping with one eye open constantly pondering if she has done something to herself."

He turns to leave, looks back at me one last time, tears rolling down his cheeks.

"I will always care for you, protect you with my life but the one thing I cannot assist you with is the battle between you and your mind. I am by your side, powerless. I have watched you fall apart, picked up the pieces. I have grown closer to you than you will ever know. If you choose to end yourself I will be left with an emptiness that cannot be filled. You mean the world to me and have made me a better person and for that I thank you. Goodbye Lexi."

With that, he turns, walking in the opposite direction.

His words cut through me like a knife. My heavy heart gives way to my anger, diminishing it instantly. I drop to the floor instantly and land awkwardly on all four limbs. Lyca begins to stand; he appears confused, unaware of what action to take. After a couple of seconds he places a hand on my shoulder, squeezes it, and for a second I think he is about to take me back. Surprisingly he releases it and follows Dion's path.

I crumple to the floor in an emotional wreck. The battle within me fierce. I am a danger to those around me, but could I honestly remove myself from this world after that? He has been my rock and I care for him more than I'd like to admit. Not only him, but Lyca has also become a close friend along with the others. What would happen to Leo? Would he remain or simply disappear? After all, he is my creation. Such thoughts had not previously crossed my mind. I was simply so set on self-destruction, that I never thought about the people I was leaving behind. They would be the ones to suffer once I had ended mine. They said I could be trained to not be a danger and it is those I have hurt with the outbursts that are the ones urging me to live, they have forgiven me. Why can I not forgive myself? I sit in turmoil a few minutes more before making a decision. Standing up I shout aloud.

"Dion! Lyca!"

They turn their heads swiftly, questioningly.

"Please help me," I mumble as my salty tears stream down my face.

Dion turns and rushes towards me, his face also streaked with tears but an enormous smile gathers, broadening as he closes in on me. He embraces me tightly. My tears flow freely as I cling to him for dear life. My heart heavy with dread but also lifted with love. After our emotional embrace, both Lyca and Dion assist me towards the house.

I have to be better; I have to make an effort for my new family. They have done so much for me I cannot even put into words how much they mean. It seems I did not realise just how much of an effect my self-destruction had on those that care for me deeply. All I can promise at this moment in time is that I will try.

"I am so pleased you decided to give it another chance," Dion ruffles my hair a sad loving smile forms as he stares at me.

"With all those soppy things you said how I could not?" I brush it off and wink at him.

ThE arT Of ReTeNtiOn

I have been allowed to recuperate for a couple of weeks now before my training begins. Amahté is more stable but remains unconscious. I am praying for the day of his return, but for now, I take care of his needs and watch over him until my friend graces us with his presence once more.

Stretching I exit my room. Winding through the enormous stairwells and hallways I eventually find myself in the main section of the house. Dion and Lyca are already there, awaiting my arrival.

After what happened they have both been overly kind and careful around me, not wanting to spark any regretful memories I assume. Although kind, it bears no use to me; the memories still burn within my brain, questioning if I have made the correct decision. The answer I always find you may ask? Yes. Yes is my answer. I have repeated this question more times in the days that have passed than one could have thought possible. I have many responsibilities, my friends, and my family. I must learn how to retain and master my abilities so it can be controlled allowing me to be able to use it against the foul creatures that wish my world amongst many others harm. That is my destiny.

"Are you okay?" Lyca asks as he stares at my blank expression.

I shake my head, my eyes focus and I smile "Yes sorry I was thinking."

"So are we ready?" I ask.

Lyca and Dion share a glance.

"What's wrong?"

"We do not wish to push; do you not think it is too soon to begin training?" Dion asks.

"Okay, I know you are only looking after me but yes, I've rested, I need to learn control, as soon as possible. Please we need to start today."

"As you wish," Lyca bows his head.

'I'm glad to see you are back to normal kiddo.'

I turn around, eying the room suspiciously.

'No, try again' Elliott chuckles.

"Oh, so you *are* still in there then?" I tap my head with my fist.

'That I am. I decided to lay low, I know you battled and that I couldn't help so I figured the best I could do was stay out of it.'

"Well, Mr. Elliott I thank you for that," I curtsy.

"I do think that was the best option until I got back my memories and saw sense," I chuckle.

Then my tone becomes more solace.

"I am sorry, you know that right? I wouldn't ever want to get rid of you and I'm sorry I ever felt that way....." I trail off.

'Lexi, no need. I do know, we are a part of each other don't forget! I know who you truly are.'

A tear wells but I wipe my eyes before they gain volume enough to fall. I smile. Changing the subject with haste I turn to Lyca.

"Are you going to show me the way then?"

His features are strained with confusion as he stares at me, listening to me chat seemingly to myself the whole journey. He still finds it difficult to comprehend the other conscious within me, but this is my body and he has to accept my decision no matter how much he disagrees with it.

After ample twists and turns, we finally arrive at the training area assigned to me. As we approach the large double doors, Lyca barks a command and they sluggishly come alive, opening the passage. I am stunned by the sight. The area is enormous, surpassing the depths of my vision; I could not even begin to guess the entirety of this enormous lair.

The black marble caresses the entire room, forming sharp rocks in certain clusters dotted around. To my left is an extra thin set of tubular beams that run about fifteen meters across. At either end is a large slab of rock which propels towards the bars, stopping suddenly just over halfway. Above much of the room are self-sustaining platforms, much like those I battled Dion on previously, the barbed marble protrudes awkwardly, awaiting to impale anything that has the misfortune to land on them. I shiver at the thought. To my right is what appears to be an enormous frame built to climb. As I stare at the strange construct, part of it moves, reforming in an altered place with a completely different course. Pieces shoot out from many places; you would have to be extremely swift to avoid all of the obstacles and falling sections from that contraption. I shake my head, gulping difficultly.

I step forward inclined to view more of this place. As my foot impacts the floor, it gives way instantly. I throw myself forwards, gripping onto the edge tightly. My hands begin to slide and I cry out for help.

Lyca leaps clear of the large gaping hole and offers a hand. I grasp tightly and he hauls me skywards. Yellow energy surrounds me propelling me upwards. As I close in on the ceiling the light dispenses, gravity takes hold and drags me earthwards. I land firmly on a platform. The wind is taken from me as I splutter.

Moments later Dion and Lyca surround me. They begin the formation of small spheres. Lyca throws his first. I manage to dodge it with ease. I smile broadly, triumphantly celebrating my small win. Lyca smiles back, cocking his eyebrows at me as I am struck in my left flank. The red ball bounces from me back to Lyca's possession.

"Never act so cockily. That is always a huge mistake. Take each defence with the possibility of more arising. When in battle the blows can be swift and battering."

Deflated I turn to Dion. What does he have in store for me? I stare at him patiently awaiting his move, eager to anticipate and react. I am thrown from my footing, landing in a crumpled mess on the platform.

"You must never turn your back on an enemy," Dion remarks.

I peer backwards. Lyca manipulates his sphere, rolling it around between his hands, increasing the size. I take on board their words. Taking a running jump I leap onto an adjacent platform. I turn to face them both. They are now in front of me.

"Very good, she does listen," Lyca remarks.

Both parties proceed to throw numerous attacks towards me, sometimes in unison, other times separate. They impact me with some, causing burns and scrapes, nothing of too great an injury. I manage to counter most of their attacks remembering my training from Dion. This time around is different; I must learn control. I must be able to control myself for fear of what I am capable of.

We fight like this for a long time before Lyca begins teaching me how to manipulate my energy. We sit on the same platform, legs crossed. Lyca forms an energy ball.

"You must draw from deep within."

He orders the sphere to levitate. He moves it in circles around my head.

"See how smoothly I can conduct the sphere. I can utilise my concentration to give it instructions. It now comes as second nature to me.

You are very much controlled by your emotions. This will be a little more difficult to gain control but it is possible."

I form my sphere, much smaller than his. I try to order it to move over to my left. Clumsily it obeys, gaining speed it eventually smoothes out. We repeat the process for over an hour to which I improve greatly.

"You are doing very well. The biggest test will come much later. When you have learned this type of control in its entirety, we must then force your emotions to run rampant. This will be when you truly learn how to control yourself, given time of course."

That thought alone scares the life from me; I am so unpredictable when I am in such an emotional state. I would not like to cause harm to anyone else. I nod in response thoughtful.

"Will I ever be able to control that side of me? When my emotions take hold..." I trail off, head lowered.

Lyca places his warm hand on my shoulder, I look to him.

"You will."

"It just feels impossible; the energy just erupts and runs rampant."

"Lexi, trust me," his eyes stare into mine, filled with confidence.

I wish that I could be filled with such confidence. I struggle to see myself as anything other than a monster.

My features must give way to my doubt as Lyca grips my shoulders. He pulls me in closer to him, shaking me gently.

"You will learn control if it is the last thing I do! I believe in you, Lexi. You are a good person. Do not let that get lost through all of this."

Lyca's words force my heart to pound as tears form. He wipes them from my eyes before they have the chance to fall. He stares into them, his gaze lingering for a few moments before he pulls himself away and shakes his head as if returning to reality.

You must be hungry," he changes the subject and puts distance between us rapidly.

"I am pretty hungry yeah," I rub my stomach. We retire from training for the day.

My thoughts spiral. I trail behind Lyca as we make our way back. Creasing my brow I ponder about our interaction. Was that strange? Did I misread Lyca's actions? For a moment there I thought I witnessed something more in his eyes than simply wanting to aid a friend. I stare off into space. Is Lyca forming feelings towards me? A pang of guilt stabs me for even thinking such a thing. I am, or was in love with Jacob....and although I would not like to admit it, I think I am falling in love with Dion. I cannot have the affection of another man; my heart will not take it. I wobble my head, shaking the thoughts from my mind. No. I defiantly imagined it. I tend to form feelings towards people that go through a lot to aid me and that was all Lyca was doing.....right?

******

A few weeks pass by rapidly. We train every day, refining my battle skills, smoothing out my control, quickening my responses.

I land on the platform and within seconds Dion is beside me. He forms a yellow blaze of fire in my direction. I manage to roll from its grip but am instantly impacted by a red wave of energy. It sends me spinning over the edge. Luckily I impact the side of a platform which I bounce from, landing safely on another. I scrape across the rough surface, tearing my clothes and skin. Scrambling to my feet I search for the next attack. A red burning ball is circling above. Dion creates an electric current which intertwines around the sphere.

"Oh dear," I puff, thinking hard.

My arms pulse blue energy as a plan forms. Encouraging the energy into my hands I form a cube of water. Encasing it, holding it together I distort the edges, allowing it to increase in size. I shake with effort and before I can finish enclosing it completely, the sphere breaks free and hurtles towards me. It splits in two, darts to either side, I have no time left. I stand firm. I have no idea if this will work but I can think of nothing else in such a short time. They hold firm floating for a few seconds before they plunge towards me like a mirror image. At the last second, I leap high into the air with the aid of my blue airstream. The spheres crash into each other. I land on a slightly higher platform and stretch my arms down, forcing more energy into it. I encase the spheres within the water and box them in. Sparks and steam fly in every direction, momentarily blinding me. I remain, eyes closed. I carry on strengthening it regardless of my sight. With a final effort, I pulsate a final blast of energy before leaping onto another platform.

I allow my contact to cease. The spheres explode as I drift from platform to platform. Peering back I notice the spheres have gone in their entirety and only dribbles of our residual energy float earthwards before dissipating.

Lyca has perched on the platform directly above, searching for me. Dion appears on the platform ahead of him, he has not noticed me as of yet but it will not take long. I must think of a way to get above them. Then I realise what I must do. Eyes closed I picture a small skeletal dragon, (the smaller the target the better) the wind blows over me as I animate the image. The flames engulf the dragon, incinerating it. Once nothing remains I open my eyes.

Nothing, I see nothing. It has not worked? Then I see Dion has finally caught sight of me. He informs Lyca and begins his descent. I panic. Lyca crashes down behind me. Dion to my side, I look from one to the other. I run at full speed, directly over the edge and towards the hungry spikes below.

My sense returns, panic sets in. Why did I do that? I hear screams above me. Then I see it. My creation zones in on my position, interrupting my descent it catches me on its back. I allow my smile to grow wide as I pat the dragon. Directing it skywards we fly past my pursuers. The dragon loops around. We head towards their position. With my assistance we create fire. The dragon spews the flames at them. Lyca is encased within the fire as it licks his clothes. Dion leaps to his assistance but I am prepared. My dragon grabs him with its foot, gripping him tightly.

The red glow tries to penetrate the flames. With the curve of my hand, I create a box around them, encasing him once more. I look to Dion then to Lyca, both helpless. Shocked but triumphant I relax slightly. That was my mistake.

A couple of seconds later a blast of yellow energy rips through the rib cage of my dragon. It roars in agony before the bones splinter. It is torn apart and we both plummet. My stomach turns as we gain speed. Thinking fast I create a tether. Dion does the same. It wraps around the nearest platform halting me. I swing out to the right. Unfortunately, I crunch into the bottom of a platform. Screaming out in pain all my energy dies. The force disturbs my concentration; I am not as advanced as I thought I was. Landing hard on the edge of a platform I scurry forwards. I practically kiss the ground before rolling onto my back.

I lift my top inspecting my injury. The deep gash in my shoulder spurts blood in my face. I fumble for a moment unsure what to do as fear embeds within me. Did the shard hit an artery? Taking a deep breath, clearing thoughts from my head I place pressure on my wound. Gathering a burst of energy I thrust it into my shoulder, yelping out in agony as it attempts to knit together. After a couple of seconds, the blood merely tickles down slowly. Holding my breath I push myself upwards. Teeth gritted I stand with a swift movement.

Lyca lands heavily before me. His wicked smile soon dispenses, concern streaking his now gaunt face. The scene before him must have the appearance of something from a horror movie. The blood strewn across my face and clothes along with the small puddle gathered on the rock formation. I chuckle as the colour fades from his face as he rushes forward.

"Are you okay?"

I smile in return, edging backwards slowly.

"No Lexi, wait! I will not attack you," Lyca coos.

A wicked evil smile crosses my face. In this very moment, I must appear to have lost my sanity, the blood splatter simply adding to my murderous look. I wink then step back once more. The platform beneath my feet has come to an end. I teeter on the edge. Spreading my arms like an eagle in flight, I topple backwards from my solid footing.

Lyca screams my name. A second later his head protrudes from the edge. The black stallion rears before spiraling past Lyca, followed shortly by Dion a little higher up. The stallion summersaults tosses its head to the side before curving his wings behind and darting towards Lyca. He dodges easily, regrouping with Dion.

I manage to avoid their advances for a quite a while, my stallion swiftly outmanoeuvring them. They grow fiercer with their attacks as if the use of my creation enraged them. The blasts of energy crack my left, to my right, even in front of me, each one closer than the last. My concentration begins to tire; after all, we have been at this for many hours.

We manage to scrape past Dion's attack, the stallion flickers. I instantly lock my gaze, unsure if what I thought I witnessed occurred. I touch him, still as firm a creation as any. Shaking my head I dispense the idea. Just as my lightning bolt cracks the platform Dion is perched on the stallion's image distorts. Before I can even turn my head he disappears. I begin my free fall, spiralling earthwards at a shattering rate.

I attempt to create something to halt my rapid descent. My attempts are weak; the tether I create merely breaks. I gather speed. Then just as the tips of the rigid rocks threaten to impale me, something hauls me from the gruesome fate. Breathing a massive sigh of relief I view my saviour, Sparkie. My heart pounds so heavily in my chest I almost feel as if it is trying to escape.

Her white fur blows gently in the wind created by her slender dragon wings as they slice through the air. A large blast of air sends my hair spiraling to my left. The source is not difficult to locate, Leo takes his place beside me. He edges close to the right of Sparkie. Their sparks leap from one another's fur as they touch. Leaning over I transfer myself onto him, thanking Sparkie with a pat.

Dion leaps onto Sparkie's back as Leo swerves around to collect Lyca. He gently places himself behind me.

"Thank you, Leo, please take us down," Lyca requests.

Leo bows his head in acknowledgement. I squeeze his neck gently, my smile widening. A rush of excitement transverses through Leo's body as he comprehends my request.

I peer backwards wearing a wicked smile.

"A little advice, I would hold on tight," I laugh.

Leaning forward I make myself flush with Leo, grasping his fur tightly. We jerk forward and I sense Lyca follows my lead.

I giggle aloud as we climb higher, looping left and right. Once we reach maximum velocity, Leo hovers a moment. I glance over the side, we are extremely high. Lyca grips my shoulder.

"No Lexi," he pleads.

I cock my eyebrow in response; leaning close to Leo once more I pat his side. We shoot earthwards, almost knocking me from my holding from the sheer velocity of the steep descent. Lyca screams all the way down. I find his terror utterly hilarious.

Finally, Leo adjusts his wings and we decrease our speed dramatically. Hovering slightly above ground I slide from his back and almost collapse with laughter as I look to Lyca. His hands are cemented within Leo's fur. His hair points in every possible direction. This, however, is not the worst part; the gaunt, terrified expression that his face beholds forces me to choke as I laugh uncontrollably.

Lyca recovers after a couple of minutes. I however cannot remove the image from my mind, fuelling my bout of laughter. He glares at me as he casually steps over my contorted form.

Eventually, I take control of my outburst as I manage to stand.

"I've never heard a burly man like you scream like a little girl before."

I glance at Dion's face, he tries to hide his laughter behind stern features, however, it seeps through and he cracks with my remark. Lyca creases his eyes towards me, staring intently. I cannot hold back my chuckle. He flashes me a forced smile before starting for the exit.

"That is enough for this session," Lyca puffs.

I allow myself to finally relax, almost collapsing from fatigue. I did not realise how drained I was until now. My head becomes fuzzy so I decide to sit a moment.

"Are you okay?" Dion asks worriedly.

I hold my head trying to alleviate my dizziness.

"Yes I just feel dizzy that's all."

Dion sits in front of me.

"When you are ready we will help you out of here. Okay?"

I nod in reply, still trying to halt this horrible feeling. After a few moments, the wave lessens and I feel as though I can move once more. Dion stands, holds out his hand and assists me into standing position. He then hooks his arm around my waist supporting me. Leo allows me to lean on him from the other side. Together we leave the training room.

The twisting corridors pass by without notice and before I know it we are back in the living space at the front of Lyca's house. I collapse on his fluffy sofa. My muscles ache in locations I would not even think possible. Dion sits down beside me. Noticing my shoulder he lifts my clothing up. My eyes begin to droop as a wave of exhaustion reaps havoc through my worn body. A sharp prod in my shoulder entices me to focus.

"Ouch!" I shout, "That hurts you know," I slap his arm playfully.

"Sorry, you have repaired most of it. I will finish it off for you."

A moment later my wound has disappeared completely.

"Thank you" I smile.

I relax once more, my eyes grow heavy.

"You know what I'm a terrible guest," I yawn loudly.

"What makes you say that?" Dion quizzes puzzled.

"I keep falling asleep everywhere and anywhere. I can't even make it to my..."

I begin to snore softly as I enter the world of dreams...Dion chuckles.

AwaKEn, My FRieND

A few months pass by in a dull blur. The training is intense but necessary and I learn how to contain myself a little more each day, growing from strength to strength. Lyca decided it would be best to integrate everyone within the training as it was very likely our group would be as one if anything sinister ever crossed our paths. We prepared for every possible and impossible situation, acting out countless battle variations.

My senses are heightened and my reactions much keener. I have also improved my thought process whilst in the thick of a battle. For instance, if encased within a situation that has seemingly no escape; I would utalise my imagination more swiftly. Providing hope in a hopeless situation as I try to claw myself away from the grips of an enemy.

The door creaks into life beside me, breaking my train of thought. Leo rushes in.

'Amahté has awoken!'

"What? Where is he?" I demand.

Before he can even respond I rush from my room and head for the living area. My mind whirls as my smile spreads across my face. He is finally awake, after the entirety of the trauma, the scars; he is finally going to be okay. Before I even realise I am in the living room. Dion greets me with a warm smile.

"Where is he?" I jitter with excitement.

"He is up there," he points towards the ceiling.

I strain my eyes, staring intensely I eventually make out his form huddled in the corner of the room. He hisses wildly at us.

"What is he doing up there?" I muse puzzled.

Dion creases his head at me, eyes narrowing. He gives me a look which tells me I should know the answer to my own question. I merely shrug my shoulders.

He shakes his head,

"Are you joking? He is clearly terrified. He obviously does not know how he got here and who we are. He has yet to see you but I doubt he will be able from that distance."

"Oh yeah..."

My cheeks burn red with embarrassment as I call to my friend.

"Amahté?"

He hisses once more in reply.

Scratching my head I rack my mind as to how I could coax him down.

"It's me, Lexi."

He does not budge. I wait a moment, he still has not moved.

Before I can think of another solution, a blast of yellow energy impacts him, dislodging from his holding. Instinctively I rush to his aid, forming a blanket of energy I aim to catch him.

I do not get the chance to be a hero as his green energy surrounds him, slowing his descent. A moment later he is upon Dion. His eyes glow, trapping Dion, his energy surrounds him, encases him, seeping through, allowing Amahté to take control.

Dion's thrashing ceases and his hands are instantly by his side. I note the terror in his eyes as Amahté closes in, preparing for an attack.

"Amahté no!" I shout.

Without even turning around he holds an arm towards me, encasing me within his spell. He giggles viciously as he opens his enlarged mouth ready to attack Dion.

"STOP!" I scream, my energy increasing in power, small fragments seep through his barrier as my eyes glow blue. A spark cracks beside Amahté startling him.

Finally, he turns to face me, enraged. The instant he realises who his attacker is he falls to the floor. All energy dispenses, freeing us.

I rush forward. Amahté peers up; his crooked smile spreads from one side of his head to the other. He cocks his head before leaping on me. He prances from one shoulder to the other repeating my name three times before licking the side of my head then continuing his actions. He repeats this couple of times before edging into my arms.

"I gather he is delighted to see you," Dion smiles, brushing himself off.

I giggle like a child as he nuzzles his head into my chest.

"I would say so."

Amahté purrs as I tickle him. I hold him close, hugging him tightly.

"I've missed you," I smile.

I sit on the sofa. Amahté leaps from my arms and attacks the long fluffy cushion beside me. He growls loudly, screeches at it before scratching it with his four arms. He pauses, waiting for the inanimate object to defend itself. When nothing happens his scratches his head and looks to me in confusion.

I laugh "That's a cushion, it's not alive."

He looks to it once more. Punches it then leaps onto my lap. He snuggles up, drifting off he begins to snore lightly. I inspect his body; he has many scars and a couple of deep wounds in his green skin that have almost healed. His arm and leg are in a cast but they are healing slowly.

His injuries do not really seem to bother him. I cradle Amahté in my arms. I kiss his overly large misshapen head.

"He is lucky to be alive after all he has been through," Dion sits beside me. He strokes Amahté's back.

"I know. I just can't believe he's here. He'll be okay now won't he?"

"I would allow Lyca to examine him to be on the safe side but I expect he should be fine."

Moments later Leo enters the room. He sniffs Amahté. Blows air from his nose in jealously. Dion is about to move over for him but he does not wait. With one small leap, he lands on Dion, winding him. He quickly shifts to the side as the enlarged Leo snuggles up close, placing his head on my lap, he snoozes lightly.

"Jealously," Dion puffs, chuckling.

A couple of hours pass by before Leo and Amahté awake. I could not disturb them, so as uncomfortable as I may have become, I allowed them to slumber. I stretch my aching limbs as I lead the way to the training room where sure enough I find Lyca. He is sparring with himself.

Amahté leaps from my arms, landing hard on the path before us.

"No! Wait!" I exclaim.

The floor beneath him gives way, instinctively he pounces from the failing ground, and it is too late. The platform propels him skyward, directly into the main training area.

"Oh no," I cry.

Without hesitation, I throw myself over the edge. The world becomes black around me as I fall, it seems to take forever before I see light again and I find myself clinging onto the edge of a platform. I struggle to regain my grip, my fingers slip. Closing my eyes I focus my energy. Forming an anchor I crash it into the middle of the rock, shards impale my arm but I ignore the slight discomfort. Feeling a little more stable, taking my time I eventually manage to drag myself from the edge back to safety.

Within a split second, I am on my feet. Having no time to waste I search for Amahté. Leaping from platform to platform, searching high and low. I find nothing. Panic begins to engulf me as I start to shake.

"Where are you?"

Then, from the corner of my eye, I notice a faint green light. The distance to the platform is enormous. I teeter on the edge, fear sets in. My heart races as I realise for seemingly the first time how high up I am. A strange sensation transverses through my body, my vision goes blurry as the dizziness increases. Unsteadily I search for the floor. Sitting down I try to calm myself. Closing my eyes I picture my friends, Amahté along with everyone else. Their comforting faces seem to assist me greatly. Succumbing to my instincts, eyes remaining closed, I stand.

Edging backwards I relax, breathing deeply. After a minute or so I cease my retreat. I can feel I am on the edge of the other side, if I had taken one more step I would have plummeted. Taking one last deep breath I concentrate. I lunge forward, my feet travel extremely fast. Digging deep I bend my knees and leap. Floating so high, eyes shut so tightly, praying that I do not miss my target. Seconds pass as though minutes, for a split second, the thought passes my mind that I have not made the distance and I am currently plummeting to my demise. A moment later I impact the ground forcefully. My wrist crunches beneath me. Although that pain is fierce, I force myself to ignore it, opening my eyes, searching for Amahté once more. He is huddled over on the corner, dangerously so; he could easily topple from the edge. A wave of adrenaline rampages through my limbs completely blocking out everything but my mission.

Stumbling forward I reach for Amahté, the platform shudders a little sending him over the edge. Pouncing forward I slide across the uneven surface which scratches my stomach. I reach out my hand, stretching as far as possible I manage to grip one of his hands. Relief sweeps over me as I plant my other hand firmly on the platform; it slips to the edge before I can achieve my grip, halting our descent. Breathing an enlarged sigh of relief I throw Amahté over my head to safety. I drag myself up with ease, most likely due to the adrenaline still coursing through me.

I lie next to him before cradling him, holding him tightly. He is still breathing; I would imagine the force of the fall most likely knocked him out. Before I can even allow myself to relax, Leo is beside me.

He nuzzles me lovingly.

'Are you okay?'

"I am now," I smile, stroking both of my companions.

'I wanted to assist you but Lyca stopped me. He trapped me, wanting to see what you were capable of if a friend was in danger.' His voice waves with anger. He growls.

"It's okay Leo, I understand, he is training me. He would have saved me if we fell." I pat his head

"Thank you."

Perched upon Leos back we are flown down to safety. Leaping from him I push Amahté to Lyca.

"Please say he's okay," I stammer, trying to contain my worry.

Lyca grips Amahté, touching my damaged wrist accidentally, I recoil as it throbs. He contorts his features.

"What have you done to your hand?"

Lyca passes Amahté to Dion without a second thought, reaching for my arm.

I recoil from him in disgust.

"Lexi, let me look at your arm," Lyca presses.

"No," I exclaim firmly.

Lyca's eyes crinkle as he narrows them at me in confusion.

"Why not? You are hurt."

"Look at Amahté first. Make sure he is okay, please?" I plead almost at the brink of tears.

"But," he begins.

Before he can say another word my expression halts his tongue. He succumbs to my wishes. Examining Amahté thoroughly he eventually turns back to me.

"He is okay. I assume all the action has just taken it out of him. He should awaken soon. I will take him to the medical room to be safe, monitor him but I do not think he is in any danger."

"Thank you," I puff with relief.

Tears begin to gather as the lump in my throat bulges. I sink to my knees. I cannot contain my emotions any longer and I burst into tears.

"Lexi!" Dion rushes to my side, "are you okay?"

He places a hand on my shoulder, comforting me.

"I...I just t...t...thought that..." I trail off.

"He is fine, do not worry yourself."

Dion pulls me from the floor. Placing a hand on my back and legs he lifts me into his arms. Holding him tightly I allow my emotions free reign. I cry uncontrollably into his shoulder as he carries me from the training room.

Moments later I find myself perched on the seat in the main living area, Dion's arms still cradling me. We remain like this for a long while, my sobbing diminishing; we embrace each other in silence.

Finally, I remove my head from his chest. I peer into his beautiful hazel eyes, we smile. Dion wipes my face.

"Thank you Dion."

I shuffle to the side of him; in the process, I knock my wrist. I hiss aloud before cursing myself for impacting my injury once again, causing the pain to return.

"Can I look at that?" Dion asks.

"Yes," I hold out my arm.

He cradles it tenderly, examining the injury.

"It does not appear broken. I think it is sprained."

Moments later a warm yellow light surrounds my wrist, diminishing the tenderness, repairing the injury. I yawn loudly.

"You should rest. I will take you to your room."

Dion stands, carrying me once more.

"No, please, I want to see Amahté."

He smiles "As you wish."

Lyca is examining Amahté when we enter.

Dion places me on Amahté's' bed. Edging myself forwards I pull myself towards him, wrapping him within my arms I close my eyes.

"Is she okay?" Lyca asks Dion.

"Yes it was just a sprain, I have repaired it. Have you been able to examine Amahté properly?"

"Yes, as I presumed he should be fine, everything appears to be well with him. He is lucky."

A moment later I feel the warmth of a hand on my shoulder before I can turn to see who it is, my eyes grow heavy and I can no longer fight sleep.

****

Blinking wildly I try to adjust my eyes to the light. It seers my retinas each time I try to open them. The agony is unbearable so I decide they should remain closed momentarily. Shuffling around I manage to sit up. I feel around, Amahté is no longer beside me.

"Dion?" I whisper groggily.

The room falls into silence once more. A sharp throbbing pounds through my mind, buckling me over. I crease on the bed, clawing at my own head as it tears through me. I fall from my holding. I impact the floor heavily.

After rocking my head for a few minutes the pain eventually subsides, leaving behind an enormous headache. I try once more to open my eyes. Vision blurred, the light is far too intense for them to remain open.

Shuffling around the floor I place my hand on an object. Carefully I move it to the side, clearing my path. Then another blocks me. Creasing in confusion I push it to the side. Then another, and another.

"What the? What's going on?" I shout.

Finally, I reach a wall, sliding across I find my way to the entrance, stumbling over various times. Touching the door I manage to open it. Confusion overruns me as I realise where I had fallen asleep yesterday, the medical room. Lyca is very particular and cleanly especially with his medical room. He would not have left it in such a state.

My imagination turns over various scenarios, terrible, sadistic scenarios. Shaking my head I force the fear from my mind, there is most likely a sensible explanation for this. I hope.

Breathing heavily I follow my instincts to where the main living room is, relying totally on my sense of direction without the use of sight. After an eternity I eventually stumble into the fluffy sofa in the main room. Breathing a sigh of relief I call out once more.

"Lyca? Dion!" I shout at the top of my lungs.

No reply. Only silence.

I am crippled by the sharp pain in my head once more. I cry out in agony.

"What's happening?" I manage to whimper as it subsides.

Searching within me I try to locate my energy. I cannot connect to anything. I plunge deeper, desperately trying to utilize something. Eventually, I source a minuscule amount. Directing it into my eyes I try to strengthen their protection, filtering out the harmful light so I can at least see. I slowly force my eyes to open. The light remains painful but bearable. I peer around, vision slightly blurred but otherwise okay.

The room does not seem any different. All items in their place, no sign of any struggle what so ever. Relief sweeps over me as I allow my body to relax.

"Just my imagination," I chuckle to myself, forgetting my troubled thoughts a moment.

An irritation on my stomach entices me to scratch. I satisfy my itch and rub my eyes tenderly. I feel something moist on my face. Confused I peer at my hands. The substance cannot be misinterpreted. Blood. My hands are covered in the thick red substance.

Dread clinches my stomach as I slowly sit up. Pulling back my top I examine my stomach. What I find terrifies me. Long, claw marks have pierced through my skin. They are not from just any animal of this I am certain. This kind of scratch can only be from one thing. A Werewolf.

ThE EnD

"No! No!" I repeat almost in tears.

My stomach churns and I empty its contents onto the floor. I crunch over wrenching for a while at the sheer disgust of the situation. Releasing my anger I pound the floor with my fists.

"How could they have found this place?!" I stammer.

I didn't think they were even able to reach this place, my mind strains as the thoughts spiral around. What am I going to do? I try desperately to gather my thoughts, intent on creating a plan. The piercing pain tears through my mind once more. I scream as my eyes roll to the back of my head.

Blindly, vision distorted I lunge for the door.

"I must…help them."

I stagger forward. Turning corner after corner. Searching the library, Dion's room, Leo and the horses sleeping quarters, I find nothing. All the while the pain begins to grow more severe. I double over in agony. My head seers and burns so intensely it forces me to my knees. Where are they?

Eventually it dulls slightly allowing me some clarity. I am stood alone in the dark, trying to regain my senses when I hear a voice.

Startled I turn.

"Lexi? Are you…?" Lyca does not finish his sentence.

The agony returns and I grasp the sides of my head and shriek aloud.

He rushes forward, catching me as I fall. We travel the corridors with haste as my insane mumblings merge into one. I hear him speak to me but cannot decipher it over my screams.

I am laid on the bed I first originated. I have come full circle, I started here and I am still here. How am I supposed to help anyone from this bed? Lyca is shocked by the state of the room but that is the least of his concerns. He manages to contact Dion requesting his urgent presence.

I push myself up, Lyca holds me down. I become angry, I no longer recognize the man before me as my sanity strains.

"Let me go!" I shout.

"Lexi please stop I am trying to help you."

My energy sparks and I begin to glow.

"I need to help Dion," I almost cry.

"Who even are you? I don't know you!"

"I am Lyca, you do know me."

"I don't!"

The pain flares and coupled with my fear, confusion and energy I begin to free myself from his grip. He struggles greatly to hold me down and he will soon lose the battle as my aura increases in size.

"We must help them," I cry, scratching at my skull, intent on clawing out the searing torture.

"DION!!!!" he shouts almost sitting on top of me.

"Where the hell is he?"

Dion casually enters the room as though nothing in the world concerns him.

His face drains of all colour; the sight he is greeted with soon forces his moment of carefree living straight through the window.

"Oh thank god, help me! Hold her hands," Lyca states desperately.

Dion stands frozen. He is in complete shock.

All the while he stands there I am almost free, Lyca grips my waist as I desperately struggle to free myself.

"Dion!! NOW!!" Lyca roars.

He shakes his head, seemingly removing the shock he hurries to my side. Taking each hand he pins them down. Although he is shaking violently I cannot remove his grip, he is much too strong and I weakened from my struggle with Lyca.

"Get off me!!!" I roar "We have to stop them."

A red light surrounds me, I can no longer move. Despite this, the pain does not dull, if anything without being able to move it seems to intensify. Lyca instructs Dion to find the restraints. A moment later he applies them to my arms and legs and the ruby red energy dispenses into nothing.

"Please, it hurts!" I cry aloud, tears streaming down my face.

Lyca twists my head towards him, squashing my cheeks with the force.

"Where is the pain?"

"My head. My head," I cry closing my eyes tightly.

Moments later a wave of energy calms my madness. It dulls the pain, clearing my mind. I can now think more clearly.

Opening my eyes slowly I finally recognize Lyca as I stare into his eyes. Lyca's expression seems puzzled. The red energy still surrounds my head. Once I have calmed he allows it to dispense.

"Okay."

Instantaneously the agony resurfaces, scrambling my brain once more. I scream twisted words that I have never even heard of previously. A language I do not even have knowledge of.

Lyca panics, he reapplies his energy. The process repeats and the pain dulls, but this time he retains his connection to the energy. I am finally allowed to see more clearly.

"What is happening?" Dion stutters.

"I do not know," Lyca shakes his head, eyes fixed on mine, "I cannot remove my aura, I cannot heal her. I have no idea."

"Lexi?" Dion asks gently trying to hide his fears, "what happened?"

"Werewolf?" I manage to choke.

Dion's expression is tainted with concern, he looks to Lyca.

Without breaking his gaze he replies.

"Impossible."

"She has imagined that from the agony; it has meddled with her mind. They cannot locate this place, we are safe."

"What makes you think that?" Dion asks me.

Grasping for my top I realise for the first time my hand is restrained. I tug at it confused.

"You hurt yourself, those are to stop you," Dion consolidates me, stroking the side of my face I have scratched deeply through my attempts at removing the unbearable pain.

"My stomach."

Carefully he lifts my t-shirt to reveal the deep scratches.

"Oh no," Lyca mumbles.

"See."

"What does this mean?" Dion asks Lyca.

He scratches his head "I am not sure, but it does not look good."

"No! We have to do something! Please let me go, we have to find the others, protect them."

Both ignore me. So when Dion's attention averts I take advantage. I manoeuvre from the grasp of the looser restraint, launching myself forwards. Then I catch sight of something on myself that makes my heart cease. My breathing becomes rampant. Terrified I begin to panic thrashing out with my free hand, I desperately try to free my other hand.

"No! No! Please no!"

I tug but it is too tight and Dion catches me quickly, restraining my free arm once more, much tighter than previously.

I strain forward as much as the belts will allow. I stare at the wound. The skin is torn with claw marks and now reveals the bright blue veins beneath. The surrounding skin has turned black and a deep red. One colour swirls around the other as if in battle. The appearance is familiar......the werewolves attack.

"W..wh...what's that?" I stammer, praying I am incorrect.

"The werewolf venom," Lyca replies simply, none wavering and seemingly without empathy.

"No! We beat it. Didn't we?"

"It cannot be beaten. We merely battled it, hoping the Ebur could counteract it. We had no idea of what would happen. This was bound to occur sooner or later. You are powerful Lexi, but not immortal."

"Please you have to help me."

Lyca falls silent, mulling over the situation.

I think a moment. Tears well up as I consider my options of which there are few. So there is number one; I can become a Werewolf and live out my life as a blood thirsty animal with no morals. I will probably tear apart my friends; rip Dion and Lyca apart with ease, and I would enjoy doing so. Then there is number two......well I could just end it all. There is not much of a choice really is there? I chuckle insanely to myself.

"If there's nothing you can do then you have to finish me off. I won't become a monster. I can't..." The tears finally grow too heavy and fall down my cheeks.

Dion is silent, utterly defeated beside me. My remark seems to spring him back into life.

"We will not!" He places an arm around me.

My eyes burn into his, tears streaking my bloodied face.

"You will!"

"No, there is still hope. Lyca?"

Lyca's head drops.

"Lyca!" Dion shouts.

"I do not know," he responds after a couple of seconds.

"This is not happening," Dion sighs resting his head on my shoulder.

I smile sadly.

"It's okay. We talked about this..."

I touch my forehead with his. My heart is completely breaking at seeing this man utterly in pieces before me. I know I have tried to hide my feelings for him, I have tried to bury them deep, and I have tried so hard to not love this man. Maybe now is the time I should let him know how I feel, allow them freedom. Maybe this is my last chance. I cannot cope with the emotions currently running though my body. I have always felt so guilty with regards to my love and who receives it, but if this truly is my last chance maybe I should tell him.

"You and the others have made my hellish existence worthwhile. I want to thank you, Dion. You don't know how much you do mean to me. I've tried to keep my emotions in check with you but if this is it then I just want to say I'll always love you… Wow that felt good to get off my chest, but in all seriousness I'll miss you so much. Well if that's even possible from where I'll be going." I scrunch up my face.

He stares into my eyes; his are filled with sorrow and agony. He does not reply he simply pulls from me disgusted at my situation. He paces, twisting his ring. He places his hands beside his head as he mulls over my fate most likely.

"Dion, say something."

He does not even look at me.

"Lyca there must be something?"

Lyca shrugs his shoulders.

"Please just think I will not lose her."

"Dion, I have grown fond of her myself, but you heard her, she does not want to be turned into a monster. Of course I want her to survive too. There is only so much I can do."

"Dion, it's okay. Just let me go."

He turns to me, rage filling his features.

"No!" He shouts.

My eyes widen as the shock impacts me; I do not think I have really ever seen him this full of rage. Dion is always such a kind loving person; he does not often grow this angry. The shock must be apparent on my facial features because he immediately softens and rushes to my side.

"I am sorry, but I am also not about to give up on you. Not yet!" He kisses my cheek, presses his head against mine one last time before leaving.

He approaches Lyca and whispers something in his ear. Lyca's features seemingly fill with a little more hope as they converge. I try desperately to listen in to their conversation.

"What's going on? I have a right to be included you know!"

The pair ignores me and continues their hushed conversation.

"She will not accept it," Lyca whispers just loud enough for me to catch.

"I won't like what? What are you planning?"

I pull on the restraints trying to free myself.

"If you won't do it then I'll do it myself."

I spark my aura around my left restraint, it is faint and very weak but I do not need much. I turn to those two; they have not taken any notice of me. I roll my eyes as I free my left arm; I get to work on my right. Before I know it I am stumbling towards the exit, moments later I am on the floor. The pair of them having practically pounced on me. I did not have a chance really.

"What on earth are you doing?" Lyca creases his brow.

"I'm leaving."

"You certainly are not." Dion pipes up.

I shuffle into sitting position, the two holding firm on my wrists. They hold them so tightly it begins to hurt.

"Why do you think you can just tie me up and hold me against my will?"

"We are helping you."

"I know you think you are but holding someone captive against their will isn't helping them."

Then Lyca says what they were both thinking.

"You are so self destructive and you are so young, you literally have no idea about anything. Yet all you want to do is to end it all."

"You have no idea what I have been through, how much my sanity has strained under all this. How dare you. You were the one that said I was beyond help. I did your treatment; I followed your rules and look where it got me! Nowhere, it just prolonged the inevitable." Tears stream down my face.

"You think I want this? You think I want to be under all of this pressure all of the time? You think I can help how my mind is wired? Sometimes the worst place to ever be is alone with only my mind for company. It can be a dangerous place. Not that you know, or frankly even care." I lower my head.

"Dion cares, I care, your friends care. We care Lexi. You have brought something to my life in such short time and I care for you more than you know."

"So that gives you the right to keep me against my will?" I shake with anger.

My hand flickers blue on and off as it tries to establish itself with my rage.

Dion and Lyca share a look.

"Yes" Lyca replies sternly.

Without a moment's hesitation he hauls me over his shoulder and slams me down on the bed, accidentally winding me. The pair replaces the restraints as I try to gather my breath to shout foul obscenities at them.

"I am sorry Lexi," Lyca places a hand on my head, "this is for the best."

A moment later the energy that Lyca had kept around me this entire time, that was keeping that terrible pain at bay, simply vanishes. The mind-numbing agony returns with a vengeance. My mind explodes as I convulse, thrashing around. The restraints hold, just. My body begins to shut down. My breathing shallow as the turmoil commands insanity. Darkness surrounds me; evil red eyes converge on my position. I scream as they close in. The sharp rows of piercing teeth surround my face. I am lost to this world.

MonSter WitHin

Eyes focus. A blur of trees. Heavy breathing. I am running I realise. From what? I try to stop. I cannot control myself. Agony creases my mind once more. Vision flutters out of focus, I fade.

Snow. My feet padding softly through it. I stumble. I plunge into the snow. Regaining myself. A flash of jet black fuzzy paws. Has something just tackled me? I question. Eager to escape the area I set off again. Vision zones out.

A nearly frozen river. Quickly I glance behind me. Nothing seems to be trailing. My tense muscles shake as I allow them to relax. My throat is extremely dry. Stepping forward I approach the icy water. Dipping my hand in. My eyes widen and panic severs logic as I revel at the sight before me. My legs waver as I lean over the water. The moon is dipping low in the sky but it casts just enough light to witness my reflection. Bright blue terrified eyes stare back at me, encased within a mass of dark fur. A wolf stares back at me. I throw my head back and scream. A howl escapes, replacing my human screams. I do not care. I howl loudly at the moon in despair.

Eventually, I cease my manic howling. Pacing along the water's edge I try to piece together this chaos. What happened? I remember Dion, Lyca, my demise. Or so I thought. Could they not go through with it? Then

I wake up to this, I edge over again, growling angrily at the reflection before me. The sound of a branch breaking behind me entices my ears to twitch toward its origin. Confused I glance around. At first, I see nothing, just as I am about to return to my despair I spot Dion. He is in dark clothing and is pressed against a tree trying to hide.

My emotions are elevated at the sight of him. He can correct this, end me once and for all. I take a step forward. Then another. I rise for my third step, plant it firmly into the snow. I try to take another. I cannot move. Shooting agony transfers through my head. My vision fades as a wolf leaps from the darkness towards me. The wolf's jaws sink into my leg before I pass out.

Limping slightly but still retaining my speed. A mountainous climb stands before me. Glancing back it appears I am around halfway up. I see nothing behind me but the blood trail I have left in my last couple of steps. Each time I push onwards I feel my hind legs intentionally spraying up snow, kicking it over my blood. Attempting to camouflage my route. I try so desperately to force myself to turn back or halt my ascent in the hope Dion will find me but I am not in control. The ravenous werewolf characteristics are clearly the driver of my body, I am but a passenger.

Is this what it is like to be a werewolf? I had imagined the mind goes insane and ravenous which is why they are so dangerous. I assumed the person turned was in control of their actions but was not their former selves and acted monstrously due to the transformation. Not like this. My conscious remains in tack but I cannot control my body the majority of the time. I am not sure which is worse. The fact that I cannot control anything and have to witness the atrocities my body will incur whilst I am alive or if I had merely gone ravenously insane. I think a moment. This reality is definitely worse I decide. I think to all the werewolves I have encountered. What if they are the same as me? Forced to bear witness to the revolting actions but unable to do anything. That would drive me insane. I shiver at the thought, I must find Dion. He can cease all of this madness.

I re-focus on the climb. I am exhausted but I still push onwards. I stumble over a rock, whimper before hauling myself upwards determination burning throughout me. After a treacherous, exhausting ascent I eventually crawl into a cave. The entrance is but a tiny crack in the side of the mountain. Forcing myself into the snow, flattening myself I manage to squeeze through the gap. The cave is small but has enough space for me to rest. I push myself into the wall, hiding from immediate sight if someone peers through the crack. Breathing rampant I tenderly lick my wound. As I lick, a blue light transfers from my tongue and into the wound. The strands of muscle stretch. Intertwining they repair. The skin and fur creeps across before joining the entirety of my fur. I lick it a couple more times before laying my head down. Eyes closed. Darkness consumes me. I fall asleep.

I awaken as I am flying through the air. I land hard, somersault a few times before stopping myself. My back legs hang dangerously over the edge. Scampering I manage to retain solid footing once again. I look back. I had only just made that leap. Moving my legs I walk forward. I can control myself I realise. Searching my surroundings I try to decipher any familiar figures. The sun is setting to my right casting a beautiful red, orange glow over the sky. I am travelling along a rocky red mountain trail. The drop beside me it treacherous. There is no way back without trying to make the death-defying leap a second time. I do not fancy my chances. Peering to my left a vertical climb, a neigh impossible feat. Only one choice. Forwards. Walking slowly, praying my friends have not lost my trail, I advance.

After a mile or so the path ends suddenly. I notice another path to my left. It twists upwards. Standing on a large rock I weigh up my options. The distance is not that great, surely I can make that. Standing on the edge

I quiver. Turning around I walk to the other side of the rock. Turning rapidly I dart forward. Hunching my hind legs I push from my standing. I clear the distance with ease and land softly. I advance, following a seemingly endless path to a destination unknown. My mind swirls. What am I going to do?

Eventually I reach the top of the mountain. Exhausted I decide to rest a moment. An hour or so passes. Feeling refreshed I continue. Still no sign of Dion. I begin to think they have lost my track. Am I doomed to roam the earth like this for eternity? To reap more havoc on innocent people without hesitation. I peer to my side, a drop either side that will certainly result in death. My paw lingers on the edge, small fragments of rock dislodge and plummet earthwards. I gulp, waver a moment before stepping forward. The pain in my mind returns, forcing me to halt all actions. I roll around the floor in agony. Vision blurs.

Eyelids flutter open. Surrounded by beautiful white snow once more. I pounce upon a deer. Snapping its neck with ease I devour its delicious meat until I fill my ravenous stomach. Bathing in the unfortunate animal's blood I roll around excited. When I realise I am in control, shock freezes me in place. What am I doing? Is this what happens? Is it slowly consuming my sanity? Will I soon be enjoying the bloodthirsty nature without regret? I shiver.

Moving forward, away from the dismembered carcass I shamefully created. Head lowered I force myself onwards. The snow grows more difficult to manoeuvre with each passing second. With each step I take the snow seems to become deeper, I struggle to forge a path through. Eventually, I must resort to leaping; the snow is far too dense. This, however, requires much more energy and after around four grueling hours I grow weary. My breathing becomes heavy as exhaustion and strain converse through my body. I manage one more leap before I can do no more. Sinking in the snow much deeper than my height I lie down.

Freezing and exhausted I give up. Curling up in a ball I try to calm my chest. Maybe I should just allow myself to be consumed by the ice? At least I would not be able to harm anyone or anything else.

A sound pricks my ear. Listening intently for its source I look up. Another loud cracking sound follows. Has Dion finally caught up to me? Excitement allows me a last burst of energy, standing I hunch my hind legs. Leaping high I slam into the side of the snow at the top of the hole. Gripping my nails into the snow I desperately try to clamber over the edge. I manage to scuttle up with my chest resting on the top, my hindquarters dangling over the edge. I rest a moment before the final haul. Just as I am about to resume my ascent, the snow beneath me begins to crumble. I cannot get a grip and moments later I smash back into the hole. A loud crack echoes through my ears and before I can even recover from the fall, the ground gives way, plummeting me into darkness.

I am covered entirely in snow. Peering around nothing can be seen. Shaking violently I remove most of the snow from my fur. Anger rises through my limbs as I throw myself against the side of the chasm. My nails grip the ice, but not for long and I am soon sliding down the edge once more. I howl in anger so loudly my ears ache. I cannot even put myself into an icy grave.

Suddenly the ice cavern is visible, a blue light permits vision. Confused I search for the source of the light. Then I realise the blue tint must be mine and examine myself. From the little I can see, my body has no light emission. I stare into the ice before me, two blue lights reflect from the uneven surface. My eyes I realise. They are glowing intensely, lighting up the surrounding area. Impressed with myself I take in my surroundings. The hole I have fallen in to is large; only a small amount of space is unoccupied by my mass. I shiver; the cold has affected me greatly. I may have a thick fur coat but it is not impenetrable. With the fact I am now wet from the melting snow matted within it, my body temperature drops. I decide to relent. I may be able to end it all here after all. Exhausted and frozen I lie in the snow, shivering violently I try to rest hoping to slip away without a thought. After all, I have never really thought about death. Of course, I have danced with death on many occasions but I have always come through the other side. This time, however, is different. I do not wish to perish. The thought twists my gut causing nervous butterflies. I also do not want to live as a monster. The room begins to darken as I think about my unfortunate fate.

My eyes flicker open. How long have I been down here? I cannot feel any part of my extremities. I am entirely numb. I watch as the temperature creates a cloud of visible perspiration with every rapid breath. Then I hear movement. I try to move my head but I am frozen in place. With all my remaining strength I try to bend around. After a couple of attempts, I hear a cracking sound, the ice loosens as I begin to move my neck. I desperately try to free my body. No use. I am frozen solid to the floor. The footsteps begin to fade as if moving away from my location. In a manic last-ditch attempt for freedom, I howl piercingly. My throat throbs from the effort but I ignore the discomfort, I merely continue my cry for help. It must be Dion, how I long to see his face one last time before I meet my eternal end. After a long while, I cease my cries. Perking my ears I listen intently. Has he heard me?

The minutes pass by so slowly but I hear the soft crunch of snow advancing on my position. Yes! He heard me. My heart skips a beat. Then instantly falls flat as a large tall woman covered in various animal skins peers over the edge of the hole. A sad expression befalls her face as she stares at me. An instinctive howl escapes. I curse myself. Suddenly her expression alters to joy. Her smile widens as she lowers herself into the ice cavern. She removes a makeshift knife from her belt and begins work on the ice around my hind legs. The work must be tiring chipping away at solid ice but she does not falter. Minutes later my hind legs are free. She quickly moves onto the lower section of my body fragmenting the ice masterfully. Before I know it my whole back end has been released and she now carves out the last section over my chest.

Finally the last of the ice is removed. I rise wearily, shaking violently I stretch my stiff limbs. I try to speak, to thank the lady even though she spoiled my plan but only a quiet whimper escapes. Thinking a moment I bow my head low, hoping she will recognise my forced appreciation. She smiles, her teeth are oddly sharp I note as she pats my head. Bending over she points to the lower part of her back, her smile remains. I stare a moment pondering on her actions before it impacts me. She wishes for me to use her to leap from my cavernous cage. The distance alone is too great, especially in my state. Shocked by her actions I obey. What else can I do? Walking stiffly I drag myself onto her back. She is extremely tall and muscular. Once perched on her back she stands slowly. The surface is now within leaping distance. Tensing my frozen hind limbs I thrust from my standing. Flying through the air I land in a bundle, roll a couple of times before finding my feet. For some reason, I am so delighted to be free. I roll around for a couple of joyful seconds before I realise the woman is staring at me oddly. Instantly I cease my actions and roll over slowly. Why is it she is not terrified of me? To her, I am a dangerous wild animal, and yet she has no apparent fear, she even assisted me from my perilous situation. I ponder a while, staring at her in a daze.

"Come." she waves a hand to follow her.

Glancing around, nothing but an endless sea of white as far as my improved eyes can see. What other choice is there? I doubt she would allow me to carry out my plan. Like a docile dog obeying their master, I follow the strange woman.

We walk for a long time. I fall behind from exhaustion but she does not alter her speed to suit mine. She does not even peer backwards to see if I have followed her. Not wishing to be alone, I try whenever I can to close the ever-increasing distance between us. Maybe this woman can help me find Dion so we can resolve this whole disgraceful situation. The only thing that keeps me going is the thought of seeing him one last time. Even if he cannot do anything and my life must be forfeit, at least I will get to say goodbye to the man who has been there for me throughout all of this chaos. The man who has impacted my feelings for him more than I ever thought possible. I owe him that at least, I must not give up until I find him, I cannot.

The snow thickens as the storm surrounds us. My black fur cannot be deciphered beneath the inches of thick snow than now cover my entire body; I must have the appearance of a polar bear. I chuckle to myself at the thought. The wind launches the snow towards us like missiles, piercing as each wave impacts our cold bodies. We trudge on regardless.

Just as I am about to fail, to allow exhaustion the control is has been fighting for, for such a long period of time now, a white structure comes into view. Forcing one foot in front of the other I drive myself forward, exhorting my body beyond its confines. Desperation and hope fuels me. The woman struggles to pry the door open. She heaves it a couple of times, slowly edging away the large pile of snow blocking the entrance. She struggles greatly as the elements seem to worsen against her. The wind repelling with enormous force, I am almost thrown from my footing. What can I do to help? Then I realise. Utterly fatigued I drag myself forward against the forceful storm. With my remaining fuel, I dig into the large pile of snow. The work is crushing and I am sure I will fail but I carry on regardless. My claws dig furiously, creating a clear path. Finally I clear enough from the door for the muscular woman to heave it open.

She pushes me inside and I collapse. I could do no more. I try to stand, to move away from the entrance but my legs waver and subside immediately. I cannot even move my head. I feel as though my mass is made of lead, every extremity too heavy to move. I have nothing left. My battered frozen carcass has given its all and more. I shiver violently as I drift in and out of consciousness.

The woman approaches me. Pulling gently she slides me across the room. The world fades once more, this time I fear for good.

ReLEnTlesS

L ight blinds me as my eyes flutter open. Shielding them as much as possible I scan my surroundings. I find a small cavernous room that holds nothing much beyond makeshift stone carvings in the form of furniture. My head throbs violently. Reaching up I cradle it. I waver a moment, hoping for my miracle cure to ease my pain. As anticipated it changes nothing so I decide to trail the origins of the light in the hope I can cease its effect on me. Reaching out my hand I crawl across the floor, trying in vain to recall the recent events. My memories are blurred. I concentrate, attempting to grasp anything. This fails and merely causes more pain; I relent. For the moment it does not matter, I must figure out where I am. I force my stiff body to the entrance, enticing my limbs to flex giving me momentum.

Placing one arm in front I grasp a rock shard, my feet shake as I thrust upwards. With a vast amount of effort, I urge forward, dragging my weak body across the wall. The process is painstakingly slow and as I struggle to keep the pace I end up in a heap on the floor. Breathing rampant I continue crawling, unable to sustain my weight any longer. As my skin scrapes away each time I drag my bare body along the cavernous floor. I realise for the first time that I have no clothing. I cannot figure out as to why I am naked but I shift this from my mind as it is not important at the moment.

I continue, my elbows and stomach leave scrapings of skin behind as I slice myself on the sharp stone. The discomfort becomes too severe which coupled with exhaustion, overwhelms me and I have no choice but to rest. I fall flat onto my chest; my cheek crushes against a stalagmite causing discomfort. I cannot afford the effort to correct my position so I endure until my breathing slows.

After a long uncomfortable stent, I manage to summon enough energy to haul myself against the wall taking some weight from my sore extremities. I examine my grazed skin. My stomach has large gouges which bleed slowly. Along the length of my arms and legs patches of red skin curl and bend away, accumulating at various incorrect locations. Taking no more notice of my small wounds I bunch up my knees then place my head on them. My breathing still rampant I rest a while. I search the depths of my mind. What is my last recollection? The discomfort within my cranium increases with pressure as I concentrate. I struggle against the searing noises before a memory comes to mind. Amahté, I recall his presence, training of some sort. The memory is fragmented. I struggle to piece it together. I think he may have been in some sort of trouble and we aided him. Yes, that is it! The last thing I recall is lying next to him in the medical room. I look around in confusion.

"So how did I end up here?" I peer into the darkness

A figure seemingly moves. I shake my head. Am I delusional? I strain to see ahead of me. I see a shadow once more. Instantaneously I draw my legs back to my stomach trying to cover up my bare body through fear and shame. Just as I think my confusion has reached its full extent, a large muscular woman steps from the darkness, her body as naked as my own. I am both shocked and terrified.

The large woman crouches, attempting to sit beside me. In fear I stumble in the opposite direction, grazing my bare skin on the wall I whimper in response.

"Who are you? What's going on here?" I manage to muster the courage to speak to her.

She smiles, her teeth sharp and unnaturally white for her rough appearance.

"I am Lupo," she extends a dirtied hand toward me.

Ignoring her gesture of acquaintance I scowl at her.

"Why have you taken me here?" I shout.

Her face creases in confusion as she lowers her hand.

Suddenly her expression alters and she laughs at me.

My anger surfaces as her laughter penetrates. I do not try to control it as my eyes glow blue in defence and rage. The energy lifts me from the floor as its power intensifies.

"Answer me!" I roar in a voice not my own.

A wave of energy is building in my hand, its spherical form growing exponentially. It takes only a split second for her to overpower me. I did not even have time to witness the occurrence, in a state of shock I stare up dumbly at the white face of a wolf.

Terror-stricken my body ceases up. The wolf bares her teeth growling viciously. I am helpless. Just as I fear for my life the wolf removes herself. My limbs relax and I manage to scamper backwards, I hit the wall, stare at this beautiful, yet terrifying white wolf.

In that moment of uncertainty, I find myself admiring the absolute magnificence of the ravenous animal before me. Her fur is long and white as snow, her eyes a striking silver colour, an utterly astonishing vision; if however, I was not about to be dismembered by the beautiful wild animal. I chuckle to myself at the thought.

Shaking my head I focus on the wolf. Her gaze is fixated on mine. Trans like we stare at each other. Seconds turn into minutes and yet the animal does not attack. Hope begins to stir as I wonder what is actually happening. Then suddenly the wolf rises on her hind legs, stretching high up she transforms into that bare muscular woman, Lupo.

My jaw falls slack as I scream aloud.

"Werewolf!!" I scramble for the entrance in a manic haze.

With rapid movements, Lupo blocks my escape. I am trapped.

"Calm down," she soothes, "I am not a werewolf!"

"You are! You must be!" I cry

"Think about it for a second, if I am a werewolf how can I go back to my human form?"

I scratch my head a moment. Thinking more clearly I realise she is correct. Werewolves are damned creatures, cursed to remain in their ravenous form, forever unable to return back to their humanity.

"Okay, so what are you then?"

"I'm Houndori." She lowers he head in shame "Well I used to be; now I guess I have to say I'm a therianthrope."

"Wait..."

A memory sparks into life. Dion mentioned the Houndori previously. They suffer a different curse to their werewolf brethren but the memory is hazy and incomplete.

"So you can just change forms?" I scratch my head trying to come to terms with the information.

"Yes. I can shape shift like you, from my human form to that of a wolf."

"So she's the same as Lyca then," I mutter to myself totally oblivious to the rest of her statement.

"Did you just say Lyca?" she hisses in my direction.

"Well....yeah...Why?" I stammer.

211

She paces up and down twisting a small piece of her wild, dirty hair. She mumbles something to herself I cannot make out the words. After a short while, she stoops down onto a broken grimy chair.

"Is everything okay?" I pry cautiously.

"Oh yes dear why would it not be? He's only the man that banished me from the Houndori and forced me to this frozen hell," she puffs.

I sit awkwardly, not knowing how to respond to her. She simply carries on twisting her hair. I pick at the floor uncomfortably.

"How do you know him?" she finally speaks.

"He helped to train me, him and Dion looked after me when the werewolf...." I trail off.

I suddenly regain all memories of late. I jump from my seating screaming at my new revelation.

"I'm a werewolf!" I scream aloud.

Lupo laughs at me hysterically.

I stare, confused by her reaction.

"You are not a werewolf," she manages to speak between laughing fits.

"But I turned. I remember it all now. I was a wolf!"

She nods encouraging me to make the connection. I simply peer at her dumbly as my emotions run wild within me.

She rolls her eyes.

"Not the brightest spark, are you? If you're a werewolf, why are you back in human form?"

"I don't know how this works!!!! Maybe this is what happens in the beginning!" I roar in anger at her comments.

She shakes her head in disappointment.

"That's not how it works, once a werewolf always a werewolf. There's no coming back from that."

"So...what am I?"

She snorts a laugh from her nostrils.

"You are a Therianthrope?" she stares intently. "A Lycan!"

The information is too much for me to handle. I cannot be a Lycan. I was impaled by a werewolf. Not a Lycan? How could this have happened? It cannot be true... I stare down at my chest. The indentations where the claws impaled me are still visible. Blue and red splintered veins surround the blackened skin around my heart. I touch the skin examining it. Could it be? Could the Ebur have overpowered the werewolves' venom? Counteracting it, allowing me to become a Lycan instead of the murderous beast I was doomed to befall.

"Wow!" I exclaim in utter astonishment.

"What?" The filthy, nude woman interrupts my thought process.

I decide to keep the information to myself. I do not know this woman and I fear to trust anyone but those I know with my revelation. Moreover, she admitted that Lyca banished her. What could she have done to deserve such a fate? I mull over the questions as I respond.

"Nothing," I smile awkwardly.

She waves the matter away as though she is not slightly interested in my withholding of facts.

"You hungry?" she asks turning to leave.

"Starving!" I respond.

She paces back and forth, twisting her hair, talking incoherently to herself. I stare at her creasing my brow, a small stab of fear pierces my gut as I watch her manic movements. She has the appearance of a person suffering from a mental illness. What will this woman do to me? Can I trust her to not harm me? I remain undecided on the matter as she throws on some animal fur and exits out into the frozen world which surrounds us. I am left to my own devices in a strange place without any clue as to what I should do next. I recall witnessing Dion following me when I was a...a...wolf... I gulp at the thought. I am unsure what my feelings about this are. How can *I* be a wolf? A wolf!! I shake my head. I must locate Dion, he can solve this problem. He always knows what to do. Yes, I need to find him! And with that, I turn towards the door. As I reach it, it flies open and the woman returns with a dead animal, covered in blood.

"Oh my gosh!" I exclaim surprised.

She shuts the door firmly before taking off her fur and tossing the animal on the table.

"Well, you said you were hungry!" she laughs as she skins the poor creature.

"Yes but...."

"But what? You think there's a store around here? Oh sorry let me just go to the shop to buy you a meal....silly girl!" she huffs as she slams the knife into the creature's neck, severing it clean off.

It rolls off, stopping directly in front of me. It has the appearance of a rabbit; its colour, however, is strange. Almost as if it was created from crystal, I can see the floor through it. Its ears are stubbed and short and its front teeth are extremely large. They almost extend down to the ground. I shiver and remove myself from the disturbing head.

"Sorry. I'm just not used to...well that," I crease my face in disgust.

She rolls her eyes at me as she starts a fire. She thrusts a piece of wood through the rabbit's carcass and begins to roast the meat on the fire. I stare at the poor defenseless rabbit, disgusted at myself for wanting to consume the roasting meat. I am starving after all.

The woman finishes cooking the rabbit and splits the meat between us. I gorge hungrily, the meal is surprisingly tasty. I quickly finish my food and return to the warmth of the fire.

"Thank you."

She nods in response, half a rabbit hanging from her large mouth. I rub my hands together. I am not used to this cold I sniff. I also despise the fact that I am naked. What on earth happened to my clothing anyway I ponder. Then I slap my face with stupidity. Of course! When I changed, the clothes would have simply fallen from their holdings. How stupid am I? I shake my head.

I sit in silence for a while mulling over everything I left behind in recent events.

"Elliott?" I whisper under my breath.

'Well it seems we are in a bit of a situation here' he laughs.

"Yep just a bit."

'What are you going to do?'

"Well, I was hoping you could help. What do you think?"

'You need to find Dion, he is one of the only people we can truly trust. He was tailing us we both saw that. Surely he can't be that far behind?'

"I hope not," I allow my head to fall loose as I cradle my knees.

I steal a glance at the door. What would her actions be if mine were to run? Would she follow? Would she block me? Or would she do nothing but wave a dirty hand in my direction uncaring of my actions whatsoever. I sit a moment, wracking my brain. I have no idea what to do for the best. Should I stay with this insane woman or should I take my chances finding Dion?

Pressing my hands against my skull I push hard, the thoughts seem to only cause my stress to rise, and with it a pain I am all too familiar with. I close my eyes a moment, trying to steady my breathing.

'I do have one suggestion. Why don't you create yourself some warm clothes? At least we won't be freezing.'

"Now that's a good idea" I whisper.

I imagine a set of warm clothes, thick waterproof trousers, a pair of hiking boots, a t-shirt and hoody along with an overly large fluffy coat. The image sets alight and I watch as the clothes disintegrate before me. The expectant wind follows spreading the ashes. I open my eyes to the clothes a crumpled mess beside me. I take no time at all to dress myself. I sigh with relief as the warmth takes over my body for the first time in a long while. I relax against the wall.

"How are you wearing those?" The woman's shocked voice interrupts my relaxation.

My heart sinks. I did not think about revealing my abilities to her. I curse my idiocy, how could we have been so dense?

'*Oh no…*'

I roll my eyes at Elliott's response,

"You think?"

I slap my forehead before allowing my hand to fall down my face. I guess it is time to involve this stranger into a small section of my existence. I simply hope I am doing the correct thing in revealing myself to her. What if she has other ideas about me? What if she tried to exploit me? What could I do to protect myself? I shake the thoughts and return her stare.

"I created them," I reply simply, hoping that would be its end.

"You created them? How?" she presses me.

I pause a moment, hesitating, unsure what will come of this idiocy, I continue…

"It's one of my abilities. I don't really understand it but my energy can somehow give life to my creations."

She stares at me her eyes creased with confusion as my words are absorbed. Suddenly her features alter. Her eyebrows raise, her face softens as she approaches me warmly, a large smile forming. She seems to glide over to me, effortlessly. The sight is strange and causes me great unease.

What is she doing? She places her dirty hand on my shoulder tenderly. Her smile firm.

"I have never known of anyone that could do that. It's amazing!" she squeezes my shoulder.

"Can you show me?" She tightens her grip. A dull ache forms under her grip.

I try to wriggle my shoulder free but she holds me tighter.

"You're hurting me!" I exclaim.

She loosens her grip as if not realising how hard she had actually been squeezing.

"Sorry," she remarks.

She turns to walk away from me and I relax a little. I may have judged her too harshly. She seems genuinely repentant at her action. Maybe she just did not realise. I rub my shoulder tenderly. She seems to be a lot more settled than previously.

Although I begin to notice she is acting a little strangely from the minuscule amount of time I have spent with her. Suddenly her ticks seem to have resolved themselves. She has straightened up her posture; she no longer twirls her hair through comfort or habit. The alteration unnerves me slightly.

She continues to mess with something behind the table, no longer pacing back and forth. She takes a seat and smiles at me warmly. I return her gesture as she begins to clean up after herself. Removing all traces of the animal we had just devoured. The more time passes the more relaxed I become. The warmth of my clothes, as well as the fire, seems to make me lethargic. My head nods as I struggle to stay awake. Yawning loudly I stretch.

My eyes grow heavy and for a moment I close them. Now I have made several mistakes in my short lifetime. But this one, right at this moment is up there with worst....for the moment my eyelids closed, Lupo took action. She grabs something from behind her table. I hear the slap of her bare feet on the ice-cold floor as she runs. My eyes open confused. Moments later she is upon me, I feel something blunt impact the back of my head. The world becomes black I am knocked out cold.

AntAGoNisT

My eyelids flutter open. Searing pain in my head causes my vision to blur.

"Ouch!" pain surges as I touch my head.

My hand returns red, I close my eyes trying to regain some sense. What happened? I try once more to view my surroundings. The room I am in is pitch black and the searing headache makes it almost impossible to think clearly. I try to stand. I am halted by something. What is that? My right arm is chained to something. A wall if I would have to guess. What have I gotten myself into now? Unable to move or even witness my surrounding I simply stay still. Hoping, praying that, somehow, this is a mistake. That this is a dream? That this is anything but that which I think it is.

I am unsure of how much time has passed. I fear I do not even care. My hope diminished as some of my senses returned. My vision has cleared for the most part and I have learned that I am unable to speak. I have not a slight inkling as to why or how, but I am mute. No words which I form come to fruition and I am chained like an animal, for the second time in my life.

I shiver as the memories of Splite rush through my mind like a whirlwind. The torture I, we endured, in that horrendous place will haunt me for the rest of my life, however short. I begin to cry and although no sound is produced my tears stream down my face. I cannot hold in my emotions any longer. I have tried to be strong, for Dion, for everyone that depends on me. I fear this may have finally broken me.

Eventually, my tears run dry. My emotions seem to drain away as I stare at the same spot in a trans, defeated, broken, captured once more.

I hear footsteps to my left. A small crack of light seeps in as a door is opened. A tall dark figure appears in the doorway. Moments later I am blinded as a light is turned on.

Shielding my eyes from the pain, I hear a voice. A voice that I recognize, my eyes spring open irrelevant of circumstance.

"Lexi?"

Dion approaches me. His demeanour, the way he moves as he approaches me is...... abnormal. Usually, his posture is perfect, I have never seen the man's shoulders slumped before, until now. He edges forwards, his face taunt and dark. I wish so desperately to speak. To find out what has occurred to him whilst I was wandering. He seems so different, all of his light and hope, diminished, if not vanquished altogether. I do not understand. Through it all, he has been my rock. I am the one with emotional turmoil, walking a thin line with my sanity that threatens to break at any given moment. Dion has always been so stable and rational. I know sometimes when we are in danger he can panic but normally he is the light in the darkness. The man before me if more like his opposite; the darkness in the light.

I lunge towards him; my chains halting me, they snap me backwards stinging my wrist. Ignoring the discomfort I reach for him. He approaches my outstretched fingers and takes my hand. Hope engulfs me as we hold hands and for a split second, I feel as though my fortune has altered. He takes my hand gently edging me backwards against the wall. Whatever has happened I know we can make it through this together. The words I so desperately want to relay to him. My heart pounds as he pushes his body up against mine. The close proximity causes butterflies. In a few moments, I will be free from my shackles. Then I hear it. A sickening click, Dion has shackled my other arm to the wall. This one is much shorter than the previous and it does not allow me to even sit down. I stare at him dumbfounded. My heart sinks. What has happened to you? Tears form as the lump in my throat almost blocks my trachea. My eyes glisten as they well up, staring into his cold, hazel eyes. My features ask the question my voice will not allow. Why?

"This is the only way. Compliance... we are a part of the losing side, we chose incorrectly, but it is not too late for you. I have shifted sides, you can too," his face is emotionless.

"Well?" His anger flourishes at my ignorance.

I stare at him, much more broken than I have ever been before. The emptiness within me increasing in size followed by the size of the hole that he just punched in my heart.

"Oh silly me. I forgot."

He waves a hand drawing out a yellow aura from my throat. He releases my vocal cords allowing me a voice. The action causes me to cough violently.

"D.....Dion," I croak.

"Will you comply?" He reprimands.

"What have they done to you?" I sniffle.

"They made me see clearly. I do not know what you are talking about."

"Please Dion, You can fight this! You need to see sense. You're already on the right side of this war. Do you think the werewolves are on the right side? They are evil creatures that ruin lives for fun. That's not you. This isn't what you believe."

221

"The Magi deserve it. They kill the wolves, why can they not do the same back?"

I stare at him dumbfounded. I cannot believe the words that are escaping his mouth. This is not *my* Dion.

"Have they brainwashed you? I didn't think you of all people could ever be turned. You have fought tooth and nail for the Houndori and the Hunters. What have they done to you?"

The flutter in my chest increases as the situation finally sinks in. If they have managed to turn the strongest, most loyal and brilliant man I know, what hope is there for the rest of us? I cannot comprehend this situation.

"Dion, please, it's me, Lexi, we have to fight this, together!"

"The only thing I need to fight is you, Lexi, you are the enemy currently. And if I cannot get you to turn I do not know what she will do to you," he laughs.

"I mean it is not like I really care that much. If she tears you limb from limb," he shrugs uncaring, "I only want to make use of your power. In case you hadn't noticed you are so unbelievably powerful. Your full potential has not even been realised yet. I should know I trained you," he cocks his eyebrows smugly. He continues.

"All of this time, all of the situations I had set you up with, the werewolf I sent to your home to destroy your normal pitiful life; forcing you into Splites' arms; the maze; the werewolf venom. Lyca also played his part to a tee."

"THAT IS NOT TRUE!!" I scream at the top of my lungs.

"See I could pretend that your entire journey was not set up....but that would not be true. I like the truth you see. I cannot keep you in the dark."

I lunge at him, the chains hold. Tears streaming down my face as my emotions run rampant.

"We had something. It wasn't all a lie. This! This is the lie! You don't know what you're saying, Dion. They have done something to you. Please, please fight whatever demon you need to, to come back."

He half-smiles whilst shrugging his shoulders.

"Believe what you want. But think on this, you are seriously one of the most powerful people we have ever come across and now you have the added strength of Lycanthropy. You are a powerful Magi and are now a Werewolf-Houndori Hybrid which has never been seen before. The power is unimaginable. Do you think that all happened by chance?"

My entire body shakes with his words. They are all lies.....surely they are all lies...

"I set up the one-eyed werewolf that plunged its venom into your heart," he sniggers, "then I took you to my dear friend Lyca to carry out the rest of our plan. I mean you might have died there and then, it might not have worked.....but it did....and now, now you are magnificent. A huge advantage in this war, you will win the war for the werewolves."

"How did you know the werewolf only had one eye? I never told anyone that?" I stammer.

"I told you! I set it up! That is how I know."

"I will never be a tool for the werewolves" I cry, utterly shattered by his revelations.

"Then you will die. You will not be a tool for the Magi either. I had hoped I could convince you....but maybe not. Maybe a little time in here alone with your new view on life might sway you. I know how unstable you are," he winks at me.

My emotions turmoil within, I cannot control them. There are too many feelings erupting all at once within one singular entity. My broken pieces form anger. The anger rises like the fire breath of a dragon. My body sparks blue in colour, the velocity of the wind sends my blue hair flying in all directions. The wind becomes increasingly intense and the chains that are binding me start to rattle, as my weightless force pulls against them. I open my eyes which also now have a blue glow. I direct my anger towards the man in my life that I was falling in love with, to find out it was all a lie. It was all a large game to create a deadly weapon for the wrong side. I direct my energy towards the coward that has pretended to love me all of this time that fought for my survival, not for love but for his endgame.

I erupt like a volcano. The blue pulse radiates from within; the room around me begins to disintegrate. The cavernous walls flake away like the ash of a fire. The ceiling cracks above me, large stalagmites fall from their holdings. One pierces through my shoulder. I feel no pain. The shard disintegrates instantaneously as the entire area is engulfed. The room vanishes from sight as my emotions peak. I can no longer see Dion; I can no longer see anything, only my aura, which does not seem to be slowing.

Suddenly a black cloud-like aura encircles me and my destruction. It pulsates as though it is breathing. Slowly it absorbs my power, diminishing me, ceasing my devastation. The black cloud converses around me, closing the gap with each pulsation until it lays itself against my skin. Like the turn of a switch, my energy vanishes and I plummet, unconscious, towards the ground.

****

Eyelids flutter open. I am back where I originated. Chained to another wall of rock, except this time I have depleted all of my strength. Now I am helpless. I peer around. The room I am contained is identical to the last. Cavernous, nothing remarkable what so ever. My shoulder aches where the shard pierced it. I peer at it, someone has bandaged it up. How nice of them I spit, removing it in anger, I toss it on the ground.

"DION!!" I shout.

"DION!!!!!"

"Yes?" He peaks his head around the door.

The sight of him causes a stabbing pain in my heart. How could he betray me like this? I do not understand.

"Just kill me...please..." I beg.

"Sorry, after what you just demonstrated there's no way she will kill you now. You are incredible. And you will win this war for us."

"Who is she?" I ask numbly.

"Do you recall the creature that haunted your dreams for a long time....two curled horns, empty eye sockets..."

"Daemonium?" I exclaim horrified.

"Yes! Well, Nyx is his right hand. She is the master of darkness, the creator of werewolves amongst other similarly evil creatures that inhabit this world. Creatures you could not even imagine, the werewolves are a blimp of evil in comparison to the others."

"I didn't think I would ever hear of that thing again," I shiver.

I sink against the wall. The chains cut into my wrists as I allow myself to dangle from them, utterly defeated. Dion has played me all of this time. How could I be so blind? Do I really believe all of this? I know this man....or do I not? Do you ever truly know someone? I cannot cope with this twist of the knife, I fear for my own sanity. Moreover, he taunts of monsters more evil than werewolves? I shiver at that thought. I am utterly and completely drained.

"You are strong Lexi, but I do not think you are strong enough to resist her..."

The most beautiful woman I have ever seen suddenly appears from thin air directly in front of me. I jump out of my skin. My heart pounds from fear.

Her arm extends as her black aura grips my cheeks, twisting my head from one side to the other. She examines me.

"You are truly remarkable Lexi."

"Such power, such potential," she squashes my cheeks together making my lips purse.

I tear my face from her grasp in disgust.

"Don't touch me!" I shout.

"Touchy aren't we!" she sniggers.

She has long black hair with a side fringe which hangs to the left of her beautiful face. She is tall and slender like a supermodel. Her left eye is a dark brown and the right one is red. I stare into her strange eyes, she does not have normal circular pupils, hers have a section missing from the bottom of each similar to an upside-down horseshoe. How can such beauty.....

"...be so evil," she finishes off my thought.

My face creases in confusion, "how did you..."

"I am a telepath amongst my many other, abilities shall we say," she smiles sweetly, yet wickedly.

My entire world has just crumbled around me, much like the room I disintegrated not long ago, and now, not even my own thoughts are safe. The one place I recluse too regularly, where all of the depths of my plans, my thoughts, my everything, is harboured, what more remains? What more can be taken from me? My heart sinks as I fight back tears.

"There are a couple more things I can take from you. Your family; well I have already taken that I guess," she peers over to Dion. "I could take your life, with your defiance to obey me this would be such a simplistic task. Your friends...."

"Already taken care of that one," Dion chirps in.

Dread engulfs my senses.

"What?" I question.

"All casualties in your war against us. It had to be taken care of," he winks at me.

Anger churns within me as the words slice into me like a knife. I begin to shake violently as tears stream down my cheeks. I close my eyes trying to cease their flow. My breathing becomes rapid as the anguish takes hold of my senses.

"My friends...No... I am so sorry for dragging you all into this mess," I babble to myself.

Dion sniggers.

"Pathetic! This is what emotions do, they make you weak Lexi."

I manage to calm myself to speak to him, my eyes remain closed.

"You don't know what you are saying. Emotions don't make *me* weak."

I open my eyes, they glow the brightest blue they have ever before. I allow my emotions to take hold of me, to empower my energy; the energy I thought depleted after my previous outburst. The chains that bind me erupt into a thousand pieces as I levitate. I feel the strength racing through my arms, down my legs, circling my whole body. The entirety of the devastating information learned within such a short time forces my sanity to strain against the power coursing through me. I begin to feel the darkness creeping up my spine, coaxing me into the eternal abyss. It hisses at me, trying desperately to take control. I feel myself slipping, allowing myself to be taken. It has to be better than this reality, surely?

As I slowly lose my grip on reality I notice the room around me is swirling, my energy has created a whirlwind around me. Yellow and black fragments of aura crack against my protective shield but they do not enter. They are simply swatted away, not powerful enough to penetrate.

"See Dion! My emotions fuel my power!" my voice morphs.

The voice I hear is not my own. I sound like all sanity has finally drained and that thought scares me. Through a small clearing passing around me, I witness the expression on the Nyx's face. She grins triumphantly at the thought of my collapse. I take a moment to think through the chaos. If I allow my madness to take hold, would I then convert to her side? The darkness within me is certainly not a force of good. Nyx would prevail. She would have my powers as a weapon against the Magi, the werewolves would have such an advantage they would surely win this war. I cannot allow that to happen. I would rather destroy myself than allow these powers to fall into the wrong hands.

That is it! Kill myself. What other option is there?

I feel my senses returning as I drive the darkness back down to its pit. It writes and hisses at me as it recesses into the depths of my soul. My emotions calm as I decide this is the only option I have. I can finally end all of this turmoil I have been forced to endure. My death could eventually save this world; ensuring this overpowered aura does not befall the incorrect side. No one person should have such power. It should be against all laws of the universe surely. Why me? Why have I been cursed with such a fate? I shake my head. It must be done before they can cease my actions.

Nyx's face suddenly alters, for the first time I see fear. I do not think her telepathy can penetrate my shield but I think she has realised that the darkness will not see the light of this day. Her features alter as she speaks rapidly to Dion. His smile fades, he begins to panic.

I encourage my energy to gather within my chest. I allow all of my emotions to burst through, all at once. Betrayal, grief, loss, love, fear, amongst many more all simultaneously pour from within. Every hidden emotion, everything I have ever forced down, locked away, I now give freedom. I do not know if this will work but I have to try. I have no options left. Tears well as I take my final fall. I will never win this battle. The words go round and round my head as my aura increases exponentially. We will all fall if I do not complete this final act. I try to compel my energy to comply, to force my cells apart from the inside. It seems to try to find another way out. Spirals of energy soar around the room. One impacts

Nyx and she flies from sight. Forks of lightning spark in every direction as I try to contain it within myself, hoping my body will eventually lose control and fall apart.

Dion approaches. I cannot prevent myself from admiring his handsome face. I do not know the full extent of his betrayal, or even if what I have been told is true. The man I was falling for, even though those feelings were twisted with guilt over Jacob. How poetic, his is the final face I witness before my demise. I laugh at the irony. He places a hand in close proximity to my swirling, chaotic hell. A warm yellow glow seeps out from within his palm, it creeps across the madness forming a barrier. His actions confuse me a little, what does he seek to achieve? They have already tried to penetrate this shell without success; it has become too powerful.

Then Dion walks forward. The action takes away my breath. He will surely perish once he breaks through. Panic strikes as he presses onwards regardless, not breaking eye contact. My head instructs me to carry out my plan, to end myself bringing him with me if I must. After all, he has tainted my life playing with the strings of my heart, snapping them one by one. My heart on the other hand belongs to him. Or at least the man I thought he was. When your head and heart are at battle with one another which should you choose? I stare down at him as the skin on his arms begins to flake away the more he presses forwards. He still glares into my soul, his eyes seem to plead, please do not give up on me.

My mind screams at me to end this madness once and for all. My emotions flood away, for my battle, is lost. My heart triumphs; I cannot allow Dion to perish, even if my love for him is misguided. I simply cannot do it. I am not a monster. I allow my energy to disperse. It blips out and erupts in every direction much like a nuclear blast would. I scream aloud as all of the power vacates. With the blink of an eye, I fall from grace. Dion catches me with ease, and for a split second, as he cradles me within his arms, I see the man I have spent such a long time with. I see a glimpse of sorrow nestled within his eyes. My energy depletes and I am left to the devices of my captors once more.

HolD My HaNd

I awake in a fully furnished room. I jolt upright in the bed I am nestled within. My heart pounding I scan my surroundings. I am in a small bedroom; the walls decorated with red tiles, a soft black carpet afoot. There is a small wooden dresser with a mirror to my right. The light reflects in from the window. I gingerly approach it. Peering outside I see nothing but snow for miles and miles.

"What's going on?" I ask aloud.

I approach the door on the other side of the room. Locked.

"Of course."

I could try to open the door with my energy but I am extremely weak; I can barely manage to hold my own weight at this moment in time. I return to the bed and slowly edge myself down. All memories of recent events come flooding back. They impact me with such velocity I simply flop on the bed and wail into the soft pillow as I become overwhelmed. I do not know how long I wept for before a voice rudely interrupts me. I peer up towards the door.

Lupo stands before me. Naked and as dirty as ever, she smiles.

I simply stare at her; I do not give a reaction. I have nothing left to say.

"I see you met the boss. She's a beautiful cow isn't she, God I hate her," she laughs, twisting her hair.

She walks across the room awkwardly.

"You know I didn't want this... but she was watching us. The moment she found out what you could do....well here we are"

I turn from her; I do not wish to listen to her excuses.

Lupo creases her brow, "she hides in plain sight you see. Well, you cannot see her ..." she shakes her head.

"You know what I mean! She is so persuasive, manipulative, she is very good at flipping people..."

The remark catches my interest.

"Flipping people? What do you mean?"

She smiles and makes a flicking action with her finger and thumb. I shake my head in response. She has seriously lost her sanity this woman.

"Hah! I knew I could make you talk."

I give her a death stare, seriously unimpressed with her remark.

"Leave me alone!"

"Yes, we are alone. Nyx isn't here, I can tell. I mean you cannot see her obviously but I know she isn't here for sure. I am getting good at spotting the signs."

"What are you talking about?" I ask confused.

Lupo smacks her forehead at my idiocy before grabbing a cover from the bed and using it as a shield. She hides herself behind the sheet.

"See I am still here, but you cannot see me." She pokes her head around the side, "get it?"

She allows the cover to drop the floor.

"Now you see me, but I was here all along."

"You're telling me she can turn herself invisible?"

"Yes! That is what I said! She has the ability to refract the light around her, rendering herself invisible!" she shakes her head at me dumbfounded.

I roll my eyes.

"So nowhere is safe from her."

Lupo nods in response.

"She can read minds and turn invisible, and who knows what else she is capable of..."

"I should have ended it all when I had the chance," I huff

"You certainly should have. She has large plans for you. Firstly you will turn, because well they all do. B. She will use your powers and C. Well, I cannot remember what C was... Oh well."

"Firstly I will never turn, or allow her to use me as a weapon, Secondly I'm going to get out of here, and thirdly....can you put some clothes on, I am sick of looking at your filthy nakedness!"

"Humour, I like it."

"It's not humour..."

"Is there a reason you're here? I would very much like to self destruct on my own."

"I thought maybe I wanted to help you. But your nasty and I have decided not to," she turns to leave.

"No, wait! Please, help me."

Lupo spins on the spot, "okay okay I will."

She approaches me cautiously placing something in my hand.

"Take this it will help you."

And with that, she turns and leaves.

I open my enclosed fist. A large ovular purple pill resides within my palm. I press the jelly inside as it surges around the casing as if wanting to escape.

"Yeah, I don't think so."

I launch the pill at the window. It rolls under the desk and out of sight.

"She is insane if she thinks I'll take that pill."

I mull it over a moment then curse myself at the action but I go and retrieve the pill from under the desk and place it in my pocket, I know not why, just that my gut was forcing me to.

I find myself alone once more. As everything falls through around me, I am in over my head. I have no idea what action to take. I wish Dion...I do not finish the sentence. My heart aches at the thought of him. I long for him to burst through those doors and save me from myself like he has done so many times in the past. This time however I am on my own. I perch myself on the end of the bed. Thinking back to all of the times Dion had aided me. Was it all one elaborate fabrication? Now that my mind is clearer I simply refuse to accept this new reality. Nyx must have done something to him. She must have! Dion is a kind loving man with a heart of gold. Can one man truly fabricate such a personality? I am unsure, but in my heart, I want to believe that all of this is simply untrue.

The door swings open. Dion stands awkwardly in the doorway. He enters cautiously.

The sight of him makes my heart skip a beat. I cannot control my feelings for him even if the truth is that he is a traitor.

"Lexi," he nods in my direction.

I ignore him. Instead, I turn to the opposite direction.

I hear him walk around the bed before he appears in my vision once more.

He places a finger under my chin. My heart breaks as he lifts my head to meet his gaze. A singular tear escapes down my cheek. He wipes it away.

"Thank you for sparing my life."

I pull away from his grip; I can no longer take the heartache.

"She must have known you would not let me perish when she told me to walk into your path of destruction."

I snap my neck around, tears blur my vision.

"Another trick to bend me to her will?"

He cocks an eyebrow, smiles, shrugging one shoulder.

"Of course, I did not think it would work. I was ready to lay my life down, but due to your kindness it was not necessary."

"Was anything real?" I ask solemnly.

"What like? Our friendship? Our forbidden romance? Hah! No, I am afraid not. I am not the man I portrayed to you."

My heart pounds within my chest as it tears itself to pieces.

"But why? Why save me all of those times? Why be nice to me? Why allow me to fall for you?" I pound on his chest.

He allows me a moment to vent my anger and pain before he grips my wrists. He stares into my eyes as my words seem to strike a chord within him. For a moment he is lost, unable to come up with an answer.

"She told me to. If I allowed you to perish, and believe me you are the most self-destructive person I have met, she would not be able to convert you to utilise your abilities."

"Why me?" I tear my arms from his holding, "what's so special about me?"

"Well think about this, you have the ability to imagine something, anything and give it life.....how useful would such a tool be in the coming war? Where you could create anything with a simple thought? Oh, there is so much destructive potential with such abilities."

He claps like an over-excited child.

"I will never help you," I stammer, broken.

"We will see."

I plead with my energy to somehow flick a switch and turn off my emotions. This betrayal seems to cause me more anguish than any of the suffering I have endured. I fear I am not able to cope with the reality of these revelations; not all at once. My literal world has crumbled, once again, around me; the entirety of my life after the fateful moment has been a fabrication. It was a fabrication to create a powerful weapon, a weapon to train and mould to their requirements. Eventually, leading to me turn on my own kind. I wish I could hand these abilities off to someone else. To pass on such a burden as this, I certainly did not ask to be special. I did not want any of this. I would have gleefully carried out the rest of my life unbeknown of such dangers residing within the world around me. The same question continuously returns to the forefront of my mind...why me?

I cease my tears; I will no longer allow this despicable man to witness my torment. I have endured enough. As if obeying my earlier request my betrayal seems to dull, my skin seems to thicken as my emotions are forced down.

"You will never break me, Dion. Nor will Nyx. *I* will not allow it. What more can you do to me? Torture me? Well, guess what, been there done that. Welcome to my life!" I half-smile.

"You may think I'm weak-minded, that I can't hold out but I'm stronger than you think. I won't break. Your betrayal has destroyed my soul and still, I won't turn. Give it your best shot!" I declare.

My words seem to penetrate. He simply stands staring at me as if slightly shell shocked. I presume they think I will simply relent to their will after such a crushing blow. I have, after all, completed more extreme acts for much less.

"You have gotten so lost in this world Dion. What happened to you?"

He stands mute, staring. I close the gap. My face is directly in front of his, eyes both on the same level only a few inches apart.

"Has she done something to you Dion?" I stare deep into his eyes, "I find it so hard to believe that the last couple of years were all a lie."

"Freedom carries sacrifice," he drones in a monotone voice.

I crease my brow at his response.

"What?"

Shaking his head he returns his senses, and without another word leaves the room. I am alone once more. I punch the bed, over and over venting my anger on the inanimate object. Taking my left finger and thumb I press them against the bridge of my nose, trying to contain myself, to think of my next move. I decide to explore the room more in-depth hoping I can locate an escape route, or else at least something to aid me. This room has nothing special and after I had explored all of the walls, floor, ceiling, even the furniture, I realise there is no way out. There are no secret escape routes to which I could pull a book from a shelf to open a hidden door. I puff in disappointment. I was seriously hoping there would be something strange here that could aid me.

I return to the bed, I allow myself to plummet, face-first onto the mattress. I lay still, head buried in the covers partially inhibiting my breathing. I care not. Then I hear a door open. I jolt upright, fearful of who may be my next visitor. No one enters and a moment later it closes once more. I approach the door. Outstretching my hand I slowly grip the handle. I turn it to the right then left. Nothing happens. The door must be locked. How strange? Did someone change their mind and simply close the door instead? Then a chill travels down my spine. I recall the conversation between myself and Lupo.

'You're telling me she can render herself invisible?... Yes! That is what I said!'

My heart stops. I glance around the room, my eyes twitching from left to right, desperately trying to notice even the most insignificant alteration to my surroundings. Is she in here with me? In my moment of panic, I raise my defences. My hands glow as my heart thuds. An overwhelming sense of dread engulfs me as I lose the ability to breathe.

My hands begin to shake as my vision becomes disfigured as though I am looking through a fish-eye lens. What is happening to me? My energy flares as my fear transpires. The field of power surrounding me grows, almost filling the entire room. It licks the walls much like a wildfire would. My heart palpitates and for a moment I fear I may be having a heart attack. Not knowing what other action to take I scream for Dion at the top of my lungs. What else could I do? Seconds later the door swings open with such velocity it bounces off the wall. Dion glances around the room as my energy threatens to lose control. I begin to sweat profusely as I hunch over in a ball. He jogs towards me concern lining his face. He closes the distance between us; gripping my shoulders he affords me a close view of his face. Despite my betrayal and anxiety, I cannot help but feel tingles run down my spine with his touch.

Over his shoulder, I can see that my energy is gaining more momentum and now escapes through the open door. Small fragments of Dion's clothing begin to chip away and disintegrate through the force. Despite my remorse, a veil of panic still befalls me and I cannot control myself. Dion reaches for my chin forcing me to face him.

"Sit up Lexi," his voice firm as he kneels before me.

"I.....I can't. I don't have control," I whisper.

Dion frowns at me straining his handsome features in disappointment. His face only a few inches from my own.

"I know an excuse when I hear one Lexi. You are powerful, do not deceive yourself into thinking you are a powerless victim to your own emotions."

Almost as soon as Dion's words penetrate a wave of relief rushes over me, my energy diminishes slowly. My heart palpitations reduce as my muscles begin to relax slightly. My body stops shaking as the last remnants leave my hands. His strong hands grip my sides as he sits me on the chair.

"You are going to be alright," he states, his voice still firm.

I nod in response to my chest feeling looser already.

"Just take deep breaths."

I close my eyes as I inhale heavily, filling my lungs before releasing it. I feel disappointed that once again I have allowed myself to succumb to my emotions.

I smile at him, "Thank you."

Dion is seemingly one of the only people that can bring me back from the brink, to calm my panic attacks before they spiral out of control. Compassion lights up his face as he squeezes my hand. He takes one last look at me before turning to leave.

He falters, "You know Lexi.... " he shakes his head sorrow filling his features, "I really am sorry."

And with those heart-wrenching words he leaves, closing the door firmly behind him. I descend into self-pity once more. Approaching the bed I burrow down like a mole and cry myself to sleep.

****

***Red twisted horns protrude the thick smog ahead of me. I turn to run in the opposite direction, the monster catches me mid-turn. It laughs a deep throaty chuckle before bringing me to eye level and with a demented grin it releases me, I plummet to the ground with great velocity.......

****

I jump from my skin as the imaginary impact jolts me awake. Groggily, with my heart racing, I peer around. Confusion taints me as I realise I am in a different room to the one I fell asleep in. I have been placed in the middle of a cold tiled floor and amidst the blackness of the room, I can decipher nothing of my location. Sharp pain in my arm entices me to touch it. A large gash seeps my blood heavily. I strain my eyes in the hope of witnessing something. What happened? Where am I now?

Almond coloured tiles decorate the floor as the white swirling tiles climb the walls and ceiling. This place looks immaculate. The darkness does not allow me much more sight than that so I have no idea what else, or who else could be in this unnerving room. The thought sends a shiver down my spine. I try to stand, my side twinges and I am forced to cradle it as I rise. As I stand a sharp pain in my ankle hinders my efforts. Shuffling along slowly I hear something scuttle ahead. I stop dead. What was that?

"Hello? Is anyone there?"

A child-like giggle is my only response. My features strain in fear as I try to locate its source. I edge onwards, fearful of what horrors I may find.

An incoherent voice booms ahead, I feel as though I recognise it but I cannot place it. For some reason, my ears seem to be muffled as though I have injured them in some way. Why am I injured? I am so confused! Although the discomfort is quite severe I manage to shuffle onwards regardless. I head towards the voice, head fuzzy, ears ringing, dazed as though I had been in close combat with an explosive.

Then in the depths of the darkness, I see him. My heart plummets as I am finally able to place the voice. A yellow glow lights up the entire room revealing his full glory. My heart sinks as I bear witness to someone I had hoped to never lay eyes on again.

"It's been a while....hasn't it," I grunt, unable to even comprehend my emotional state.

His head jerks to the right, twitching violently under the black mask.

"It would seem so. Just over three years, yes? I had hoped we would cross paths once again," he grins menacingly.

As I approach I notice someone tied to a chair off to my right with their back towards me.

"Another torture victim I see?" I scowl.

He turns to his left. Then he removes his mask showing me his true face after all of this time, I finally get to witness my captors full form. His skin is tight and disfigured. In a way, he has the appearance melted flesh; even his eyeless sockets seem slightly drooped as though licked by flames. He has no defined nose, simply two slits like that of a reptile.

"Wow, your even uglier than I imagined," I insult him, disgusted by his actions towards me those years ago.

"Well, you do not look so healthy yourself!" he snarls.

"Have the years not been kind to you?" he sniggers. "You should have just stayed with me," he shrugs, smiling wickedly.

I do not allow my anger to rise; I will not permit him to get the better of me. I simply ignore his comment and approach his latest victim. I stare at him emotionless, every minute emotion within drained away the moment I realised who occupied the same room as me. I simply feel numb to the world, as though, I have turned off my emotions somehow.

"Why am I here?" I question as I shuffle along, face stern.

"Are we to repeat three years ago? Because that did not work out so well for you now did it?"

"I have endured your torture. I have come out of the other side, and I have endured much pain and turmoil since. It will take a lot for you to break me. I'm guessing you work for Nyx?"

"Oh yes, clever girl! I have always worked for her. She wanted you all of those years ago, I guess she finally got her wish," he laughs cynically. Then his head twists violently to the left, twitches.

"Lexi! I am so glad to see you. How have you been?" Splite's kinder personality shines through.

"I have been better, but thank you. It's nice to see you too."

I know this seems an oddity, the feeling of such hatred and anger for Splite, yet I can easily share pleasantries with his softer side. It is a strange circumstance with him, through all the torture and agony, his left side was always kind and nice to me, he looked after me, repaired the injuries he inflicted with such tenderness. I shake my head at the strange reality. This atmosphere does not last however, moments later his left side is ripped from control and his head jerks to the right, his features altering with the change.

"Why did she want me all those years ago? I was nobody!"

"Oh she saw your potential alright, she can see many things. She knew she had to have you on her side. Your powers are marvellous."

"Well I guess this way is better."

"How so?" he scrunches up his disfigured face.

"Well, you see all of those years ago I may have cracked. She may have been able to manipulate me, to turn me to her side. I was much weaker then," I force an emotionless smile that scares even me.

"Now? She hasn't got a chance. I would rather die. No amount of torture, emotional turmoil can be worse than what I have endured."

He stands still, silent, not knowing how to respond.

"So I guess that's on you! I'm surprised she has let you live actually. What a huge mistake you made allowing me to escape your prison," I wave a finger and tut at him.

His anger flourishes and he grabs a long kind of sword, pointing the tip to my throat. I stare into his empty sockets, emotionless, I do not flinch. Then he smiles. He digs the blade into his victims left wrist. He slices deep, scraping open his artery. Blood begins to spurt out of the gaping hole. I am almost beside him now. I do not let his actions break me, although I feel sick inside I will not let it show. Who is this poor soul that is about to bleed out in front of my eyes?

The figure is slumped forward, not moving at all but I can see he is large in stature. Just I line up with him, my heart plummets as tears form rapidly. His latest victim, bleeding profusely, battered almost to death.

"LYCA!" I scream, no longer hiding my emotions.

My sanity strains as I stare helplessly at the once ferocious man that saved me countless times, made me stronger, became my friend, is now clinging onto life because of me. I grasp his arm desperately trying to cease the blood flow. He has torn too much of his artery for my feeble attempts to be successful.

My energy flares into my hand as I try to heal his fatal wound. A yellow light surrounds me, halting my action.

"No! PLEASE," I struggle.

Tears stream down my face as I watch my friend's life ebb away before me.

"Splite please help him!"

He sniggers "You were so cocky, so self-assured. I had to bring you back down to earth. You think you will never accept her deal. Yet you are begging me for his pathetic life."

"You are not so strong when your friends are threatened are you?" He rolls his eyes.

"WEAK! You are weak" he paces around Lyca, ranting and raving.

"Splite! Please. I am not strong, your right I am weak. You have me, please just help him and let him go."

"Oh my dear, you have no idea. He will be our leverage, if I permit him to live of course. If not, I can retrieve one of your other so-called friends, you are running shockingly low of by the way."

"Okay! If you heal him I will give in. I will not fight just please, spare my friends lives....." I cry uncontrollably.

"As you wish…"

Splite waves a hand, the yellow energy releases me and darts into Lyca's arm, collecting his large pool of blood, the aura forces it back into his artery and nits the pieces back together. Moments later his skin lies still and all evidence of foul play has vanished. Splite turns to me, his disgusting smile larger than ever. Nyx and Dion blink into sight directly to his right. They have been here this whole time.

I drop to my knees as I stare into Dion's uncaring eyes, which I can no longer call his own. This is not him; he just stood there while his friend bled out. He did nothing. Everything drains from my entire body all at once, leaving only a husk.

Defeated, utterly broken and with nothing left to fight with. I finally relent, allowing the darkness to clamber from its depths. It is the only way I know to enable me to become what they want me to be. I am not a monster, but my darkness might be. The thin line I have walked all of my life, balancing with great difficulty to stay on the correct side of sanity, I must now take my fall from grace, allowing it full reign. It clambers my spine eagerly racing for control. One of my biggest fears is about to become reality. It latches on; I feel the darkness spread, engulfing me.

My body convulses, my eyes turn black as they increase. I grasp my face as pain tears through my mind. Seconds pass and the pain dulls. As I slowly rise, I remove my hands. With blackened eyes, I turn to them.

"So where do we start?" I grin disturbingly...

Printed in Great Britain
by Amazon

24731159R00145